Liar, Liar

Liar, Liar

A Cat DeLuca Mystery

K. J. Larsen

Poisoned Pen Press

Poisoned Pen Press

First Edition 2010

10 9 8 7 6 5 4 3 2

Library of Congress Catalog Card Number: 2010923841

ISBN: 9781590587256 Hardcover
9781590587270 Trade Paperback

Poisoned Pen Press
6962 E. First Ave., Ste. 103
Scottsdale, AZ 85251
www.poisonedpenpress.com
info@poisonedpenpress.com

Printed in the United States of America

This is for our parents,
Harold and Arlene Larsen,
with much love.

Acknowledgments

We'd like to express our heartfelt thanks to everyone who made *Liar, Liar* possible. First of all to Barbara Peters, editor extraordinaire, who took a chance on three sisters' dream. Barbara wrestled a clumsy manuscript into coherence and the best of the story is hers. To our sister, Lynn Higbee, for her tireless research and support. To Cheri McManus for invaluable guidance and advice. To our long suffering family who brainstormed with us, read chapters and suggested changes. We couldn't have done it without you.

A special thumbs up to the wait staff at Connie's for their colorful stories and a fine cup of coffee. To Officer Kohnson and the blue and white-shirts of Bridgeport who patiently answered our questions and offered valuable counsel. Any inaccuracies in Chicago Police Department procedure reflect only the story teller's privilege.

Doing the work on this book and getting to know the neighborhood of Bridgeport has been our great joy. The exceptional, hardworking people make this one quadrant of Chicago one of the sweet spots on earth. Thanks for sharing it with Cat and her Pants On Fire Detective Agency.

Chapter One

The mark in a cocoa colored suit stepped out of the Bridgeport Bank into the bright sunlight. He leaned against the doorway and slipped on a pair of shades. I adjusted my binoculars to enjoy the view. My eyes wandered south over his hard athletic frame. This man was eye candy and I'd been craving some sugar since I started surveillance three long days ago.

He jogged across the street, past my Honda to the parking lot. I ditched the binoculars, propped a weekly tabloid in front of my face, and whispered into the recorder.

"4:03 pm Wednesday. Subject exited bank stuffing a wad of bills in his money clip. Question: Is he meeting person of interest tonight? Using cash to avoid a paper trail?"

I stretched my neck and peered over the magazine. The man shrugged off his jacket. His silk shirt hugged an impressive chest. I watched him open the door, ease his fine ass onto creamy leather, and roll away in a shiny black Porsche Boxster.

"Wednesday, 4:06 p.m. Subject left parking lot. Heading north on Archer." I fired up my silver Accord and shadowed after him.

The hot guy in the Boxster is Chance Savino. A.K.A. the lying cheating bastard who's married to my client Rita Savino. I met Rita last week when she burst through my office door, electric blue eye liner rolling down her cheeks. The ugly tears flowed from her conviction that her "no good husband" had his hand up someone else's skirt.

That's where I come in. My name is Cat DeLuca and I'm a private investigator. I don't snoop for insurance companies and I won't find your lost Uncle Harvey. I do what two years of unholy matrimony taught me well. I catch cheaters.

I trailed the black Porsche as it bulldozed across town. Rush hour had started early and traffic slowed to a standstill. I cranked up the stereo and blared my horn with the rest of Bridgeport. I wanted to wrap this job up and go home to a bottle of wine. I had my own personal meltdown to attend to.

My birthday.

Next week I turn the big three-oh. And to top it off I don't have a date for my own party. The guys I meet in this business are not the type you want to go out with. If they were I'd still be married to Johnnie Rizzo, the two-timing—wait, make that six-timing—cheating bastard. Unfortunately the only sex I'm seeing these days is through the lens of a camera. And trust me, in this business, sex is not a spectator sport.

A collision on Loomis and 31st blocked the intersection. I crept through the gridlock tailing the Boxster off 35th until it jerked to a stop in front of an abandoned building.

The windows were dark and a weathered, sun-bleached sign grew out of the tall grass. It said FOR LEASE. I parked half a block back in the shade of a birch tree and pulled out my high powered specs.

I got a close up of Savino's dark wavy hair and broad shoulders. He stretched back in his seat and laced his fingers behind his head. My client's husband was waiting for somebody but it wasn't his afternoon delight. This deserted office building was no Hotel No-tell.

I ducked behind my scandal sheet and relayed the subject's position into my recorder. Pushing back my seat I raised my legs, wrapping them around the steering wheel. I do a lot of surveillance and I can usually wait longer than most people can be good.

My Honda is an arsenal of cold pizza, Mama's cannoli, and Tino's Deli sausages. The sausages are for my sidekick, Inga. She's an overgrown, energetic beagle and she rules the backseat.

I tossed her a sausage and snagged myself a cannoli. Cannoli is an Italian pastry. It soothes like Sex On The Beach, with or without the alcohol.

Something vibrated in my Levi's and Hank blasted "Your Cheating Heart." I dragged my cell phone from my pocket.

"Pants on Fire Detective Agency," I said. "We expose Liars and Cheats."

The voice grated like nails on a chalkboard. "Tell me the truth, Cat. Is my husband sleeping with his secretary? Cuz I'll kill that hootchie."

It was a fair question and one half a dozen clients might ask. But the voice was a dead giveaway.

"Ms. Jones."

"Call me Cleo."

"Your husband is not sleeping with his secretary, Cleo. Did he mention his secretary is sixty-three years old?"

"He's a liar!"

"And a cheat. Your husband is sleeping with your sister."

She gasped. "My sister the lesbo?"

"No, your sister the ho. Come by my office later for the pics. And there's something else."

"There's more? You're killing me!"

"Your husband plans to leave you. He's funneling funds to an offshore account."

For the first time since I met Cleo, she was stunned to silence. "There must be a mistake."

"No mistake, girlfriend. The man is sucking you dry. I have the account numbers here for your lawyer."

The voice squawked like a cat skimming hot coals. "We never had this conversation. Destroy the evidence and forget I hired you. When I kill the bastard it'll look like an accident."

I shoved the last bite of cannoli in my mouth. "My lips are sealed."

My eyes wandered across the street to the black Porsche and I shrieked like Cleo. My eye candy wasn't in it. I swept the street with binoculars. How could this happen? But I already knew the answer. It was the voice—that crazed Cleo voice—that threw me off my game. There was no call for Cleo's husband to cheat on her, but why he didn't choke the squawking life out of her while she slept is beyond me.

My passenger door jerked opened and a giant blue eye filled the lens of my binoculars. I screamed and untangled my legs from the steering wheel.

"Looking for someone?"

I dropped the spy eyes and checked Rita Savino's husband with a professional eye, tripping briefly over the baby blues and lean hard physique. He smelled musky and clean and his short cropped hair rivaled the color of dark chocolate. His skin was tanned to a soft caramel and that yellow silk shirt fit him like melted butter. Liar, liar, I reminded myself and dabbed the drool from the side of my mouth.

"You're in my car," I said frostily. "Get out or my dog will attack."

Inga licked his ear as the cheater helped himself to a cannoli.

"Hey. That's my supper."

"You've eaten two already."

"Have not," I lied and licked the powdery sugar from my lips. "I'm calling the cops."

"Good. Then you can tell them why you've been following me all day."

Damn.

"I didn't spot you at first but I smelled your donuts. They gave you away."

"They're not donuts. They're cannoli and I've been tailing you since Monday."

His brow arched in surprise. "You're good. But your donuts are better." Savino slurped the last lick of cream from the cannoli and winked. "So, who's paying you to tail me?"

I flung a business card and he read aloud, "Pants on Fire Detective Agency. We Expose Liars and Cheats."

He glanced over. "You're Caterina DeLucky?"

"It's DeLuca. I'm Cat and that would make you the Liar and Cheat."

"You're not serious."

"Your wife is. She hired me."

"*Ha*!" He followed with an eye roll.

"Did you think you fooled her? You have all the classic signs of a wandering husband. You don't wear your wedding ring away from home, you sniff around other women's donuts, and you drive a Boxster. What is it, Chance? A mid-life crisis or a need to compensate."

"I like the car. It performs well."

"And you don't?"

"Do you want to find out?"

It was my turn for the eye roll.

"Do you have a picture of this woman I'm rumored to be married to?"

"I don't need her picture. I've got yours."

His eyes fell to the file on my lap and he snagged it before I could stop him. "Not a flattering photograph."

"Your wife must like it. She gave it to me."

He scrunched his lips. "Look at this picture, DeLucky. It's not something a wife would keep of her husband. It was taken on a street somewhere without my knowledge. Your client isn't my wife. She hired you to check me out."

I snatched the file back. "You flatter yourself, Chance Savino. Your wife filled this form out. She describes your height—six four. Weight—one ninety. Eye color—bro…"

I stopped short and closed my eyes. "Damn."

"I'm glad you noticed. Yours are the color of emeralds."

My skin felt hot and I drew in a breath. Chance Savino was everything I hated in a man. Unfaithful, a player, and God knows what else. But he was smoking hot.

"Blue, brown, what's the difference," I flashed back. "Your wife made a mistake. A woman forgets things when her husband does the horizontal hula with somebody else."

"*Ha!* You're hilarious. When do you meet her again?"

"Thursday at Marco's. It's Lady's Night. Two-for-one margaritas."

He pulled a bill from his wallet and my mouth dropped. I didn't know President Cleveland had his own money.

"This is a retainer. I don't know what this woman's game is but I want you to find out. She's probably a business competitor but don't take any chances. Don't let her know you're on to her."

My voice rose an octave. "I'm not on to her, I'm on to you. As far as I know, this could be Monopoly money."

He stepped from the car, leaned in the window and winked. "Wait here, DeLucky. I'll be right back."

Chance Savino moved like hot smoke. He sprinted toward the vacant building with the FOR LEASE sign. For a suspended moment my mouth gaped and my eyes fixed on his hard muscular ass.

"Wait!" I screamed and jostled the door open. A box of cold pizza fell to the floor. I hightailed it out of the car and dashed after him, yanking up the straps of my sling backs as Chance Savino disappeared inside the building.

"Hey, I'm not taking your money!" I chased after him at a dead run.

I was two steps from the door when the earth rocked and the building exploded. The sound was deafening. I flew out of my Dolce & Gabbana's and was hurled backward in a raging blast of glass and debris. Heat scorched my lungs and the words FOR LEASE whirled at my head. I gave way to darkness and the strange sensation of breaking into a thousand Monopoly pieces.

Chapter Two

I woke with the certain knowledge I'd been hit by a truck. My eyeballs throbbed when I pried them open and strained to focus on the man leaning over me. His face was obscured but I stared into unforgettable cobalt blue eyes visible beneath scrubs, cap, and mask.

"You're dead," I mouthed.

Relief flooded his face. "Wanna play doctor?"

My brain struggled to make sense. If Chance Savino was dead then… My eyes widened.

I glanced around the sterile room. It wasn't exactly what I had expected on the other side, but playing doctor with the hot Boxster guy sure wasn't hell either.

Savino's eyes crinkled at the edges. He laughed soft and low in his chest. "Go back to sleep, DeLucky. You're going to be fine."

"DeLuca," I mumbled and plunged back into dreams.

I was named Caterina after my paternal grandmother. She was a small Italian woman who scared the crap out of young children. People say I have her green eyes and chestnut hair but at five ten I'm a foot taller and I don't scare anyone. God knows I've tried.

The DeLuca men are Chicago cops: my dad, uncles, brothers, and cousins. Most are honest and hard working, but a few have deep pockets and drive Ferraris. Like my Uncle Joey. He knows people. I went to him once when a client's husband nearly beat her to death. He broke bones and caused permanent blindness in her left eye after she accused him of molesting their daughter. Amazingly the man had a change of heart. He apologized and bought an insanely huge life insurance policy. Later when they had found enough body parts, she cashed it in. There were other times I consulted with Joey but trust me, you don't want the details.

The DeLuca women have less interesting lives than the men. We're expected to marry early and breed more cops. If you ask me, the world has enough cops and Chicago has enough DeLucas.

I faded in and out of consciousness for a day. A host of divine white beings hovered around me and I smelled pasta. The next day, the jackhammer in my skull ran out of gas. My eyes focused and the sea of hovering faces lost their halos. I wasn't dead. These people weren't even close to heaven. They were my loud, obnoxious family. Papa, mama, three brothers, and one whacko crazy sister.

Mama clung to my hand. "What you have put us through, Caterina, you should be ashamed." She sobbed, pulling tissues out of her bra.

I was mildly surprised my mother wasn't serving up dinner. That's what she does. Food with a healthy side portion of guilt.

I squinted through the maze of faces. "Where did he go?" I asked groggily.

"Who?"

"The Boxster guy. He was here."

"Nobody's been here but your family and nurses. And the doctor."

"That was him, mama. He wanted me to play doctor with him."

My sister snickered. She doesn't like me much. She thinks our parents like me more. I think she was switched at birth.

"You played doctor when you were six with the neighbor boy," Mama announced. "That's not a nice dream for a good Catholic girl who should be married and having babies like her sister."

That would be crazy Sophie, the baby factory. As if on cue, an infant squawked and a swarm of nieces and nephews scaled the bed. Two fought over the remote and one swung from the IV pole. The jackhammer was back at full throttle and I closed my eyes. When I opened them again, I had two mothers. Double the pasta, double the guilt.

"I don't think I want kids," I muttered sullenly.

"Nurse," Mama shouted with a hint of hysteria. "My daughter has lost her mind!"

One of my sister's demon children pulled the plug from my oxygen and blew in the hose. I gasped.

"We eat!" Mama announced and the mass exodus gathered around the window. She opened two large grocery bags and there was a rush for paper plates. My meaty twin brothers, Vinnie and Michael, squeezed out the kids. They're always first in line.

Mama waved a spoon at me. "I was at Mass when the call came about somebody trying to kill you."

"Oxygen," I choked.

"You gave me no time to cook. I stopped at Tino's on my way over."

"Can't breathe over here."

"You take dirty pictures, you make people mad," Mama said. "Bad enough your father was struck down by hoodlums. I still have nightmares."

Three years ago, Papa was shot in the caboose by friendly fire but Mama tells it differently. Papa got a medal and early retirement. He's a bit of a Chicago legend but the rookie cop who nailed his ass is on permanent traffic duty. Papa is now the Chicago Police Department liaison for the local schools. He warns kids about drugs, lets them wear his hat, and he pulls his pants down just far enough to show off his scar.

Mama gripped her heart. "Bad enough I should worry about your brothers when the phone rings. You are not a cop, Miss Caterina."

"I'm not breathing, Mama."

"You're a snoop, a busybody. What people do is not your business."

I was saved by a knock at the door. "Someone call for a nurse?"

"I fix food for you." Mama piled the nurse's plate. "With extra meatballs."

The nurse removed the bouncing devil child from my chest and reconnected the oxygen. "Is that better?"

"Auuugh," I said.

Mama crossed herself. "A man died, Caterina. That's what comes from sticking your nose in other people's business. You should go to confession."

My voice sounded strangled. "Who died?"

My brother Rocco balanced a plate with one hand and pulled a scratch of paper out of his pocket. "The FBI ID'd the body. A guy named Chance Savino."

"It wasn't Chance," I said. "He was here."

"Playing doctor?" Rocco grinned. Rocco's the oldest and we're barely a year apart. He's probably my best friend.

I shuddered. "The body would've been badly burned by the fire. How could the FBI make an ID so quickly?"

"Hey, I'm just glad it wasn't you, sis." Rocco sat on the bed beside me. "I hate to agree with Mama on this but your work is too dangerous. I made some calls and I can get you a job in dispatch. Pay isn't great but people don't want to kill you either. You can start Monday."

"I have a job. Where's Inga?"

"She's at your house. Your neighbor's feeding her. Not that she's hungry. She was so scared by the explosion she ate a whole pizza."

"You should know better," my sister snapped. "Cheese plugs a dog like a cork."

The nurse took my vitals. "How are you feeling?"

"Caterina's crazy," Mama said. "She has foolish dreams."

"It's to be expected after a concussion."

"She's dreaming about dead people."

"He's not dead, Mama."

The nurse looked at my pupils. "I dream about Elvis and I don't even have a concussion." She gave me a quick wink and turned to Mama. "Your daughter will be fine, Mrs. DeLuca. She just needs to rest."

"I want to go home." I sat up in bed and Fourth of July fireworks exploded in my head. I collapsed on my pillow.

"The doctor is keeping you one more night, to be sure there are no complications from blunt trauma."

I started to protest and the nurse's hand shot up with a needle that could kill a horse.

Yowzie.

"I'm giving you something for pain. There's a nasty gash on your head. In a few days you'll be good as new."

Mama clapped her hands. "She can start dispatch on Monday."

My brother Rocco was a dead man.

The afternoon shadows outside my window had lengthened.

"What time is it?" I exaggerated a yawn.

"After five," Mama said.

Damn. I was supposed to meet Rita at Marco's in less than two hours.

I yawned again. "I should rest now. I'd like to sleep this headache off."

I feigned a soft snore. When the last toddler was dragged into the hallway I threw off my covers. I held my head, located the floor with my feet, and wobbled to the closet. My bloodied jacket, jeans, and tee shirt were stuffed in a clear plastic bag. No shoes in sight. My Dolce & Gabbana's must have been a casualty in the explosion. On the top shelf lay a brand new, fuzzy pink robe with matching bunny slippers and a card from Rocco and Maria. I instantly forgave my brother for the dispatch thing.

My battered cell phone and a crisp Cleveland nestled in my jacket pocket. I punched a number and on the third ring a bored, nasal voice answered.

"Yellow Cab."

I slipped into the hallway and darted for the elevator, fuzzy and pretty in pink.

"I'm at the hospital," I whispered, "and I need a ride."

Chapter Three

I live on the south side of Chicago, too close to my parents but not far from U.S. Cellular Field and the White Sox. Bridgeport is a closely knit blue collar community with a small town feel. It's where I grew up with three brothers and a sister. They're all married now and raise families close by. Chicago is two-hundred thirty-four square miles of nesting possibilities but Mama sucks us in like the Bermuda Triangle.

My house is a corner brownstone with a fenced yard and a garage in back. I got it at a steal. My Uncle Joey handled the negotiations. You have to wonder if there's a body in the basement. I didn't ask. I signed the papers and told Father Timothy to bring holy water in gallon jugs. He soaked the shit out of it.

I quit a promising career in the fast food industry and went to work for myself. Revamping the front bedroom into an office, I built a separate entrance for my clients. Got myself a P.I. license and launched Pants on Fire Detective Agency.

My silver Honda was parked in front when the taxi driver dropped me at my door. He gave me all his change and a huge grin in exchange for my Cleveland. I wrestled a spare key from a pot of geraniums and slipped it in the lock. Inga body slammed me at the door, knocking me off my feet and slurping my face with kisses. When I latched onto her collar, she pulled me up and dragged me to the kitchen.

I pushed the red button flashing on my answering machine. There were four frantic calls. One from the big mouth hospital police and three from Mama.

I shuffled to my bedroom, dropped my pink robe and hospital gown over my bunny slippers, and stepped into a shower. My arms and legs were bruised and scraped raw in places and the hot water stung my skin. I worked my fingers across my scalp, discovering a tender area the doctor had stitched, and kept it dry. My shoulder throbbed and my ribs ached when I breathed. I had survived my flight well. It was the crash landing that needed work.

I dressed quickly in a short black skirt and button-down white dress shirt, then cinched it with a scarf for a belt. I hid the bruises beneath black stockings and slipped into a short kitten heel, not wanting to test my balance. A fluff of my hair covered the gash in my head and an overdose of perfume scourged the stubborn scent of antiseptic. I raced Inga to the Silver Bullet and zipped across Bridgeport, applying mascara and Dr. Pepper Lip Smacker with one hand, jabbing my cell phone with the other.

I held my breath and hoped Papa would answer. Mama has a short fuse. She can be ruthless and withhold cannoli.

"Tony DeLuca."

I felt a rush of relief. "Papa, it's me. Tell Mama I'm fine and—"

"Is that Cat?" Mama wrestled the phone from Papa's hand. "Caterina DeLuca, where are you?"

I yawned loudly. "I couldn't sleep in the hospital. I need to be home."

"You're there now?"

I avoided a direct lie. "I'll rest better in my own bed. Call off the cops, I know you have them looking for me."

"Are you in bed now?"

"I haven't brushed my teeth yet or flossed."

"Cat, if you're at home I'm calling 911 right now. Because you aren't answering your phone and somebody stole your car. Are you dead in there?"

I considered my options.

"Listen to me, girl. You have a concussion. You're out of your mind. Tell me where you are and your father will bring you home."

I gave it up. "OK, mama, I'm working. I'm meeting a client before I go home. I didn't want you to worry."

"You don't have clients. You're a dispatcher now."

"I'm a Private Investigator with a promising career."

"You're a snoop with no insurance. You won't be so lucky next time someone bombs you."

"Nobody bombed me."

"This is how you treat your Mama? You're killing me, Caterina. I'm holding my chest. My heart feels funny. It's a murmur, maybe worse!"

"Your heart is fine, Mama. The doctor says it's gas."

"It's your dirty pictures and people blowing you up. You're breaking my heart."

"Call off Search and Rescue, Mama. I'll call you tomorrow." I hung up.

I pulled into a parking spot on the street a few doors down from Marco's. A green BMW coasted by and my antenna shot up. The car looked like one I noticed earlier on my ride home in the yellow cab. It's nothing, I told myself, and blew the red flags off. When you follow people for a living you get paranoid. It's a professional hazard.

My conversation with Mama jacked my headache up a notch and I needed a stiff drink. I told my sidekick to guard the car and followed the live music through Marco's doors at seven-oh-seven.

Rita Savino hadn't arrived yet and I didn't know if she'd show. I'd followed her cheater husband for three days and didn't catch a whiff of the other woman. I didn't have answers, but I had a few questions.

Like what did Chance tell her about the explosion? Who was he meeting that day? And why did the FBI say he was dead?

Something else was bothering me. I've caught cheaters who've sworn they don't know the cheatee in bed with them. But this was the first time a husband had pretended not to know his wife. What's that about?

I took a seat in the bar with a clear shot at the entrance. I remembered the day Rita Savino flounced through my office door. She was a thirty-something redhead with skin like silk and smoky eyes to die for smudged with tears-stained eye-liner blue. She carried forty more pounds than any woman wants and wore a Mickey Mouse watch and bell-bottom jeans clear down to the pennies in her loafers. You could pluck her like a plum from the sixties.

I'd handed Rita a box of tissues and she mopped her face.

"Chance Savino is a lying cheating bastard," she sniffed. "He smells like Red Door."

"Red Door?"

"It's a perfume." She twisted the blue tissue like it was his neck.

I lifted the waste basket and held it up until she pried the tissue from her hands. Then I took her hand and dragged her to the kitchen.

"You need coffee," I said.

"Do you have herbal tea?"

I tried not to stare. "I got Coke, wine, and cake."

Rita slumped onto a chair. "I'm good."

"The cake is gooey and chocolate," I said cutting myself a fat piece for my mid-morning snack. I poured one cup of coffee and sat at the table beside her.

"Your husband's a schmuck," I said. "What are your plans?"

"I'm leaving him. And I'm taking his balls with me."

Yikes. "You should really try the cake."

"Will you help me?"

I nodded.

More tears rolled down and bounced off her chin.

"What do you want me to do?"

"Follow Chance. Keep a journal of everywhere he goes and everyone he meets. Tell me everything about Miss Red Door. Who is she? Where do they meet? Is she hideously thin and gorgeous?"

I licked my fork. "I'll get you some nice 8 X 10 glossies to show the judge. They'll fatten your divorce settlement."

The plump, blue-streaked cheeks smiled. "Bring me the glossies and I'll buy the champagne."

A loud pop jerked me into the present. My waitress sucked the bubble gum back into her mouth. "Some jerk beat you up?"

She sported black spiked hair with fuschia tips and her pierced tongue did things to bubble gum I hadn't thought possible. I winced. Staring did nothing for my headache.

"Excuse me?"

"Your makeup ain't cuttin' it, sweetie. Somebody knocked you around."

"I lost a fight with a sidewalk."

"Leave him, honey. No man is worth it."

"It was a sign. It said FOR LEASE."

She lowered her voice. "I know someone. For a small fee the jerk won't bother you again."

"Thanks. But I have Uncle Joey."

She shrugged and smacked her gum. "What can I get you?"

"Something for pain."

"Aspirin or Tylenol?"

"Both. And a grande margarita to wash them down."

Two tacos and a second margarita later I figured my client had stiffed me.

I paid the tab and padded the tip, my contribution to the emerging art on my server's shoulder. The tattoo could be an exotic flower or a tiger eating small children. I didn't ask. With the tongue thing going I didn't want to encourage conversation.

I gathered my purse, vaguely aware of eyes boring into me. I jerked my head toward the door. A crowded party of diners waited for a table and behind them, head above the rest, cobalt blue eyes held mine. Catching my breath I bolted after him, pushing past staff and a sea of waiting customers. I dashed into the street but Chance Savino had disappeared like a mirage into the night.

"It was him." I clenched my fists and kicked a rock.

A voice argued in my head citing concussion, tequila, and the general insanity running rampant in my family.

"Maybe I'm losing my mind. Maybe I'm crazy like my sister." People were staring.

A cool April wind shot through me and I stumbled numbly to my car. Inga wagged her tail in the back. I slid behind the wheel and bleakly pondered the future. Nothing made sense. I finally gave up, started the engine, and headed home.

Four blocks from my house lights were on at Tino's Deli. Tino Maroni is a round bear of a man who gives candy to the neighborhood children. His capanota is unrivaled in Chicago and a reasonable woman would kill for his recipe for tiramisu. The deli is open odd, unpredictable hours. Sometimes late at night you hear voices in the back. Some speculate a high stakes, illegal card game. Others say he's a fence. Tino rolls in money like he won the lottery. I wonder about it sometimes, but it's not my business.

I rolled to a stop and Tino met me at the door. He grabbed my face in his hands and made a tsking sound. "Caterina! Back from the dead!"

I did a grimace. "You spoke to Mama."

He pulled me inside. "She told me everything. You took dirty pictures and the man tried to blow you up. The explosion made you goofy in the head. You escaped the hospital and now you're a dispatcher." His face broke into a wide grin. "Good you should come to me. Hospitals kill you with their food."

My head throbbed. The shot the nurse gave me had worn off. I needed another margarita.

"Almost everything Mama told you wasn't true. Nobody blew me up. It was a gas leak."

Tino shook his head and narrowed his eyes. "It was a professional hit. The Feds found plastic explosives."

I was stunned but I didn't doubt him. Tino knows what goes down in the neighborhood. Usually before the cops.

"What about the body they found?"

"They say his name was Savino. I didn't know him."

"It's not Chance Savino. He's the guy I was following. I've seen him twice—well at least once," I amended, "since the explosion."

Tino's face hardened. "This Savino won't hurt you again."

"He didn't plant the bomb. I'm sure of it. But even if he did it wasn't meant for me."

Tino studied my face for a measure of sanity. He was unconvinced. "Are you certain this Savino is still alive? You've had a concussion. Maybe you're…"

"Crazy?"

Tino smiled. "I'll look into it."

I stretched my arms around his generous belly and hugged him. "I stopped by to pick up some Sopressata and a treat for Inga. Something not too spicy."

"Ah." He made a clicking sound with his tongue. "I heard about the pizza."

I waited while he wrapped sausages and my eyes wandered outside. I stiffened.

"What is it?"

"I'm not sure. I think that green BMW has been following me since I left the hospital. It's probably just my imagination."

A shadow passed over Tino's eyes. "Wait here. I saved something for you in back."

He left and I heard the murmuring of voices. A moment later he returned with a bag stuffed with deli boxes.

"When your Mama called, I cooked a little something for the wake."

"Uh, thanks, Tino."

"I threw in a nice bottle of Chianti. Come, I'll walk you to your car."

Tino opened the car door and tossed a sausage to Inga before dropping the bag on the passenger seat. I slid a sideways glance across the street. Two bouncer type gorillas emerged from the shadows and pulled the driver out of the BMW. They shoved him against the door and worked him over with a series of one-two punches. My stalker groaned and dropped to his knees. Tino gave me a kiss on both cheeks, shut the door, and waved me cheerily away.

I arrived home exhausted and began peeling off my clothes at the door. I slipped into an oversized tee and brushed my teeth, skipped the floss, and sank into bed as the phone rang. I winced.

"Hey, Mama. I'll call you tomorrow."

The voice on the other end was strained. His breath came hard and heavy like he had run a marathon or just gotten the crap beat out of him.

"You're gonna pay," he sucked air. "There won't always be someone around to save you."

A chill cut through me and my mouth turned cotton. "What do you want?"

"Forget what you saw. If you're smart you'll stay out of this."

And I thought I was crazy. "What the hell are you talking about?"

"You heard me. Cross me and you won't see your next birthday."

I dropped the phone like a snake and ran through the house, checking the locks on my windows and doors. I positioned pepper spray and stun gun on my nightstand and stuffed a pistol under my pillow. Diving under the covers, I curled into a ball, and skirted a troubled sleep with every light in the house blazing.

Chapter Four

The DeLuca family isn't crazy about the FBI. Not since 1998 when the Bureau turned down my cousin Frankie because of mental instability.

"The feds are stupid," Mama says. "The DeLucas are too good for them."

Being nuts isn't frowned on so much by the Chicago Police Department. My cousin Frankie embarked on a promising career there. On Frankie's behalf I'll say he's less scary since discovering Prozac.

The commute was heavy the next morning when I merged onto the Dan Ryan. I didn't see my stalker but the hair rose on the back of my neck as if someone walked on my grave. He was behind me all right. I scratched my neck and let him be for the moment. I wanted to be first in line when the FBI opened their doors for business.

I skipped up the FBI steps, shimmied through the metal detector, and set off what sounded like a three-alarm fire. I clamped my hands over my ears and groaned. I forgot I was armed. I don't usually carry a weapon but my crazy stalker was creeping me out.

"Oops," I said.

The agent jumped me, wrestled my hands behind my back, and yanked the gun from my holster. I was still deciding who to scream at with my one phone call when my permit checked out. No one was more surprised than me. The gun came from

Joey who's not exactly a stickler for red tape. It's not that my uncle's gifts can't be legitimate. I'm just saying it's a crap shoot.

Everyone got to have a gun at the FBI but me. A stiff female agent with cold hands frisked me. She said she'd hold my weapon until I left. I gave her my business card for Pants on Fire Detective Agency. She eyeballed me frostily. That woman's pants hadn't seen a spark since George Sr. was President.

Special Agent Larry Harding kept me waiting an hour. I suspected he wanted me to know how important he was. I checked his mouth for donut crumbs and spotted a chocolate glaze.

I followed Harding's tall frame through the maze that led me to his office, a small box of a room with a tiny window obstructed by boxes stacked to the ceiling. I guessed they were cases he hadn't solved yet.

Agent Harding's glasses tended to slip down his flat nose and he peered at me over the lenses. His eyes formed dark narrow slits and his thick bristly hair was shaved close in a flattop. He wore a four-button slim-cut suit over his wiry frame and a maroon dress-for-success tie.

"Nice shoes," I said. "Gucci?"

He ignored the question and motioned to a chair. I sat down, crossed my legs, and rotated my sandals in little circles.

He glanced at a slip of paper in his hand. "I understand you have questions about the explosion in Bridgeport, Ms." he looked again. "DeLuca. How may I help you?"

"You can tell me what you're doing about it."

"Doing about…?"

"The bombing," I said.

He raised a brow. "Gas leak."

"I was told it was plastic explosives."

"It was a gas leak."

I digested this a moment. "And the person who died?"

He reached down opening his bottom drawer and pulled out a file. "A business man. We're guessing he was interested in the property. His name was Savino."

"It wasn't."

"Wasn't what?"

"It wasn't Chance Savino. He made it out safe. I've seen him."

Harding frowned. He glanced at the file again and ruffled through a stack of folders on his desk. He pulled one out, opened and shut it again quickly.

"You're *that* Caterina DeLuca," he said like he was seeing me for the first time. He cleared his throat. "You're mistaken about Savino. He wasn't as fortunate as you. However, I'm happy you survived the gas leak."

"Bomb."

He didn't look that happy.

Harding glanced at his watch. "So, if there's nothing else."

"There is. Why is the FBI interested in a gas leak?"

"We're not."

"Then how come you have two files. And why does somebody out there think I saw something."

The bushy brows darted. "Did you?"

I shrugged. "Someone thinks so. A man has followed me since I left the hospital. He threatened me to keep quiet."

"Would you recognize him in a line-up?"

"Yeah. He's the guy who had the crap beat out of him."

Harding opened the file and shuffled pages. He cleared his throat. "The identity of the body was confirmed through dental records."

"So fast?"

"We're the FBI. We made it top priority."

"I'd like to see the corpse."

"The family opted for cremation."

"That was convenient."

"Unfortunately he was well on his way."

My eyes shot to the file on his desk. "May I look at that?"

He snapped it shut. "Sorry. Classified."

"A gas leak is classified?" I rolled my eyes. "Is there *anything* in that file you can tell me?"

Harding peeked inside. "It says you suffered a concussion, escaped from the hospital, and..."

"Mama called you, didn't she?"

"You're experiencing psychotic episodes."

"What?"

"Apparently you see dead people."

I wanted to throw myself on his desk and rip the file from his hand. Being the only person in the building without a gun, I didn't like my odds.

Harding's eye twitched. "Good day, Ms. DeLucky. We're finished here."

"Aha!" I clapped triumphantly. "That's proof. You've seen Savino. He's the only one who calls me that."

Harding's mouth did a mean imitation of a gold fish. Nothing came out.

I hiked my shiny black DKNY bag up on my shoulder and headed to the door, turning back to smile.

"Next time you see Savino, tell him he owes me a cannoli."

◇◇◇

The green BMW wasn't in sight when I skipped down the FBI steps. In case he was watching I waved. Unless the guy's a total moron he would have changed cars by now. I decided to find out.

He did change cars but he was still a moron and no match for Special Agent in Charge Pants on Fire. I spotted the cream colored Lexus within four blocks, lost him in four more, and headed north on Lake Shore Drive to the address Rita gave me in Evanston.

The Savino house was a modern Tudor, white with blue trim and a red door. I parked in front and tried Rita's number one more time. She didn't answer. That never happens when the client pays in advance. I slathered on my Dr. Pepper Lip Smacker, fluffed my hair, and tromped to the door. Three days of newspapers littered the porch. I didn't bother with the bell. I used my lock picks to let myself in.

Plush white shag carpet. No blue tears here.

Creamy white couch. No wine, no pizza, no dog.

Silk flowering plants. No oxygen.

The room was picture perfect but something didn't smell right.

Not that I expect every house to smell like coffee, pasta, and a wet dog. This house reminded me of a Street of Dreams home. There wasn't a picture, magazine, or discarded piece of mail. No pantyhose hanging in the bathroom. No laundry basket by the washer. I couldn't come up with a stick of electric-blue eyeliner. The master bedroom drawer revealed a week's worth of men's socks, tees, and briefs. All starchy new and fresh from the package.

Two Armani suits hung in the closet. One brown, one black. A leather jacket, scattering of shirts, slacks, and tees. Bathroom toiletries were stuffed in a travel bag under the sink. A person who stayed here could be packed and gone in less than five minutes.

I dropped onto the side of the bed and smacked my forehead with the palm of a hand. I'd been duped. The house was a ruse, a sham. Rita Savino didn't live here. For that matter Chance didn't either.

My client had lied to me. She wasn't married to the smoking hot guy in the black Boxster. She wouldn't recognize his naked ass if I blew it up on an 8 X 10 glossy.

I whipped out my trusty fingerprint kit. All I needed was one good print of this guy. It was time to find out who he really was. I dusted every surface including the ice trays in the freezer. Nothing. The place was wiped clean, every trace of Chance Savino gone.

I stomped back to my car, pissed. My liar, liar client wouldn't return my calls. Chance Savino was playing dead. Even the FBI thought I was crazy. I opened the back door and tapped my foot on the grass. Inga jumped out and did her business on Savino's lawn. I felt a little better. We made a quick schlep around the block and returned to the car.

Holding the phone away from my ear, I punched in Rocco's number.

"Where the hell are you?" my brother hollered. "Have you lost your freakin' mind? Ditching the hospital with a concussion?"

"Hello to you too."

"Don't hello me. You've lost it, Cat! Totally lost it! You're gonna give me a god damn heart attack. And you know how crazy Mama gets."

"Are you done?"

Dead silence.

"Meet me at Mickey's," I said. "I'll buy lunch."

The way to calm any DeLuca is with food. I figured this was going to cost me big.

Located in downtown Bridgeport, Mickey's has been a cop hang-out as long as anyone can remember. The food is decent, the drinks are strong. If you like cops the company's good. I drop by when I need help on a case or wanna scoop out the rookies. The one thing I can't get at Mickey's is a date. The DeLuca men see to that.

Rocco was draining a beer when I passed through the swinging doors.

"You look like shit," my brother said.

"That's what I appreciate about this family. All the love and support." I snagged the menu.

I ordered the cheeseburger and fries and Rocco settled for the most expensive thing on the menu. A sixteen ounce rib-eye with all the fixings. He caught me up on Maria, the kids, and soccer. Rocco's the girls' coach and I go to as many games as my schedule will allow.

"Enough about me. How's your head?"

"Scrambled."

"There's a room for you at the hospital. They keep the really good drugs there."

I scrunched my mouth. "I need your help, Rocco."

"Name it."

"The FBI is staging a cover up. They're calling the bomb a gas leak."

"It *was* a gas leak."

I shook my head. "Plastics explosives."

"You're saying the FBI is lying."

"Through their shorts."

"Why would they do that?"

"Conspiracy."

"You do know you have a concussion, don't you?"

I made a face.

"Are you eating your fries?"

"Take them," I said. "A man was murdered in that explosion and it wasn't Chance Savino. I saw him at the hospital."

"Of course you did. Pass the ketchup."

"Now I have some creepy stalker guy tailing me."

"Where's the steak sauce?"

"He called me at home threatening me to keep my mouth shut."

"You really shouldn't be driving."

"He's all kinds of pissed cuz Tino's guys beat the crap out of him."

A fry fell from Rocco's mouth. "*Tino* saw this guy?"

"Of course he saw him. I stopped by on my way home."

Rocco pushed the plate away. "Where's this asshole now?"

"I shook him after I left the FBI."

"You went to the FBI?"

"Special Agent Larry Harding is an arrogant ass. So are you."

"Huh?"

"You didn't believe me until I told you Tino saw my stalker too."

"Tino doesn't have a concussion." Rocco threw the napkin on his plate. "OK. I'm on board."

I started over at the beginning. From the first tear Rita spilled in my office to the oddly sterile house in Evanston.

"What kind of man fakes his own life?" I demanded.

"I don't know, but you're not spending another night in that house alone. You're staying with Maria and me and that's final."

"I'm not afraid of the stalker guy," I said without conviction. "Inga will tear him to shreds."

Rocco gave me a raised eyebrow. "You're the only person on the planet who mistakes her for a guard dog."

"I won't tell her you said that."

I handed him a folded sheet of paper. "Trace these license plate numbers for me. And here's the address on the Evanston house. It would be interesting to know who owns it."

"It's too bad you didn't get a print on Savino."

"It's bizaare. Like he didn't touch any—" I sucked air.

Rocco smiled. "I know that look. Whach'u got?"

I shot a goofy grin. "I got Savino. He opened my passenger door."

Chapter Five

I had two more stops to make and I intended to drag them out as long as possible. The sun was in a westward dive and I dreaded going home.

My first destination was to a modern architectural masterpiece in the heart of downtown Chicago. Thirty stories masked by glass and steel where I tailed the black Boxster Monday morning. Savino's office was on the twelfth floor. I intended to charge up there and get some answers.

Monday I wasn't so lucky. The trick was getting past the two guards stationed in the lobby. The information desk featured a bleach-bottle blonde with a Betty Boop boob job. The elevator was defended by a steroid freak of a giant who missed his calling in the WWE wrestling ring.

I tried to bust through Monday without success. First I mixed with a group of office workers back from lunch. We crammed into the elevator and the freakish giant plucked me out like a whore in a church choir. Later that afternoon I tried stealing unnoticed up the staircase. Betty threw herself in front of me and her cohort hoisted me over his shoulder and planted me on the sidewalk.

Today I planned a more direct approach. I would ask for a pass.

I changed my clothes in the car. I had switched from blue jeans into a dress, pantyhose, and a pair of Jimmy Choo's. I now freshened my makeup and added cat eye frames and a candy apple wig.

I walked to the desk. "I'm here to see my husband," I announced.

"Name and company?" she bubbled.

"I'd rather go up and surprise him. Today is his birthday."

"You should've brought balloons. Everybody loves balloons." Betty picked up the phone.

"Name and company?"

I crossed my fingers behind my back. "Chance Savino, Open Passage, Inc."

She dropped the phone. "Chance Savino is your husband?"

"So?"

"First of all Chance wasn't married."

I narrowed my eyes. "Did you date my husband?"

"We had drinks. And second," her voice caught, "he's dead."

"So that's why he didn't come home last night."

She called to the person behind me. "Next!"

"Wait," I said. "This is so sudden. I don't know what to say."

"Don't say anything. Next."

"I'd like to go upstairs and clear out his office."

"You don't have a pass."

"You could give me one."

"I could."

"But…"

"I won't."

"I demand to speak to your Supervisor."

"Tucker," she screeched.

The Bulk barreled toward me and his nose twitched. He was picking up a scent.

"I know you."

"Do not."

"Do too."

He had me. I saw it in his eyes. He picked me up and threw me over his shoulder like a sack of potatoes and carried me out the door.

I smoothed my dress down and stomped back to my car. I ditched the wig and cat glasses and headed across town to my last stop. The Morgue. Somebody died in that explosion and it wasn't Chance Savino.

I was hoping someone could answer my questions. Like, how badly was the body burned? Where was it found? And did the coroner examine the corpse before the FBI whisked all its secrets away?

Business at the County Morgue is never slow. In my experience the people who work there aren't like the actors on TV. They're like the brainy sci-fi geeks in high school who can't dance unless the Star Trek theme is blasting.

I fixed a somber and grieved expression on my face before ringing the bell. It was after five and the door was locked. A kid about seventeen leaned against the rail and jammed to his IPOD. I knew he didn't work here. This boy could dance.

After a few minutes a man wearing a white polyester shirt and a greasy black comb-over opened the door. He reminded me of the nerd who sat next to me in Biology. The guy who threw himself over tests so I couldn't copy his answers.

"May I help you?"

I reasserted my stricken look. "My husband was brought here the other night after a terrible accident. I'd like to speak to someone who saw him."

"Who was your husband, ma'am?"

I blew my nose hard. "Chance Savino."

He sighed. "The man who died in the explosion?"

"The same," I sobbed.

He crossed his arms. "I didn't believe the first woman who said she was Chance Savino's wife and she was a hell of a lot better actress than you."

"I doubt that," I snapped holding up my fingers. "Three years, drama club."

He gave a little snort. "Take your questions up with the FBI. They warned us you people would come by."

"What people?"

He ignored me. "Your break is over, Billy."

"I got four minutes."

The door slammed and I turned to the kid. "You work here?"

"Community Service. Judge gave me forty hours in Hell."

"What for?"

"Reckless driving. Said I should see the stiffs that drive too fast." He shrugged. "You gotta die sometime."

"But not today." I found my keys. "Take it easy, Billy."

He grinned. "For the record, you're hotter than the first Mrs. Savino."

"You saw her?"

"Yeah, red hair. She wore it up like my English teacher. The blue makeup around her eyes was a little smeared. She was a better crier, I'll give her that."

He was describing my client. The Mrs. Savino wannabe.

"What did he tell her?"

"Same thing he told you. Take it up with the FBI like he doesn't know anything."

"Oh."

"He's lying."

"What does he know?" I prodded.

"It's like I told the first Mrs. Savino. They were talking about the guy but they didn't know I was listening."

"What did you hear?"

"They said he had a snake tattooed around his neck and the rattle was a tiny skull."

"Nasty. Anything else?"

"He wasn't all burned and he wasn't blown apart. The blast threw him out of the building."

Like me. I was so busy whining about my headache I hadn't thought about how lucky I was to survive the bomb. Mama was right. I should go to Confession for being a putz.

I sat beside Billy on the rail. "I was there when the bomb went off. It was so loud I thought it shattered my head. Maybe this guy didn't even know what hit him."

"He didn't."

"How can you be sure?"

"Dude had a bullet in his brain."

"Oh my god."

"Yeah, that's what I said." Billy grinned. "You know the first Mrs. Savino let me test drive her new Mazda."

"I'm guessing she has more insurance." I pulled a twenty from my wallet. "Take a cab."

Chapter Six

The creamy Lexus wasn't parked outside my door when I got home. I thought that was a good sign. Inga raced me to the kitchen. I walked to the fridge and pulled out the bag Tino had prepared for my wake.

I pulled out two plates from the cupboard.

"If you get farts you're banished to the guest room."

I set Inga's food on the kitchen floor and carried my dinner and a glass of wine into the living room, and settled on the couch. I scanned the channels for something to watch. There was too much drama, too much blood, too much my recent life.

I settled on a White Sox-Twins game and dozed off in the third inning. We were tied when I woke at the bottom of the eighth. I stumbled to the bathroom, peed, and brushed my teeth.

A low growl escaped Inga's throat and my fierce companion crouched low, hair raised on her back. My toothbrush fell in the sink. Was someone lurking in my closet?

Did I say lurking? I crouched after her, my Colgate mouth white and foamy. My gun was on the couch defending my wine, but I grabbed a towel rack and can of extra-hold sticky hair spray, determined to beat my stalker senseless and glue his eyes shut with John Freida. My heart pounded in my chest and I realized I wasn't breathing.

"Get 'im, Inga," I whispered. She skulked past the closet door and charged onto the bed. Gnawing her teeth into the quilt she snarled and shook her head fiercely.

I forced one foot in front of the other full with dread. "Leave it," I said. She dropped the quilt and the growl in her throat deepened. Something was in the bed and whatever it was the hairspray couldn't help. I took two deep breaths and flung the covers aside, exposing a bloody mass of guts and hair. The stench of death filled my nostrils and my head reeled. It was a filthy disgusting rodent, a giant rat sliced open from neck to tail, innards spilling on my sheets. The creep's final unforgivable gesture was made with the Tuscany silk scarf I bought in Italy last summer. It was tied to the rat's tail.

My knees went wobbly on me and I tasted vomit mixed with toothpaste. I shuddered. He had been here in my bedroom, going through my things. *Forget what you saw or you'll be sorry*, he told me last night on the phone. Well I was sorry, all right. Sorry I couldn't remember what it is I was supposed to forget. At least then I would know what the hell was going on.

I marched into my office, flipped the light switch, and groaned. I smelled his fat cigar. A Starburst candy wrapper had just missed the waste basket and Chance Savino's file had disappeared from my desk.

Heavy footsteps sounded on the porch and I heard a rattle of keys. I sucked in my breath. The door knob jiggled and a succession of keys twisted in the lock.

"Get him," Inga, I hissed. The beagle danced by the door and wagged her tail.

Some watch dog.

I ditched the hairspray and dove for the couch and my gun. My hand shook and I crept toward the door and leveled my gaze through the peephole. A rush of relief surged through me and my breath caught a sob. I threw the door open and fell on my brother Rocco.

"My god, sis, you're foaming at the mouth."

He pried my fingers from the gun and closed them around a bag of Chinese take out. I nodded wordlessly and pointed toward the bedroom. Rocco disappeared inside. He swore viciously, kicked something hard, and emerged with every stitch of bedding in his arms, rat buried deep in a bundle of linens. He delivered them to the garbage and I morphed into the mad cleaning woman, sterilizing any surface the intruder may have touched with Lysol. When I was finished I found Rocco in the kitchen and he pressed a drink in my hand.

"What are you doing here?" I said. "I thought you were that monster. I almost shot you."

"I was looking for the right key. I told you I wouldn't let you stay alone."

I took a deep breath and willed my hands to stop shaking.

"Besides I was glad to get away. Maria's sister's here from Jersey and they giggle like school girls. I don't remember you and Sophie being like that."

"We weren't. Sophie played with dolls and I climbed trees with you. There's a glitch in my girlie genes."

The screwdriver settled my nerves quickly, maybe because I'd drained most of the OJ at breakfast.

"I don't think you'll find a rat in the guest room," I said, "but I wouldn't crawl into bed with the lights off."

"Good tip but I'm taking the couch tonight. If that asshole comes back I'm nailing him."

I cracked a couple beers and nuked the take-out. Rocco ate like a great hunter just in from the kill. The squid on his plate looked like something I'd seen on my bed. I wished he'd ordered vegetarian.

"I ran the plates for you," Rocco said.

"Yeah?"

He paused to suck a chicken bone dry. My stomach lurched.

"The green BMW was a bust. Stolen plates." He tugged at a back pocket and came up with the paper I'd given him. "This is interesting. The Lexus and the black Boxster are licensed by two separate companies with offices in the same building."

"On Michigan Avenue."

He looked impressed.

"The place is a fortress. I stopped by twice and couldn't get past the front desk."

He wasn't impressed any more.

Rocco daubed barbequed pork in Chinese mustard and chomped it with his teeth.

"Jackson and I'll drop by tomorrow before our shift. Unofficially, of course."

Jackson is Rocco's partner. He's Samoan and built like a government machine. In a world of Fords and Chevys, few argue with a tank.

"Do you think that's wise?"

Savino's office was hell and gone from Bridgeport's 9th District. Rocco had no business flashing a badge downtown. Chicago cops are serious about the turf thing.

"No one will know we were there." Rocco dragged a notebook from his pocket and flipped a few pages. "The Lexus is registered to the Harbor Reach International Corporation. The business began in the midnineties. They deal in commodities."

"I think I have one of their commodities in my trash. What about the Boxster?"

Rocco read from his notes. "Licensed by an import export investment company. Owner C.J. Savino."

"Chance."

"Looks like Savino did extremely well until his untimely death three—"

"He did *not* die three days ago."

Rocco held up his hands. "Hey, I'm just reading this."

"Sorry. What happened when you ran the print off my passenger door?"

"I ran it three times but it locked me out. Savino's file is classified. Requires a level four security clearance."

"Talk to the captain."

"I'm not authorized to investigate this case. It belongs to the FBI. They tied our hands."

"And they aren't doing shit." I took a steadying breath. "Why is an investment company interested in me?"

"It's not you. It's what they think you saw before the explosion."

"I didn't see anything."

"Maybe not. If you did, it might come to you later. The events that occur just before an accident or head injury are often lost."

"Tell that to Ratman."

I poured myself another drinkr. "What about Savino's house."

"The plot thickens. The house was purchased in '87 by a J. Smithe. Funny thing, Smithe doesn't pay taxes."

"I'm guessing he's not a church."

"Smells like government. Probably Feds. These are people you don't want to antagonize."

"Too late."

"Harding is supposed to be a decent guy. How'd you piss him off?"

"I pissed off the whole department. I'm an equal opportunity pisser."

Rocco raked his fingers through his hair. "Do me a favor. At least think about taking the dispatch job Monday. The pay sucks but the health insurance is great."

"I already thought about it. If I took the job why would I need insurance? No one blows up a dispatcher."

Chapter Seven

I awoke early the next morning less sore and ready to kick ass. I studied myself in the mirror. The bruises were starting to fade. All in all, I looked more like myself again.

I had tossed much of the night trying to make sense of what I knew. That was the short list. The long list was what I didn't. The person who could fill in the blanks was somewhere in this city. What I knew about her was the shortest list of all. Her name wasn't Rita Savino.

The number my client gave me rang a disposable cell phone. Her clothes were unmemorable and penny loafers could be purchased anywhere. However, sometime in the night I remembered a crucial detail. The day Rita came to my office she dropped her keys on the floor. As I bent down to scoop them up for her, a shiny brass key chain caught my eye. It read *KIDS FIRST VOLUNTEER*. The Kids First Project is a popular Chicago based charity. I had a lead to track my client down.

I wiggled into jeans and a light cable knit sweater and slapped a red *SERVICE DOG IN TRAINING* vest on Inga. We're a team. She's my partner at the Agency. The vest doesn't improve her manners but it gets her through most doors.

I tapped a finger to my lips and we tiptoed past Rocco snoring on the couch. I snagged my keys off the counter and we sped across town in the Silver Bullet. We drove through Starbucks before pulling into the Kids First Project parking lot. A sign above the door read *CHANGING THE WORLD ONE CHILD AT A TIME.* I had no idea how many volunteers took on the world this early but I brought six Foo-Foo coffees and a box of Mama's cannoli.

A slightly stooped white haired man welcomed me in the lobby. The volunteer workshop was in the warehouse and he gave me directions. I offered him a coffee.

"Is that decaf?"

I shook my head and handed him one. "How about a cannoli?"

He scooped up a decadent pastry and grinned. "Don't tell the wife."

I zipped my lips. Without coffee and cannoli a person might live forever. But what was the point?

I followed a maze of twisting hallways past administrative offices and a vending snack room to the warehouse. Three early volunteers were at work preparing donations for distribution. They were sensible women and snatched my caffeine and cannoli like a lifeline.

The woman in charge had big, jet black, dyed hair and wore a pair of tortoiseshell glasses half way down her nose. Her name was Gloria. She explained the warehouse housed two charities. On one side was the Kids First Project, the other was its sister company, International Relief.

I flashed a smile. "I'd like to volunteer here sometime. I dropped by to check the place out."

"Stick around 'til eleven," a woman smiled. "One of our volunteers cleans tables at McDonald's. She'll bring a big bag of leftover Egg McMuffins."

McDonald's? Inga's ears perked and she pranced in a circle. She's such a food whore.

I served up another round of cannoli. "I met a woman in a coffee shop who volunteers here. She said it makes her feel good to help the kids and all."

"Oh it does," they agreed.

"She said the other women who volunteer here are—" I searched my memory—"*fabulous*! That's it! She said you're fabulous."

"We are," they laughed.

"Who is she?" Gloria asked.

"Who?"

"The woman you met."

I sighed regretfully. "I forgot her name. I was hoping she'd be here today. She left her scarf at the coffee shop. An Italian Tuscany silk." I recalled my own tied to a rat in the trash and forced a smile. "I'd like to return it to her."

"You can leave it here," someone suggested.

Gloria wagged a finger. "Honey, don't do it. It'll be boxed and shipped to Mexico."

"Well darn," I said all disappointed.

"What does this gal look like?"

"Um, let me see." I tapped my chin. "Dark hair"—

"It could be anyone."

"She's about my age."

"It could be us twenty years ago."

"She wears—what would you say—electric blue eyeliner."

"Rita Polansky!" The group cheered in unison.

I smiled. "Rita sounds right."

Gloria pulled a little black book from her purse. "I'll give you her address, if you like."

"I like."

I fairly skipped my way back through the maze and the old man eyed the cannoli box wistfully.

I handed it over. "The last one is yours."

At the door I paused and studied the pictures on the wall. There were more than a dozen. A fat bald man with the mayor at a homeless shelter, hamming it up with the good ol' boys at the Capital, cheering a Bulls game with the chief of police, shaking hands with Nelson Mandela.

"Who is that guy?"

"You mean Eddie Harr? He's my boss. Maybe the richest guy in Chicago."

I studied the pictures on the wall and wondered if this was the guy my client was investigating.

"Seems to be well connected."

The old man grunted. "Seems to."

Prying info from him was like pulling teeth.

"You're lucky to have such a great boss," I gushed. "I mean look at this charity. All the work he does with the poor. Eddie Harr must be a really decent guy."

The old man took the last cannoli from the box. "Couldn't say one way or the other, ma'am. I ain't never pissed him off."

◇◇◇

Rita Polansky's apartment was in a four-story brick building with a slam dunk view of the great Chicago El train. I took an archaic open cage elevator to the third floor and padded down a long threadbare carpet to the end of the hall. Apartment 302 served up burritos for breakfast. 305's door was riddled with bullet holes and double dead bolts. My client lived in 309. She'd laid out a welcome mat at her door. Rita Polansky was definitely not from Chicago.

I hung an ear to the door. Rita was at home all right—I could hear her moving about inside. I considered knocking, but only briefly. One peek through the peephole and my liar, liar client wouldn't open the door. I decided to piss Rita off and let myself in. The welcome mat convinced me she was too civilized to shoot. And she had told too many lies to call the cops.

I did my magic with her lock, scooted my butt inside 309, and closed the door behind me. Rita's world was a jolt back to the sixties. The orange lava lamp and wing-back olive green swivel chairs screamed retro like the electric blue eyeliner she wore. The home was tidy except for a few discarded Starburst candy wrappers twisted in bows. And there was one penny loafer with a lucky copper coin discarded on the hardwood floor.

I heard Rita in the bedroom opening and closing drawers. Getting dressed, I decided. I snooped around the corner to a gingham-checked kitchen. A slew of blue glass jars lined the counter filled with brewer's yeast, lecithin, and organic soy protein powder. Yuck. An assortment of herbs and vitamins spilled from an apple box on the table. I snooped around the cupboards for a snack and couldn't find a cookie or decadent chip. Apparently Rita Polansky was a plump health nut. It's a bitch to get fat on granola.

I trotted back to the living room and waited for her to come out. Plopping down on a swivel chair I spun around fast until something glittery caught my eye and I jerked to an abrupt stop. A shiny penny gleamed in the morning sun. It was fixed on the missing loafer and the luck was choked clean out of it. The foot beside the one in the loafer had lost its shoe. I followed the chubby white leg until it disappeared behind the couch.

I felt my heart sink down to my stomach. My breath came in short strangled gasps. With slow, careful steps I crept on gumby legs to peer behind the couch. Rita Polansky wasn't in the bedroom dolling up after all. Her unseeing eyes gawked back at me. A kitchen knife jutted from her chest.

Something clattered in the bedroom and I stared at the 9mm in my hand. How did that get there? I was alone with a psycho nutcase killer. I steadied the bobbling barrel with my free hand. I can do this, I pumped myself. The DeLuca blood runs through my veins. Chicago blood, cop blood. So maybe I don't have a license to kill or even to break into an apartment. Chicago cops are always good for a cover up.

The killer shuffled from the bedroom, his head down thumbing through my client's wallet. His eye caught my Sketchers and Levi's first. He froze.

"You!" I choked and the room spun a bit. I honed my gun on the hot guy with the black Boxster. He wore trousers, a dark green turtleneck, and a black leather jacket. Dammit, he was fine.

He recovered quickly. "DeLucky! What the *hell* are you doing here?"

"What am *I* doing here? I'm catching you in the act with your wife!"

"She's not my wife."

"Whatever she was to you she's dead. And you murdered her."

"She was dead when I got here."

"Liar, liar!" I waved the 9mm at the body.

Savino frowned. "Do you know how to use that thing? Put the gun away before it goes off."

"If it goes off it won't be an accident. You're going down, Savino."

"I never saw this woman until ten minutes ago. I arrived just before you."

"Save it for the cops. I caught you stealing money from her wallet."

He threw me a "you've got to be kidding" look. "I was checking her ID. I want to know her angle. I'm trying to figure out why she had me followed."

I juggled my purse, struggling to unzip it with one shaking hand.

He removed a license from her wallet. "Her name's Rita Polansky."

"Tell me something I don't know."

"I didn't kill her. Look at the body."

"I'm a little busy eyeing her killer." I moved craftily to the coffee table and rummaged through my bag. "Stay there, I'll have my phone out in a minute."

"Let me know if I can help. Here's her press card. Polansky's a reporter for the Chicago Tribune."

"Aha!" I opened the inside zipper with my teeth. "So that's why you killed her. She was onto you and your—"

"My what?"

"Whatever it is that makes a man fake his own death."

"You're the detective, DeLucky. Consider the evidence."

"I am."

"Her jewelry box is open and emptied. Her watch and rings are gone. The people who did this wanted it to look like a robbery."

"*Hah*!" I squeaked. "If Rita's jewelry's gone it's bulging from your pockets."

He grinned. "The bulge you see is not her jewels. Check my pockets if you wish."

I threw the purse away and mumbled. "Great, I left my phone in the car."

"For godsake I couldn't have done this, Cat. Her body's not even warm."

I waved my gun. "Drop to the floor with your hands behind your back." I made my way to the Mickey Mouse telephone next to the lava lamp.

Savino stretched out on the floor. I slid around him, my weapon trained on his back. In an instant he struck. His right hand seized my ankle, jerking me off balance. He yanked me down, tearing the gun from my hand. My head bounced hard on the hardwood floor.

"Ow!"

He sat on me. I sputtered and struggled to jolt him off.

"I don't want to hurt you, DeLucky. You're so damn hot-headed you won't listen."

"I wish I'd shot you," I lashed back at him.

He jerked me to my feet, pinned my arms, and dropped me in front of the body. "Look at her."

The pool of blood was dry around the edges and the stain on the knife looked black and crusty. Her body was a grayish blue, and her eyes vacant. Her mouth was slack and gaping. Rita Polansky had been dead at least ten hours. Okay, so Savino was telling the truth. Maybe he wasn't the murderer, at least not this time.

"OK. She's been dead a while. Maybe you came back again."

"Really? You're not serious?"

"Fine." I admitted grudgingly. "So you didn't kill her."

He threw out his arms. "Thank you."

"But her death is still on you. If Rita didn't care about your stupid secrets she wouldn't be dead now."

"And what secrets would those be?"

"I haven't figured that out yet." I pulled my eyes from his well defined chest. "But I will."

The dreamy cobalt blues smiled. "I'm sure you will. Just don't get yourself killed over it." He snatched two satin ropes from the velvet drapes, secured my ankles, and tied my wrists behind my back. When he was finished he leaned close, his breath tickling my ear.

"If I could trust you I wouldn't have to do this. The knot is loose enough. If you don't jerk it tight you'll free your hands in no time."

I twisted my bound wrists furiously. He moseyed to the door. "One more thing, DeLucky. You might want to stop trying to convince people I'm alive. They'll think you're nuts." He walked out letting the door swing shut behind him.

"Too late," I screamed.

I was free in five minutes and spent the next ten tossing Rita's apartment. Not that I expected to find anything. Both the killer and Savino had had their shot before I got there. I came up empty for anything that would explain her death, but I found letters and a photo album of her family. Rita was the middle of three daughters. She attended high school and college in Oregon and her parents and siblings still lived there. Their recent letters talked about her big story and hopes for a Pulitzer. I put her letters away and looked hard into the unseeing eyes outlined in electric blue.

"I won't let the people who did this get away," I promised.

I hated to admit it but Chance Savino was right. The killer wanted to stage the murder as a robbery gone wrong, but the ambitious reporter was killed to silence what she knew. Her watch and jewelry were taken away, but so was the one thing that could speak for her, the hard drive to her computer.

I wiped away my prints and slipped from the apartment unnoticed. I'd been doing this surveillance gig a long time and felt confident I wouldn't be remembered.

At a busy intersection I placed a call from a payphone.

"911. What is the nature of your emergency."

I disguised my voice with a really bad accent. "A voman eez dead in her apartment," I said spouting the address.

"What is your name, ma'am?"

"Ze Cleaning Voman."

Click.

I made my next call from a payphone a few blocks away.

"Chicago Tribune. How may I direct your call."

"You have a reporter by the name of Rita Polansky. I'd like to speak with her supervisor."

"One moment please."

"News desk. Stephanie Mills speaking." I could hear gum popping between syllables.

"This is the Detective Sasha Lewis from the Chicago Police Department. My call concerns one of your reporters, a Rita Polansky."

She popped a bubble. "Her supervisor is in a meeting. Is Rita in trouble?"

Not any more. "I'm sorry to inform you Ms. Polansky died last night in her apartment."

"*Really?* Omigod!"

"Really."

"She choked on granola, didn't she? I mean, the way she *wolfs* it down…"

"The cause of death is under investigation."

"I can't believe it," Stephanie sniffed. "She was such a health nut."

"Ms. Polansky's family arrived early this morning from Oregon. They'll gather her things and take her home for the funeral. Maybe you've met them?"

"No. She hasn't worked here that long. I can't believe she's gone, this really sucks."

"We'll have more answers in a few days."

"Thanks for calling. I didn't know the cops cared that much."

"Oh we care. Chicago cops are all heart."

Chapter Eight

I took Inga for a three mile run. I get a cloud of doom around dead people and when I lie a lot. I had to shake a double whammy.

When the run didn't help I drove through The Sugar Shack and ordered two coffees, a doggie treat for Inga, and a dozen gooey donuts. The coffee was still hot when I pulled into my driveway.

Balancing the drinks in my hands, I clenched the bag with my teeth, and bumped the car door with my booty. Rocco met me on the porch, arms folded, eyes narrowed to slits. "You shouldn't go out alone with that psycho—" he began, and his eyes lit on the donuts. He snatched the bag from my mouth.

"Sweet!"

Forgiven again. I followed my brother inside and kicked the door behind me. I removed the lids from the coffees and joined Rocco at the dining room table.

Rocco held up a sugary white finger. "Do you hear that?"

I listened. Nothing. "What?"

"Silence, Cat. Sweet uninterrupted silence. I read the entire newspaper for the first time since the kids were born."

The paper was scattered in a mess across the table.

"I see that." I shuffled it together in a pile and smacked him over the head with it. The DeLuca men are like Mama made them. Dependent, messy, and helpless in the kitchen.

Rocco stuffed an apple fritter in his mouth. "I'm eating my whole fritter. No squalling babies, no kids climbing on my lap."

I smiled. "You hate it."

"Give me a few days."

He dug deep in the donut bag. "Jelly filled," he gloated, still gnawing on his fritter.

I sank my teeth into a maple bar and melted inside.

"Where'd you run off to at the butt crack of dawn?"

I wiped the sugary glaze from his cheek. "I was looking for my client. The one who's not married to Chance Savino."

"The dead man?"

"The dead man who *isn't* dead."

"Right." He shot up a brow.

"It turns out Rita Savino is Rita Polansky, a reporter for the Trib."

"Did you talk to her?"

"Yep. I did all the talking."

"Why's that?"

"She's dead."

"Holy shit."

I told my brother everything except maybe the part where I was scared. Rocco sucked in air. "What is wrong with that head of yours? You could've been killed."

"I wasn't."

"You were tied up by a dead man. Give it up, Cat."

"No can do, bro. I made a promise and I'm keeping it." I didn't mention the promise was to a corpse. You don't want to go from crazy to committed before lunch.

"Let the cops handle it."

"I'm way ahead of the cops. Rita was working on a story. She got too close and they killed her."

"Who is they?"

"The bomb people. The rat people. Who knows how many people there are?"

"Back up. The explosion was a gas leak."

"Uh uh."

"The guy in the Lexus could be acting on his own."

"No way. Ratman was delivering a message. I'm a detective, Rocco, this is what I do."

"No. I'm a detective, you're a hootchie stalker. The only thing you investigate is who's doing who and how they're doin' it. This is murder. It's my gig. You're way over your head."

I stomped to the bathroom, grabbed my bag of make-up, and disappeared into my bedroom. I dug deep for something I hadn't touched since Halloween.

"You'd be a damn good dispatcher," my brother shouted through the door.

"Stuff it," I barked back.

I made my face and doused my scraped skin with Bactine. I slipped into black pantyhose and a clingy little black dress I bought last year for my great uncle's funeral. There was a crusty spot on the front of the dress and I spit washed it away with my finger. It was probably red wine or chocolate cake from the wake. Uncle Barney was a fat boozer.

"What's wrong with your eyes?" my brother said when I joined him. He was working on a lemon crème donut.

"Electric blue eyeliner. You like?"

"It's hideous. Where are you going?"

"To the Tribune. Maybe I'll learn something about the big story my client was working on."

"Take someone with you. I don't want you alone until we catch this asshole."

"I'm not alone. I have Inga."

My brother growled and I kissed his cheek. "Meet me later at Mickey's."

Inga and I made our way across town to the Tribune Tower, a neo-gothic skyscraper near the Michigan Avenue Bridge over the Chicago River. I glided through the doors and fixated on a suit exiting the elevators, his attention focused on a sheaf of papers. He looked important enough to get me upstairs and too busy to ask questions.

I blinked feverishly, recalling the day my childhood dog, Spooky, was hit by a car. Blue tears stung my eyes. Don't tell me I'm not a good crier.

I clacked across the stone floor and cut him off at the pass.

"Excuse me."

He nodded vaguely, his attention focused on his papers.

My voice caught. "I'm Amber. I'm looking for my sister's office."

This time he glanced up. He took a step back.

In my experience men are usually terrified if a woman cries, has PMS, or chases 'em with a hatchet. "Who's your sister?"

It was too painful to speak. I choked on the name. "Rita Polansky."

He shifted uncomfortably. "Sorry. I just heard."

He reached into his jacket and spoke into a pager. The elevator doors parted, and a woman in a gray tweed pant suit waved me inside. When I looked back again the suit was gone.

I read her tag. Her name was Alice.

"Where to?" she said.

"Rita Polansky's office."

"Everyone liked Rita," Alice said. She punched a button and the elevator jerked sharply, groaned, and a hard jolt shot us upward. When the door opened I breathed.

Alice took me to Rita's office and introduced me to Rita's friends. They were good criers too and hugged me tightly. They packed my sister's worldly possessions in a box for me to take home to Portland. There were organic chocolates, herbal teas, an autographed picture of Rita with President Obama, and an *Award for Integrity in Journalism* plaque.

"I can tell you're Rita's sister," a redhead gushed. "You got her eyes."

A woman with round glasses gnawed on a lip. Her voice was low and throaty.

"I had lunch with Rita last week. She was working on a big story."

"What story?"

She shrugged a shoulder. "But she said some people wouldn't like it."

"What people?"

"Dunno." She threw her hands up, then shook her head. "She was worried someone might want her laptop. She began leaving it at work. I guess it belongs to you now."

Laptop? Score!

Rita's friend pulled a bobby pin from her hair and patiently worked the lock on the desk.

I clenched my hands behind me. I wasn't sure Rita's sister from Oregon should know how to pick locks, and I resisted the temptation to throw her out of the way, snag the laptop, and run. Her patience paid off and she dropped Rita's laptop next to the box with the chocolates.

I looked at Rita's coworkers and a blue tear splashed on my chest.

"My sister loved you all." Sniff. Sniff. "Thanks for making her feel at home in Chicago." I seized the laptop in a vice grip.

"Don't forget the organic chocolates," the red head said.

I reached for the box of effects and a pair of elephantine hands pinned my shoulders.

"Not so fast, Cat."

You could've heard that bobby pin drop.

Busted. My eyes dropped to the floor and I turned around slowly. My eyes traveled up checkered polyester pants, white dress shirt, tummy over his belt like the home of the Whopper, and a red-blond beard. A serious honker sprouted nose hairs that screamed for a trim.

"Harry!" I gulped. "I can explain."

Harry Kaplan raised a bushy brow. He was one of my first clients. He had been convinced his wife was cheating on him. I wondered if he got the therapy I recommended.

"Cat?" A chorus of confused voices echoed. "She said her name was Amber."

I smiled weakly.

Harry slapped an expansive arm around my shoulder. "Cat is Amber's nickname. Rita introduced us last fall at the National Media Conference in Seattle."

"Hi, Cat," the redhead giggled.

Harry waved above his head. "Back to work everyone. We have a deadline."

I inched behind him, ready to bolt, but he snapped out an arm and snared me.

"Your sister's death was a terrible shock. There must be something I can do."

"There's not."

"Nonsense."

"I should go now and grieve."

"I've got tissue."

Harry dragged me in his office, slammed the door shut, and closed the Venetian blinds. First chair I saw, I grabbed, slipped out of my pumps, and propped my feet on his desk.

"Thanks for covering for me, ol' pal."

Harry sank into his overstuffed chair. "What the hell are you doing here?"

"I came for Rita's laptop. Don't try to stop me, Harry."

Harry snorted and glared at me over the rim of his glasses. "Stephanie called me out of a meeting. She said Rita choked on tofu."

"You can't choke on tofu. It's smooth as silk."

"Here's another funny thing. I called the Chicago Police Department. They never heard of a Detective Sasha Lewis."

"I can't believe that, Harry. It's a huge department."

"Not that huge. Maybe a dozen cops responded to the 911 call to Rita's apartment. No Sasha."

"That's odd." I pressed a hand to my throbbing temple.

"Nice name, though."

"Thanks."

Harry opened a drawer and pulled out two glasses and a flask. "Rita was a good kid, Cat. What the hell happened to her?"

I looked bleak. "She was dead when I found her in her apartment this morning. Stabbed in the chest."

"Did she…"

"It was quick, Harry. She didn't feel a thing." I didn't know if that was true but it felt good to say it.

"Thanks."

I offered Harry one of his tissues. "Now let's cut the crap, Harry. You told Polansky to hire me and I want to know why."

"I did not!" The bushy eyebrows shot up and down.

"You're lying, Harry."

"Damn the eyebrows." Harry's shoulders sagged. "Rita *might* have said she needed a detective. I might have mentioned your name."

"I've been blown up, threatened, chased all over town, and someone put a dead rat in my bed. Yes a *rat*!" My voice rose precariously. "With my Tuscany silk scarf around its tail."

"Sorry, Cat. I—"

"Maybe if you'd told me the truth from the beginning I could've helped and my sister wouldn't be dead now."

He looked at me over the rim of his glasses. "She's not really your sister you know."

I shot him a withering look.

Harry sat up, frowned. "It was Rita's idea to keep you in the dark. She said it would be too dangerous for you. It was better if you didn't get involved."

"Involved! Tell that to the rat in my trash."

Harry collapsed in his chair and covered his face with his hands. I hadn't seen him so distraught since he punched out the priest he accused of pursuing his wife. *She is too much woman for one man,* Harry lamented. *How can I fault her when every man desires her.*

Looking back, I still didn't get it. Harry's wife is a kind and generous woman with a face that screams Bow Wow.

When Harry hired me he explained that his wife had no desire for sex and must be having an affair. I followed the plain, exhausted woman for a while and finally just came out and asked her. She said she had four young children and didn't want to get pregnant again. I drove her to Planned Parenthood and took the kids for a long weekend. I also told Harry to help more at home, hire some Merry Maids, and see a shrink for beating up a priest.

"The story Rita was working on has been canned. It's over. Go home and forget it happened."

"I can't believe it."

"What?"

I stared at him hard. "Oh my god, they got to you."

His bushy eyebrow shot up and down. "Did not."

"Your reporter was murdered and you're letting them get away with it."

"I told Rita to back off but she wouldn't listen. I've got a wife and kids. Do you have any idea what they'd do to such a desirable woman?"

I started to respond but thought better of it. "Who got to you?"

"Maybe I got a phone call. So what? It's over, forgotten."

"I'm not forgetting, Harry."

The phone rang and Harry listened, grunted, and hung up.

"The cops are on their way up, Detective Lewis. You may want to slip out the back."

I leaned across his desk and kissed Harry's cheek. "I'm taking my sister's pictures, organic chocolate, and laptop with me."

Harry shrugged. "You'll never crack the code."

I opened the office door to a chorus of "good luck, sorry for your loss, Cat." I waved to my new friends.

"Watch your back," Harry said.

"Gotcha."

"And don't get yourself killed. I need you to take the kids for a long weekend this summer."

Chapter Nine

I knew Harry would buy me some time. But someone in Rita's office was certain to blab to the cops. I put my money on the big-mouthed red head. I hot footed to the service elevator, exited through a side door, and flung Rita's worldly possessions in the trunk. When this was over, I'd mail them to her family in Oregon.

I turned my wheels toward Bridgeport and wondered about the secrets that cost my client her life. I hoped she shared them with her laptop. Ratman thought I witnessed something before the fireworks. I've wracked my brain over and over to get nothing. The truth is my secrets aren't worth killing a rat over. But at least I know how to keep them.

One of my first cases involved a Senator's wife who became suspicious when she noticed charges on her husband's credit cards for lingerie she didn't receive. She hired me to find out who had. The conservative Senator courts the moral outrage vote and his wife wasn't about to let a second rate hootchie blow her chance at First Lady.

I closed the case in ten days and delivered the 8 X 10 glossies to my client. Not that he was good the first nine. The Senator was surrounded by an entourage of associates and I couldn't get close to him. The tenth day I slipped in his hotel room, scooted under his bed and waited. The Senator returned early and alone. He placed a call to his wife and left a brief impersonal voice mail for his secretary. Then he plunked on the foot of the bed and kicked off his shoes. His pants dropped to the floor and his briefs tumbled inches from my face. Then he stood, scratched his hairy butt, and sauntered to the bathroom.

He took a long steamy shower. The Senator knows the words to more musicals than a singing waiter off Broadway. I don't recall the songs he sang but "I'm Going to Wash that Man Right Out of My Hair" would have been a good choice, because a Senator stepped into the shower, but a hairy ho in pink satin lingerie shimmied back into the bedroom.

I don't know what the Senator's wife did with the pictures I gave her. She paid me well and sends other sensitive cases my way. I heard her husband heads a Congressional Committee on Family Values. The memory of his fat ass in lace cheers me to this day.

At a red light I glanced in a mirror and scared myself. Rita's big unseeing eyes stared back at me. I burned rubber to a corner Starbucks and scrubbed every trace of make-up from my face.

I bought Inga a biscotti and me a cinnamon dolce latte with extra whipped cream. Then I called Uncle Joey.

"Sweetheart. Your Mama said you lost your mind in the explosion."

"I'm fine. You know how she worries."

"Your Mama says you're a dispatcher now. She said they'll fire you if you don't show up to work."

My head pounded at the temples. "You know I'm a private investigator, Uncle Joey. I have a successful business."

My uncle chuckled. "That's right, Cat. You can always depend on people to cheat."

"What else did Mama say?"

"Father Timothy will be calling on you soon."

I groaned. "Of course he will."

"So what's on your mind, kid?"

"I'm hoping Joe Jr. will hack into a laptop for me. It involves a case I'm working on."

"About the explosion in Bridgeport?"

"I think so."

"Bring it over. Junior's leaving tomorrow for Cambridge. I'll put him on it right away."

"Thanks, Uncle Joey. Your boy's a genius."

"I think his Mama was screwin' the judge. The DeLuca men ain't that smart."

I laughed. "Tell Joe Jr. I'll pay him."

"Save your money. I'll take care of it. You can pick up your laptop tonight."

"Thanks."

I counted to ten before dialing Mama.

"Caterina, is that you?" Mama has caller ID but she doesn't trust the little box.

"It's me. I talked to Uncle Joey. You have to stop telling people I've lost my mind."

"What? I should lie for you?"

"I had a concussion, Mama. Not a lobotomy."

"Are you a dispatcher."

"Nope. I'm a snoop."

"You lost your mind. Come over tonight. I made cannoli for you."

"Cannoli?" I was fresh out.

"I made your favorite. Dipped in dark chocolate."

I weakened. "Well, I'm dropping by Uncle Joey's house later."

"Stop here first and I'll send some for Joey and the kids. Don't let your Aunt Linda eat one. She's too thin. She doesn't fool me. There's a fat Italian woman inside her and I won't have her throwing up my cannoli."

◇◇◇

Mickey's was packed and happy hour in full swing when I plowed through the door. I was met with a few wolf whistles and a hand slapped my behind. I spun around to a half-dozen goofy grins. Cops are cheezy like construction workers but with more dangerous tools in their belts.

I covered my ass and scuttled to Rocco's table, dodging servers with baskets of juicy burgers and fried chicken.

"You don't look so good," Rocco's partner said.

Jackson's toughly built frame wears the hell out of a tight fitting black turtleneck, and his chocolate eyes matched his jacket. My brother Rocco is no slouch, but his untamed hair has a mind of its own, and his eyes were tired like he slept on the couch.

I made a face and slung my purse on the back of the chair. "Did you eat?"

"We ordered," Rocco said. "You're having the special. Barbequed ribs."

"Good enough."

Rocco's radio blurbed static and a screechy voice spat out numbers and a street address. He groaned disparagingly. "That horrible voice took your dispatching job."

"With that great insurance, it'll screech forever."

The server brought three baskets of gooey ribs, fries, and a pile of extra napkins. I ordered a salad with a side of ranch and when the waiter returned with it I popped the question.

"So what happened at Savino's office? Did you make it past the lobby?"

"No problem," Rocco said. "I can't believe you let that guy carry you out of there."

"He *what?*" said Jackson.

"Never mind." I pointed to a glob of barbeque sauce on Rocco's tie.

"Damn." Rocco wet a napkin and smeared it around.

"What happened upstairs?"

"Savino's office is sweet," Jackson said. "Full bar, leather couches. Fancy appetizers in the fridge."

"You went in?"

"How else could we eat the cheese and crackers?"

"We scored with some eighteen-year-old Scotch," Jackson said.

"You *stole* his booze?"

"It's not like he can take it with him."

I looked at Jackson blankly. "What?"

"I mean now that he's gone."

I kicked my brother. "Didn't Rocco tell you? Savino isn't dead."

The partners exchanged glances.

"Right," Jackson said.

"You guys are so lame," I said.

Rocco grinned. "The office looks like any other office, until you look deeper. No address book, no appointment calendar. There's not a goddamn sticky note anywhere."

"No paper trail," I said.

Jackson licked his fingers. "There's a high-end computer but the hard drive's missing."

"OK." I whipped the air with a fry. "Here's the question. Did Savino clean house before or after the explosion? And did he plan to stage his own death?"

"You're scaring me," Jackson said.

"Concussion," Rocco mouthed.

"Should she be driving?" Jackson didn't bother to whisper.

I exaggerated an eyeroll. "What about the other office. My stalker had their Lexus."

Rocco removed the fry from my fingers. "It's called Harbor Reach International. Looks legit. The driver could be a nut case acting on his own."

"He's not that smart," I said.

Rocco chewed. "The rat gig is a no brainer. It just takes a strong stomach."

"And a twisted mind," Jackson said. He dragged a notebook from his pocket. "Harbor Reach International is an import-export business with interests around the world. They have a good public image. Their stocks are up—"

"Yada yada yada," I snapped. "What about blowing up buildings? They killed some poor Joe Blow—"

"Savino," Rocco mouthed.

"I saw that!"

"We got nothing shady on Harbor Reach or its owner." Jackson turned a page. "Name is Eddie Harr. He's loaded."

"Aha!" I gasped. "My client had something on Eddie Harr. Maybe something that got her killed."

"You can't prove that," Rocco said.

"Can too. I'm a detective."

Jackson choked on a laugh.

"If Rita had told me the truth, I could have saved her."

Jackson opened his mouth to say something and I shot him my full evil eye. He closed it again.

Rocco smeared more sauce around his plate. "Even *if* Eddie Harr is involved…"

"That's a huge *IF,*" Jackson said.

"Eddie's too big," Rocco said. "You can't take him down."

"I don't care how big you are. You ruin somebody's perfectly good Tuscany scarf, you gotta pay."

Jackson shook his head. "Is this about the scarf?"

"I loved that scarf."

"Geez, Cat."

"And also you can't kill people."

I jabbed the salad with my fork. Maybe they were right. Eddie Harr had an army of thugs along with a pocketful of politicians. I was out of my league here. Sure I was a detective but my cases were the stuff soaps are made of. My clients aren't supposed to be murdered. They're scorned lovers who have their panties in a bunch.

Rocco buried his face in his hands and shook his head.

I beamed a smile. "Maybe you're right and I can't bring Eddie Harr down. But I bet I can wipe the arrogant smirk off his face."

Chapter Ten

My parent's house in Bridgeport is much the same as it was when I was a kid with a few upgrades. The large oak tree with the rope swing has been replaced by a cedar swing set for the grandkids. Papa's new deck and Viking outdoor kitchen was the talk of the Moose Lodge for a week. The community hasn't changed all that much in thirty years. Mrs. Gigliotti is still the neighborhood gossip. She runs to Mama who spices it like a good Italian meatball and spreads it over the south side of Chicago.

There were way too many cars at my parents' house when I dropped by for cannoli. I wanted to make this fast, pick up the laptop at Joey's, and pop by Tino's Deli on my way home. With this kind of crowd, getting away might be trickier than I planned.

I scooted around the back and caught Mama in the kitchen. "You'll stay for supper," she beamed. "Father Timothy is here to see you."

Uh oh. "This isn't about my concussion, is it? Because when it comes to crazy, you and I are in a dead heat."

Mama sniffed, affronted. "Is it crazy to want to help my daughter when she talks to dead people?"

"The man isn't dead. I saw him again this morning."

Mama crossed herself.

"Ask Rocco."

Her face glimmered with hope. "Rocco saw this dead man?"

"Not exactly. But a man doesn't have to be dead just because the FBI says he is."

Mama squinted. "Who else was there when you saw this dead man?"

"You mean like a witness?"

"A witness would be good."

"His wife was there."

"Ah!"

"Or I should say the woman who wasn't his wife."

"You have a witness, Caterina. Saints be with us."

Yup. You know there's a priest in the DeLuca house when saints are called to supper.

I hedged. "Now that I think of it she may not be the ideal witness."

Mama's eyes narrowed to slits. "And why would that be Caterina?"

I sighed. "Mostly because she's dead, Mama."

"Dead?" Her voice was a hoarse whisper.

"Checked out, stabbed in the chest, off the planet dead."

"Father Timothy," Mama screamed. Her pitch reached a shattering level and just like that all the saints scattered.

The priest appeared and hauled me into the living room. I didn't want to go with him but it's hard to argue with a man who knows all my shit from the confessional. At least since I was fifteen and met Stanley Swank behind his Papa's store.

"Sit, Caterina. Please."

"No," I said, and sat. I looked around the room. Papa, Sophie, the twins, their wives, Uncle Joey, and a slew of running snot-nosed children added to the chaos. From across the street I could feel Mrs. Gigliotti's high powered binoculars piercing the window.

"My child, we're here tonight because your family is worried about you."

My head spun around. "*What?* I'm here for the cannoli."

"I understand you've suffered a recent concussion."

"Uh, I was feeling OK until now."

"Your family has seen some troubling changes in you."

"Cat talks to dead people," Sophie blabbed. "She's scaring the children."

Sophie's a big fat tattle tale. Her bratty children ran around my chair. "Auntie Cat's a witch!"

I went rigid. "What's going on?"

"Out of the mouth of babes," Sophie said.

Mama sniffed. "The explosion was awful. The building blew like a bomb."

"That's because it was a bomb."

"Cat's delusional," Sophie said. "It was a gas leak."

Mama yanked her hankie from her bra. "My little girl flew through the air and a slab of concrete crushed her head."

"It was a sign. It said FOR LEASE."

Mama wrung her hands. "And now my Caterina is crazy. She doesn't go to her dispatching job. She takes dirty pictures."

"Pornography?" Father Timothy gasped.

"It's a sickness," Sophie smiled.

The priest shook his head. "It's been too long, Caterina, since your last confession."

"Whoa," I held my hands up. "What's happening here?"

Papa gazed longingly at the door. "This is your Mama's Interfering."

"Intervention," Mama said.

"Holy crap," I said.

"I just came for the food," Uncle Joey said. "You know your Aunt Linda can't cook."

"No one cooks like Mama," the twins declared.

Their wives ground their teeth and Mama lit up like Christmas.

Father Timothy captured my hands. "Take the first step, my child. Acknowledge you have a problem."

I wrangled my hands back and looked around the room at my whacko family. I had a problem all right. It was too late to be adopted.

Mama tapped her fingertips to her temple. "Caterina forgets she has a job with benefits."

"She remembers enough to know she's not a dispatcher," Uncle Joey said.

Papa twisted around in his chair and tugged down his pants. "You see this scar? I was gunned down on the streets of Chicago."

"Papa is a hero," the twins breathed.

Mama made the sign of the cross. "There is a curse on the DeLuca family. My husband is shot on the street. A building falls on my little girl."

"It was a sign." I cradled my head.

"Sign of the Beast," Mama said.

"How many fingers do you see?" Sophie shouted.

I gave her my middle finger. "One."

The twins sniffed the air. "Meatballs," they said. "We should eat."

"Stuff a sock in it," their wives said.

"No one eats until Father Timothy fixes Caterina," Mama said.

The room hushed. Every head turned expectantly to the priest.

"Recovery is a process that takes both time and prayer."

The twins groaned.

"Caterina is dealing with several issues here. The concussion may account for her mental instability."

"Instability?" I said. "Will you look at this gene pool?"

"Apart from the concussion there uh, appears to be some uh, moral and spiritual issues as well."

"Pornography." Sophie's eyes gleamed.

Father Timothy stood and stretched to his full height. His eyes skimmed the door. He wasn't fooling me. He longed to split with the saints.

He raised his arms in a benediction. "Tonight you have helped Caterina take an important first step in recovery. You've given her love and support. She knows she will never be alone. Her family is with her always."

"Kill me now," I said.

Mama looked confused. "Is that it? Is she a dispatcher?"

Papa scratched his scar. "He fixed her."

I held my head and rocked.

"She looks good," Uncle Joey said.

"How do you feel?" Sophie shouted.

"Hungry!" the twins said.

Mama plucked a dinner bell from her bra. "It's a miracle!" she announced. "We eat!"

Everyone cheered. Mama beamed. Her first intervention was a success.

The twins made a beeline for the buffet and Mama splashed chianti and punch in frosted glasses. Sophie hunched over the buffet table piling a fat plate for the priest. She's such a kiss-ass.

Father Timothy searched my face. "I hope this was helpful, Caterina."

"It was…" I swallowed the stinky word on my tongue and started over. "I don't know what to say, Father."

"We'll talk at Confession," he smiled.

I managed a crooked smile back and escaped to the kitchen.

My chocolate dipped cannoli stood in the fridge beside Mama's Italian cream cake. I cut off a large chunk because it's faster and cheaper than therapy. Then I slipped out the back.

Inga and Joey were waiting at my car. I unlocked the door, dropped my booty on the seat, and threw my uncle a look.

"*What?*" he said all innocent. "I said you looked good."

"I was *ambushed*. You could've warned me."

"I intended to. Right after supper."

"Ugh!"

He laughed and swung Rita's laptop out from behind his back. "Joey Jr. cracked the code."

I grabbed the computer and hugged it against my chest before propping it on the seat. Then I lifted the fat chunk of Italian cream cake to Uncle Joey's face. He breathed in the wonderful coconut and pecans and his eyes glazed over.

"For you." I kissed his cheek. "I have Rita's laptop now. Therapy isn't so urgent."

He looked perfectly happy.

"What did Junior say about the laptop."

"He said it was almost too easy. Call him if you run into problems. He's flying out tonight to Cambridge. He wants to check out some university."

"That would be Harvard."

"Whatever. Junior doesn't need a fancy education to be a good cop. It's in his blood."

"It's in *your* blood."

"Damn straight. My grandfather, Agostino DeLuca, worked the Valentine's Day Massacre."

"Wasn't he a bootlegger during the prohibition?"

Joey smiled. "He and Scarface did a little business during the prohibition. My grandfather was a good cop. I never wanted to be anything else."

I regarded Uncle Joey silently and spoke the unthinkable words gently. "Did you ever consider that maybe Joey Jr. doesn't want to be a cop."

Uncle Joey laughed. "Right. What else would he do?"

◇◇◇

As planned, I dropped by the deli for pizza and beer on my way home. Tino chuckled when I cruised through the door.

"How'd the intervention go?"

I made a face. "*Et tu*, Tino?"

He grinned. "It could be worse. Sophie wanted an exorcism."

"Of course she did." I followed Tino back to the kitchen. "Mama had a great time and Father Timothy thinks I'm addicted to pornography."

"It's not a sin to take dirty pictures if you don't enjoy them."

"Tell that to Father Timothy."

"Why listen to me?" he laughed. "I'm the sinner that enjoys them."

Tino popped a couple of pizzas in the oven and carried a bottle of wine and two glasses to a small table by the window.

"How's your head?"

"It's better the nights I don't attend an intervention."

"I hear you've been making trouble for the Feds."

"*Me?*"

"Sniffing around, saying Savino's not dead."

"He's not dead. I saw him this morning."

"Where?"

"At my client's apartment."

"Your dead client?"

I didn't blink. Tino knows everything. "What else did you hear?"

Tino leaned slightly forward. "Your client went after some very nasty people."

"She had a big story."

"It didn't work out so well for her."

"They didn't have to waste her." I swallowed hard. "They could have scared her off, put a carcass in her bed."

"Whoever it is, they—"

I cut him off. "They polished her off because her life wasn't worth a dead rat to them. Her cousin's not a D.A. and the Polansky men aren't Chicago cops."

Tino shrugged. "Just remember, choose your enemies carefully. These guys have deep pockets. Plenty of cops and politicians are in them."

"I'm getting that message."

Tino topped our glasses. "By the way, I asked around about Eddie Harr. Seems he fought his way out of the Projects. He made some dirty friends on the way up."

"How dirty?"

"The usual. Prostitution, drugs, guns, murder for hire. Eddie Harr owes these guys big time. The word on the street is they won't let him forget it."

"Anything else?"

"The Feds think they have a leak."

"Really?"

"That's all I heard, though. No details."

"Thanks, Tino."

"You're a damn good detective, Cat. Don't make the same stupid mistake that reporter did."

"What mistake is that?"

"She didn't shoot first."

The bell jangled. A customer walked through the door.

"Back to work," Tino said.

He boxed my pizzas and stuffed more sausages in a bag for Inga. Soon she'd look like one.

"I know someone who'll stay with you a few days," he said. "If it doesn't work out with Rocco let me know."

"I'm fine."

"Wait." He scooped a fistful of chocolates and tossed them in my bag. "Life is uncertain…" He gave a crooked smile but his eyes were troubled.

"…always eat dessert first," I said.

◇◇◇

Rocco met me at the door. He grabbed the pizzas from my hands.

"Thanks for coming to my intervention!" I said sarcastically. "You could've defended me from Mama!"

"Like that's gonna happen," he grinned.

"Coward."

I grabbed two beers, a fistful of napkins, and followed Rocco to the living room.

"How did it go?" Rocco said as he sank his teeth into a fat slice of pepperoni and gooey cheese.

"Father Timothy is convinced I'm a pervert," I said. "He thinks I lost my good sense in the explosion."

"That's ridiculous," Rocco countered with his mouth full. "You've never had good sense."

"Exactly!"

Rocco's cell beeped. He nodded at his shirt pocket. "Get it, sis. My hands are greasy."

I threw a napkin at him, pulled the phone out, and put it on speaker.

"Hey."

"Rocco. It's Captain Maxfield."

My brother swallowed quickly. "Yes, Captain."

"I just got a strange call from Special Agent Harding of the FBI. Know him?"

Rocco gave me a sharp look. I scrunched my face.

"No, sir," he said.

"He was calling about you."

"Me?"

"He said you ran a background check on a Chance Savino."

"I did."

"Who the hell is he?"

"Savino's the guy the Feds ID'ed from Tuesday's explosion."

"So he's dead."

"Yes."

I kicked Rocco and shook my head.

"Harding claims you're compromising an FBI investigation," the captain said.

"They're investigating a dead man?"

"He wanted me to give you a message."

"What's the message?"

"Stop."

"That's it?"

"There was more. I cleaned it up for you."

"Is the order coming from you?"

He snorted. "Harding's an asshole. Be discreet, DeLuca. The department doesn't need the grief."

"Yes, sir."

Click.

I tucked the phone back in Rocco's pocket. "That went well."

Rocco raked a hand through his hair. "Damn, girl. The FBI is like the IRS. You don't want those people knowing your name."

"Larry Harding can bite me." I took a bite and chewed thoughtfully. "Why do you suppose the FBI is protecting Savino?"

"They're not. Savino's dead and the FBI is handling the case."

"There's more. The FBI is faking Savino's death. I'm thinking he's a snitch. A total scumbag ratting on his scumbag friends."

Rocco tapped his head. "I'm thinking concussion. Feds are jerks. They turned down Frankie, you know."

"I know."

Suddenly I wasn't hungry anymore. I tossed my slice of pizza back in the box.

"You done?" Rocco said.

"Put a fork in me." I hiked Rita's laptop under my arm.

Rocco waved his pizza. "Sweet dreams."

I carted Rita's laptop off to bed. "This baby sleeps between Inga and me."

Chapter Eleven

My brother is one of those annoying people who wakes up way too happy. I'd spent thirty minutes glaring into my coffee cup when he skidded across the kitchen floor in his socks. He poured a cup and sat down beside me at the table.

"Mornin' sis. Why so glum?"

"Gee, Rocco, I wonder. I have a crazy stalker, everyone thinks I've gone loony, I'm almost thirty, and I'm living like a nun."

"Whoa. The nun part? Too much info."

"You can cancel my birthday party," I said. "Say I see dead people. My family's scheduling an exorcism."

"Everyone knows that already. Why do you think they're coming to the party?"

I dumped a spoon of sugar in my cup. "Can't blame a girl for trying."

"Got a plan B?"

"O yeah. I need a smoking hot dress and a pair of Ferragamo pumps."

"You are such a girl."

"Thanks. I'll take that as a compliment." I paused to sip my coffee. "One more thing, I need a man."

"Huh?"

"I can't go to my party alone, Rocco. I'm looking for a guy who's clean, who'll start the evening sober, and doesn't consider public transit his home."

"No wonder you're in a dating slump. Your standards are too freakin' high."

Rocco kicked back his chair, skidded to the back door, and stepped into his shoes.

"I'll grab breakfast with the family before I head to the precinct."

"Tough guy," I smiled. "You miss the kids. I knew you'd buckle."

I locked the door behind him, topped my coffee, and lugged Rita's laptop to the office. I booted her up and held my breath until the screen lit up. Joey Jr. had worked his magic. I was in Rita's world.

I clicked onto her Hotmail. She had a boyfriend named Sam in Oregon. He was a social worker for child protective services and a vegetarian. He wrote sappy poetry that could crack the bolt off a chastity belt.

A note to Sam written two days before the explosion read: *I met with FBI guy today. Rattler wants out. Will testify in exchange for witness protection. Something's gotta blow soon. Miss you, R*

Reply: *Don't get caught in the fireworks. Love, Sam*

Rita's last note to Sam ended with: *Duped. Rattler needs out. Will explain tonight. Love you more, R*

Rita probably didn't have that conversation.

I blinked and called up her recent Documents. The list of stories was ambitious and the names gave nothing away. "Yogi" was a piece about National Park funding. "Wesson's Disgrace" was an oil company scandal.

Rita Polansky was hilarious.

My next click of the mouse hit pay dirt. My client marked the document "Forever." As in *Diamonds Are.*

I rang up Rocco. "About six months ago Rita was at O'Hare doing a story on airport security. Customs stopped a man coming in from Australia."

"Your dead man?"

"Chance Savino. He had a stash of diamonds in his pocket. Bunched in a black pouch. The agents shuffled him to a back room and Rita hung around for the story."

"And?"

"They let him go. The official version was a misunderstanding. But Rita schmoozed an agent and off the record, Savino walked. With the diamonds."

"Who gave the order?"

"The agent said it came from 'high up.'"

"Like that narrows it down. What did Polansky know about Savino?"

I searched the screen. "He did eight years in the Navy with the Seals."

"He wasn't a wimp."

"He's a thief."

"And?"

"He's rolling in the money. Rita has tax records and credit card statements. He travels frequently to Australia and cave dives all over the world. Oh, and he golfs once a week with a congressman."

"Where does Eddie Harr fit in?"

I scrolled down the page. "Rita stumbled on Eddie when she checked out some business associates. He's an American success story. Parents were immigrants, came with the clothes on their backs. I'll catch you up on the rest tonight."

I disconnected and continued reading. Eddie's financial assets were outlined with his business interests in Japan, Australia, and South America. Extensive charity work, political and social connections were well documented. There was nothing to link Eddie to any crime syndicate.

The bulk of Rita's research focused on Eddie Harr. My gut told me Rita had something big on him but I wasn't finding it. One of Rita's co-workers said she feared her laptop would be stolen. Maybe the FOREVER document was a red herring. A safety net. In the wrong hands it wouldn't convict her.

If I was right the real story was buried somewhere else in the computer's memory. Harry said I wouldn't crack the code. Maybe he wasn't talking about her first password. Harry doesn't know my cousin Joey Jr.

I followed my rumbling stomach to the kitchen and reviewed what I knew. One. Ratman had been on me since I left the hospital. Two. Rita Polansky believed Eddie was dirty. Ergo, Ratman works for Eddie. Dead people make a convincing argument.

I foraged the cold pizza and a coke from the fridge and plopped down at the table. Rita's secret would have to keep a few more days. Joey Jr. was away looking at schools.

I didn't have a clue how to find Chance Savino but he'd probably show up soon enough. When he did I would scream for a witness.

Eddie Harr was a different story. Finding him was a cakewalk. His residence, businesses, clubs, and hangouts were listed on Rita's laptop.

I finished off the pizza and made a plan. I needed a different car, one my stalker wouldn't recognize. I gave my mechanic a call. My Honda could use a tune-up.

Jack and I go back to my first car when I was sixteen. Grandpa gave me his '70 Cougar and Jack put flames on it. He's kept my cars purring ever since. His shop is always busy and at his prices he could be the richest guy in Bridgeport.

I dressed quickly and was finishing the last touches of mascara when Jack showed up dangling car keys. His grease-stained hands are short a few fingers. He lost them in engines years ago before he quit drinking.

Jack's nephew waited in front of the house. We went to high school together and he did graduate work in Joliet prison. Devin revved his engine and I waved.

A blue '67 Mustang glistened in my driveway.

"Sweet."

I reached for the keys. Jack jerked his hand back.

"My loaners are out. I'm trusting you with Dorothy. She was my dad's car before he…"

"What?"

Jack pointed up.

My eyes followed his short nubs to the heavens.

"No worries." I snatched the keys from his hand. "Dorothy's not going to join him."

Jack waggled a nub. "Not one scratch, Cat DeLuca. Dorothy is a family heirloom, and I've given her some extras. Only one lady my dad loved more. Olivia."

"Olivia?"

"A 1953 Bel Air Convertible. My dad lost her in a game of poker. The guy put her in his garage and never let my dad buy her back. It almost broke him."

"Okay, Jack. Geez. Not one scratch."

"Anything besides a tune up?"

"There was a pizza incident. My car could use a good detailing. Inga sheds and slobbers on the windows."

"That beast doesn't ride in Dorothy."

I ruffled Inga's hair. "You can't come today, girl. Our mechanic is evil."

Jack grunted. "Evil? Wait 'til you get my bill."

I tossed Jack my keys and waved goodbye to Devin. Five minutes later I was on the road headed for Eddie Harr's good-times neighborhood. He lived there with his third wife. I saw her picture on Rita's laptop. She was a silicon-stuffed Barbie with fish lips and way too young for an aging fat and bald guy. I hoped she was old enough to vote.

Eddie's street was fortified with stone walls and iron gates. I parked Dorothy across the street and waited for the first cop to cruise by and shoo me along.

A floral delivery truck pulled to the gate and I buried my face in a map. The driver spoke into the speaker and the gates magically opened. He drove in and exited a few minutes later.

Ten minutes later a carrot orange car with a glasspack muffler and two wide white stripes rumbled to Harr's gate. The driver leaned out the window and the morning sun shone on his recently battered face. I cheered. It was Ratman and the '69 Dodge Charger he drove was likely his own.

I shot a few pictures and jotted down the license plate. I tied my hair in a loose knot, grabbed a White Sox cap, and jogged across the street. Ran the long perimeter of the Harrs' marble wall, stopping to stretch at the edge of the iron gate. My jeans, sweater, and sandals weren't exactly running fare but I stretched my quads and threw in a few lunges. Ratman stepped from the car and sauntered to the door.

A beefy butler jerked the door open and shoved a brown cardboard box with bright yellow tape in Ratman's arms. Ratman carried the package to the trunk of his car. I raced back to Dorothy and scrunched low and out of sight when the Charger exited the gate.

I let a few cars pass before easing away from the curb into the traffic behind Ratman. He was the best lead I had and I wasn't about to lose him.

I called Rocco. "Hey, I need you to run a license plate for me."

"Dammit. Is someone outside watching your house?"

"I don't know. I'm not at home."

His voice was wary. "Where are you?"

"Hmm. I'm not seeing a street sign."

"Tell me you're not alone."

"OK. I'm not alone." I slathered Dr Pepper Lip Smacker on my mouth.

"All right then. Who's the guy? One of your sleazy cheaters?"

"The sleaziest."

"You could be dispatching," he grumbled.

"And living in your garage."

"Yeh, yeh. At least you're working again. Gimme the license."

I read the numbers from my notebook and waited. A few minutes later Rocco called me back. Ratman had a name. It was Charles Ross.

Charlie cruised across town to Eddie Harr's Kids First Project. He pulled around the side of the building and parked with a few scattered cars. It was Sunday and the lights were off in the lobby. I drove past the warehouse, made a Uey, and parked Dorothy in a lot across the street.

Charlie lugged the box with the yellow tape from the trunk and entered the warehouse through a side entrance. I grabbed my camera and flew across the street, darting wildly across the long open lot to the orange Charger with wide white stripes.

My heart pounded in my chest and I pressed my face to the window. A missed French fry and a dozen Starburst wrappers littered the floor. Each twisted in a bow. Like the ones I found in Rita's apartment.

He was there. A sickening knot twisted my gut. Ratman killed my client. I gauged the length of the parking lot. It was a long terrifying run to Dorothy.

The side door shot open and I sprinted for cover. Hugging the front of the building I dived for the shrubs bordering the front entrance. I caught my breath and parted some branches with my fingers. Charlie leaned against his car and lit a cigarette. He lobbed the smokes and lighter to a pencil thin dude with a goatee.

"Mitch, this is a genuine reproduction of the General Lee."

"Yeah? When you gonna sell me this real fake?"

"When you gonna shave that ferret off your face?"

"I ain't."

"Well I ain't sellin' either."

"Betchu I can jump through the window like the Duke boys," Goatee said.

"Betchu won't."

They smoked cigarettes and swapped lies about women. Charlie liked big boobs and Mitch went for tight booty. Tits and Ass. Right. Like those guys saw much of either.

I crouched low behind the flowering bush and my legs went numb. A spider crawled down my back and the 9mm in my jeans poked at my skin. I glared through the brush debating whether to shoot them both.

Charlie took a last hard drag of his cigarette and flicked the butt away. He ducked into the Charger, and the bright white stripes bounced over the railroad track and disappeared down the road. Mitch finished his smoke and ambled back toward the warehouse. I jumped to my feet and shook away the spiders.

Yuckos! I waggled the pins and needles from my legs. Swinging the camera around my neck, I plucked my phone from my back pocket.

"Is that you, Cat?"

"It's me."

Mama giggled. "The phone's been ringing off the hook all morning. Everybody enjoyed your little party last night."

I choked.

"It's too bad you left the party so early. Your track teacher stopped by—"

I gasped. "Mr. Berring?"

"And your friend Sherry—"

"That bitch slept with my husband."

"Who didn't, dear? I'm sure she's sorry now that you're unstable."

"Geez, Mama."

"That's what Father Timothy said. Hmm. Someone else stopped by. I can't remember who."

"Please don't. I need you to pick up Inga for me. I might be working late tonight."

"Your voice sounds funny, dear."

"That's because my teeth are clenched."

"That's it. It was Dr. Gambetti."

I cradled my head. "You invited my dentist?"

"You should call him if your teeth are sticking together."

"Rurrrrrr—"

"Don't worry about Inga. She'll—Ooh, someone's ringing in, dear." She giggled. "It's Father Timothy."

Click.

Chapter Twelve

I slipped my lock pick in the door. The lock was trickier than most but so am I. A dozen photographs of Eddie Harr's fat face greeted me.

I followed a trajectory of night lights down the darkened corridor to two doors at the end of the hall. The room to the left was the workroom where I had schmoozed the volunteers with mama's cannoli. A second door straight ahead led into the warehouse. I made out voices and a forklift from the other side. The workroom opened with a twist of the wrist. I slipped inside and closed the door behind me.

At once the forklift zoomed louder and the voices lost their muffle. I froze. The large bay door, closed tight the other day, was wide open. The forklift driver charged past and heavy footsteps stomped toward me. I hit the floor and wriggled to safety behind a stack of brown cardboard boxes.

A whistle. "Damn the boss' wife is smokin' hot." It was Mitch's voice. "I thought she was the boss' daughter, ya know?"

An older voice barked. "Put Mrs. Harr's package in that pile over there. They'll be sorted through later."

I sucked my breath and shuffled into a small ball. If Mitch caught me I intended to have a heart attack.

"I can't figure why a sexy dame like—"

"People got reasons."

Mitch howled. "And Mrs. Harr's got millions of them."

The older man stopped him cold. "When you work for Eddie Harr you mind your own business and keep your mouth shut."

"I didn't mean…"

"And dammit, don't shake the package."

"I wasn't—"

Smack.

"Geez, Pop. Why'd ya go and hit me."

"Gimme that. Don't make me sorry I got you this job."

I poked my head from behind the boxes. The old man jerked the package from Goatee's hands, plopped it a few feet from me, and stomped away.

Goatee skirted after him. "I didn't mean nothing, Pop."

I snagged the box with bright yellow tape and ripped it open like Christmas morning. The current Mrs. Harr had crammed in a rich assortment of expensive linens, 800-count bed sheets, and designer place mats for Chicago's disadvantaged youth. There was a Gucci silk jacket and designer clothes, everything new with tags. Eddie's latest wife buys more pretty things for herself than she can possibly use. I stuffed the contents back in the box. Damn, I got nothin' here.

"Nash!" the old man shouted and the driver turned off the forklift.

"I'm sending my boy out for burgers. You hungry?"

"Gimme a whopper and coke. Supersized."

Goatee hawed. "McDonald's supersizes. Burger King—"

Smack.

"Geez, Pop."

The old man called to the driver. "I'm stepping outside for a smoke. You comin'?"

"Nah. I'll finish loading this truck first."

The forklift started up again. I jolted across the workroom to the large bay door and pressed flat against the wall. Nash and I were alone in the warehouse until Pop finished his cigarette. Not much time to figure out what Rita Polansky was after when she volunteered at the Kids First Project.

Nash flashed by with a load of boxes tagged with green stickers and zoomed onto a truck backed into the loading dock. I knew green stickers meant the boxes go to Chicago area families.

Volunteers sort through the donations and slap red stickers on boxes targeted for International Relief. The stickers, Gloria had said, are placed on the right upper half of each box like a postage stamp and Gloria okayed each box before it left the workroom.

I didn't catch the discrepancy at first and wouldn't have if I hadn't got the drill from the volunteers. There, scattered among a whopping number of boxes to be shipped out of the country, were a dozen or so bright red stickers slapped on the left side.

Holy crap, I hoped Pop was a chain smoker. I bounded under the glaring florescent lights, my Valentino Strappy Napa sandals skating precariously across the slick cement floor. I skidded to a stop. My trembling fingers scratched away packing tape exposing a flurry of fabric. I dug further, shoving double fisted hands deep inside, and my knuckles smashed against something cold and hard and familiar.

My heart pounded wildly in my chest and I yanked an assault rifle from the box. Rita said Eddie Harr was a hood who rose to the top with a big boost from organized crime. The relationship was sealed long ago. Maybe Eddie Harr was paying back a debt or maybe he was a common crook. But I knew he was running arms. And I knew why he killed Rita.

Ding ding ding. The forklift signaled Nash backing out of the truck.

I snapped a hasty photo and jammed the contents back in the box, sealing the tape with a slap of my hand. I lunged to safety behind a mountain of International Relief. My heart hammered in my ears and I forced myself to breathe.

"Nash!" Pop's voice bellowed. "I'm back."

The forklift died. "This load's a go. Where's my burger?"

I glimpsed around the stack of boxes. Nash jumped to the ground and pulled a pack of smokes from his pocket. The old man supported his back against the big yellow machine and Nash propped a foot on a step. The moment they flashed their backs to me I kicked my Valentino's into my hands and took off running. My bare feet flew across the cold concrete, my eyes fixed on the loading dock. I didn't look back. The camera around my neck smacked my chest and my 9mm dug into my waist. I hit the platform at full speed, hurtled to the ground, and slapped the sandals on my feet. I high tailed around the back of the building, easing into a jog when I set my sights on Dorothy.

I was in the final stretch and almost home free. A long black Caddy spun into the parking lot. The darkened windows obscured the big shot in the back seat but Godzilla was behind the wheel. The car burned rubber and effectively cut me off at the pass. I dug my heels in the asphalt to avoid clambering over the hood.

Godzilla climbed out of the big Cadillac. It was a little small for him but so was a tank.

Uh oh. I made a show of checking my pulse and moving my legs.

"Move your car, you're screwing up my run."

A man, fat and fifty, stepped from the car. The pinstripes on his tailored suit didn't make him look taller or thinner. I recognized him from the pictures in the lobby but this time he wasn't smiling. Rita described Eddie Harr as "powerful and paranoid." Right now he just looked pissed.

"You're trespassing."

I faced him, hands on my hips. "And you broke my time. I'm training for the Chicago Marathon-"

"In *those* shoes?"

I dismissed the question. "I turned around in your lot. Is that a problem?"

"You weren't turning. You ran a straight line from the warehouse."

"I made a big circle. So what?"

I side stepped and Godzilla grabbed my arm.

"Tell your gorilla to let go of me or I'll call the cops."

"I'm curious. Do you always run with a camera?" He nodded and Godzilla jerked the camera from my neck and passed it to Harr.

I lunged to snatch it back but Godzilla pinned my arms.

"You can go now," Harr said.

The blood pounded in my ears. "Give me my camera," I hissed.

Harr's face turned to stone. "I caught you on my property running from my business where I have a camera that looks exactly like this one. Press charges if you wish and I'll press charges for trespassing and breaking and entering. Our lawyers will sort it out."

I was livid. I suspected my mouth was foaming. "Jackass."

He climbed into the car. "If I catch you here again you won't walk out on your own."

I didn't walk now either. Fueled by rage I ran in my Strappy Napa sandals across the parking lot and onto the street. I ran passed Dorothy and kept running like I was marathon champion of the world. I'd return later for Jack's car. And I'd bring Chicago's finest with me.

I stopped at the first sandwich shop I came to. I ordered a coke and a Murphy's Red Hot and called for back-up.

"Yello."

"Rocco, it's me."

"Where are you? You're not doing anything stupid are you?"

"Uh, no. Maybe. Okay. Yes." I nudged the phone away from my ear, prepared for my brother's scream. "This morning I staked out Eddie Harr's house."

"You *what?*" he screamed.

I worked my tongue in my cheek. "I was there. Charles Ross showed up and a guy gave him a package."

"Who the hell is Charles Ross?"

"Ratman."

He expelled a breath. "You're out of your freakin' mind."

"I followed Charlie to Harr's warehouse and he left the package there. So I let myself inside—"

"Breaking and Entering."

"—and I found the box. Lots of linens."

"Ooh. Linens? You're scaring me, Cat."

"I snooped some more. Eddie is shipping small arms out of the country with the International Relief project."

"Holy shit. How many weapons are we talking about?"

"How should I know? I was a little busy trying to avoid being spotted."

"That's exactly why you're not qualified for this kind of work. You don't have the sense to call for back-up."

"What are you waiting for? Go tell the captain."

He hesitated. "You're sure about this, Cat?"

"Of course I'm sure."

"What about the person who was with you today. I'll tell the captain there's a witness who will verify your story."

"Uh, nix on the witness."

"You lied to me?"

"Please talk to the captain, Rocco. I'll hold."

I drank another coke and waited for my brother to come back. When he did his voice sounded awkward.

"Cat?"

"Yeah."

"The captain wants to know if you're still unbalanced."

"What!"

"It's just that after the concussion there was some concern for your sanity. The conversations with the dead guy. There's been talk, Cat."

"O my god, Rocco, you're my brother. You're supposed to defend me."

"I did. But then Mama invited the captain to her intervention party. He had a late meeting, but he dropped by later for Mama's buffet."

"Auuugghh!"

"I think you should talk to the captain yourself."

"Fine," I snapped. "Put him on."

"You should talk to him in person. I'll see you when you get here."

I hung up on him.

"Damn." I called him back.

"Yello."

"Uh, I need a ride."

"Where's your car?"

"With my purse. I'll explain when you get here. And I need you to pay for my lunch."

Chapter Thirteen

The sun hung low in the sky as we drove across town and over the tracks to the Kids First Project warehouse. Rocco parked next to Dorothy and cut the engine. It had taken an hour to light a fire under the captain and three to shake a signature from the judge. Now we waited for the cavalry to show.

Two cars were parked in the warehouse lot and I was betting their owners didn't drive a forklift. One was a brand new Mercedes finished in lemon with killer rims. The other a long black caddy I remembered well.

Rocco pushed his seat back and stretched his legs. "I hope to hell you know what you're doing."

"What I'm doing will get you a promotion, bro."

"Or a gig working Security at Kmart."

"You always have a job at Pants on Fire Detective Agency."

"Mmm. Taking dirty pictures and talking to dead people. A tempting offer."

A parade of flashing blue and red lights spun toward us and my heart raced with anticipation.

"We're going in." I shoved the door open.

Rocco reached across and pulled me back. "Not you, Cat. Captain's orders. He's overseeing the search and he doesn't want any screw ups."

Captain Bob Maxfield and my dad were beat cops back in the seventies. He was at my Baptism and I remind him of that whenever I need a favor.

"That's not fair, Rocco. It's my case."

"No, if this was your case it would involve panties and Vaseline. Stay in the car. If this goes down bad you don't want Eddie Harr to even dream your sticky fingers are involved."

"Uh—"

"What?"

I grabbed my Dr Pepper Lip Smacker and slathered it on. "Nothing."

When I told Rocco and Bob my story I somehow skipped over the part where Harr caught me in the parking lot and wrestled the camera from my hands.

Flashing cop cars and the local ATF whirled into the parking lot, screeching to a halt at the warehouse door.

"Show time. Stay," Rocco joined the others across the street.

Flashing lights circled the building and covered all exits. Captain Bob Maxfield, surrounded by an entourage of uniforms pounded the door.

"Chicago Police," the captain shouted. "We have a warrant to search the premises."

The door swung open immediately and three suits filled the doorway. The short fat one in the middle was Eddie Harr. Godzilla on his right was the camera thief. And the tall thin guy studying the search warrant would be Harr's lawyer.

Uh oh. Not good. Eddie knew we were coming and he was ready for us.

The seven dwarves in my head mounted a full fledged assault. The search took less than an hour and Eddie locked up. The black caddie and new lemon-colored Mercedes with the killer hubs drove away.

I was greeted with dead silence when I mustered my vibrato and joined the cluster of guys surrounding the sour-faced captain.

"What happened," I protested. "You let them get away."

"Why the hell did I listen to you," the captain shook his head. "For chrisake, Caterina, see a doctor."

Rocco fell over himself apologizing. "Let me say again how sorry I am, captain."

"We'll be damn lucky if Harr doesn't sue the city."

I faked outrage. "What? Are you saying you didn't find the weapons?"

"We didn't find weapons because there are none. Everyone can go now. Sorry to cut into your evenings. Stop by Mickey's. The first drink is on me."

Rocco snagged my arm and dragged me across the street as I pulled my keys out of my pocket.

"Terrific. I'll be directing traffic in the morning if I still have a job."

"I think I know what happened. The muscle who stole my camera looked at my pictures and moved the guns."

Rocco stopped in his tracks. "What! They were onto you? Why didn't you mention this before?"

"My concussion must have affected my memory." I rubbed my temples.

"Do us both a favor. Forget this shit. Buy a new camera and take your dirty pictures. Liars and cheats are getting away as we speak."

"A murderer is getting away too."

He opened my door and stuffed me inside. "Follow me. We're going to Mickey's."

"Uh, not tonight."

"O, you're going, sis. You owe me big time and you're buying."

I winced. "Everyone's mad at me. They wouldn't even wave."

"Buy them enough drinks and they'll get over it."

Rocco stomped to his car and I started Dorothy. In my headlights a small wrapper blew in the wind and caught my windshield. It was a red waxy paper, twisted in a tie.

"Wait!" I shouted and shoved the door open, caught the candy wrapper in my hand, and skipped to Rocco's door.

"This candy wrapper proves it. It was Ratman who dropped it—uh, I mean Charlie Ross."

"Right."

"I found a wrapper in my office and one in Rita's apartment twisted exactly like this."

"Yeah. Only a killer would twist a candy wrapper that way."

"That's what I'm saying."

My brother growled. "Follow me. I need a drink."

"Rocco, wait. Don't you want to bag the evidence?"

"Cat."

"What?"

"Shut up."

I drove Dorothy across town lying to myself it would be a slow night at Mickey's. The parking lot was jammed. I parked Dorothy on the street beside a fire hydrant.

Rocco met me at the entrance and pushed me inside. "Cat's here!" he shouted and a flood of groans rocked the room.

"Hey, guys," I called. "After you left we found a candy—"

Rocco jabbed me with an elbow and I sucked my breath.

"The next round of drinks is on me," I choked.

"And the next round is on me," Uncle Joey called. "Give Cat some slack. She has a concussion."

"You saying she imagined the weapons?" someone said.

Uncle Joey shrugged and called to the bartender. "These guys are hungry. Bring them whatever they want."

I was forgiven. I found an empty seat at the bar and ordered Absolut on the rocks.

"And easy on the rocks," I told the bartender.

A rookie cop sidled up next to me, his uniform still crunchy new from the package. I gave him the once over. Not bad. He had a nice smile and his carrot top hair and pale blue eyes gave him a boyish look.

"Cat is it? Nice name."

"It's not real popular tonight."

He laughed. "This was my first big bust. I'm Tommy. I just moved here from Wisconsin. Maybe we could go to dinner sometime."

He was sweet. A few months on the force would change all that.

"I'd like that. I can show you all the hot spots of Chicago."

Four large DeLucas closed in. I watched Tommy get the deer in the headlights look.

"Gotta go. My friends are calling."

Tommy slouched to his table. He didn't have any friends.

"Hey, give a girl a chance to get lucky. He was cute."

My cousin Tony grunted. "Gimme a break. He isn't even Italian."

"You say that like it's a bad thing."

The White Sox played on the big screen and Uncle Joey kept the drinks coming until some of the guys thought they were celebrating my birthday.

Captain Bob slapped an arm around me. "Cat, when did you get here. I haven't seen you since…" he racked his brain.

"Forever. Another beer, Bobby?"

"You're tho beauteeful," he slurred.

Rocco yanked Bob off my shoulder. "All right, captain. Time to get you a taxi."

It was late and my head began to throb. "Thanks for the birthday party, guys," I called. "Nood Gight!"

"You're not driving either," Rocco said. "You've had too much to drink."

"Shull Bit," I countered. "Where's my keys?"

I emptied my purse in front of me. My diaphragm rolled down the length of the bar and dropped in front of the chief.

"For me?"

The room snickered and my cheeks flamed hot. Uncle Joey pried the diaphragm from the chief's hands.

"You really don't want to take that home to your wife," Joey said.

Rocco waved my keys. "Looking for these?"

"You kole my steys!"

"C'mon sis, you're riding with me," Rocco said. "We'll get your car tomorrow."

Tommy stepped from the shadows. "I'll drive your car for you and take a cab back here."

Rocco tossed Tommy the keys. "You can follow us, but you're not going inside. *Ever.*"

"He's cute!" I sang.

Tommy settled his tab at the bar while my brother dragged me to his car. Tommy stepped outside. His easy blue eyes glistened in the glow of the street light. He spotted Dorothy beside the fire hydrant and walked toward her, flicking buttons on the key sensor to disable the alarm and unlock the door. Jack had spared no expense on Dorothy.

"Schanks, Tommy!" I twisted around and waved giddily for the rookie to follow.

Tommy waved back, keys flapping above his head. His finger skimmed over the ignition key and Dorothy's engine caught with a blinding flash of fire. The explosion was deafening, whooshing Tommy off his feet, hammering him against the wall. Glass and metal pelted the street. The fire hydrant shot off like a rocket.

In seconds the street was filled with cops pouring from Mickey's. I body slammed the door and screamed into the street. I shoved and pushed my way through the crowd. I dropped beside Tommy. He was conscious. His boyish face twisted with pain. The squeal of sirens wailed in the distance.

Rocco pulled me back.

I stood in the jetting fountain of the busted hydrant and the cold numbing spray washed over me.

"You have really pissed off the wrong people, Cat," Rocco said.

Eyes wide with shock, I turned to my brother. He pulled me to him. I buried my face in his shoulder and sobbed.

Chapter Fourteen

"Well, you've obviously pissed somebody off." The captain was glaring at me across the table at Mickey's with six of Chicago's finest standing behind him. The moment Dorothy blew, the boys in blue had taken over the scene. Blockading the street. Keeping passersby and the curious behind yellow tape. Calling in the evidence teams and ambulance. It's an amazing thing to see how fast a cop can sober up. But I've lived with cops all my life. They drink hard. They click into cop-gear harder.

Every one of them was looking at me with a direct, hard gaze. I could tell they didn't like it that Rocco's charming-if-annoying sister had just had an attempted hit made on her. But they were fuming, too. Their new rookie had almost bitten it. That doesn't sit well with cops. They're proprietorial. If anybody was going to get a chance to mess with the rookie first, it would be them.

"Think, DeLuca," the captain said. "We've already been through the first two years of men who want you dead. Since you've started the agency, there's got to be one or two that really stand out."

"What can I say?" I said, batting my eyes. "I have this power."

"This isn't the time, Cat. Cut it out!" Rocco was on his last nerve, big brother that he was. I'd lost mine with Dorothy but I wasn't going to let them see that.

"Listen. I've already told you. You can have a copy of my cases. All the info is in there, including follow up reports on some crazy cheater-behaviors after the case was closed. But if you'd just listen to me, and I'm speaking as a trained detective here..."

I waited for the belly laugh to subside.

"It's possible the bomb has nothing to do with the Pants on Fire Detective Agency. We need to consider Eddie Harr. We were at his warehouse tonight. He's running guns—"

"Enough!" The captain barked. "There are no guns!"

I could see a lot of eye-rolling from the cop gallery behind him.

"Let me explain something to you, DeLuca."

The captain started talking like he was addressing a five-year-old. I resisted sticking out my tongue.

"The Chicago Police Department may not all be made up of Mensa members like yourself, brain surgeon that you are. But we have a certain protocol we follow. A certain line of suspects with motive, if you will. It's proven to be amazingly effective in the past. It goes something like this. When there's an attempted murder investigation, our first line of suspects is the next of kin. You know, the husband, the wife, the extended family members. I believe this first line of inquiry could be amazingly effective in your particular case. I can't imagine any next of kin who would not be driven to kill you. I'm just surprised they've waited this long. While I will forever be puzzled about this, they truly have my undying respect. I, personally, would have wrung your scrawny neck long ago."

Grind, grind.

"Sweet-talker," I said.

"Tell me about your ex."

"Johnnie Rizzo?"

"Is he jealous? Have you driven him insane?"

I flapped a hand. "Puh-leeze."

"Would your death benefit Johnnie Rizzo in any way?"

"Absolutely not," I said and a long forgotten detail flashed in my head. Shortly after we were married, Johnnie and I each took out a life insurance policy. Three hundred thousand dollars each. I had no idea what Johnnie did with his. I just knew Johnnie Rizzo was still my beneficiary.

"You're remembering something," Rocco said.

"It's nothing." I slapped my pockets. Where was my Lip Smacker? "Bob can continue yelling now."

"Let's just say that it's not one of your long-suffering clan," the captain continued in his best condescending voice. "Our next line of inquiry might be, oh, I don't know. This might sound foolish to you, but it just *might* be, one of the hundreds of men IN THE CITY OF CHICAGO THAT YOU HAVE TOTALLY PISSED OFF BY SNEAKING AROUND AND TAKING PICTURES AND RUINING THEIR MARRIAGES!"

Grind, grind, grind, grind, grind, grind, grind.

Yada Yada Yada.

It was almost dawn when Rocco and I stumbled into the house. An officer followed us home and I turned over my case files.

"You're not sleeping here another night, Cat," Rocco said.

"I won't be bullied from my home," I mumbled without conviction.

"Stay with Maria and me."

"And innocent children? That's crazy."

"Then stay with Mama and Papa."

"You want to blow up our parents?"

Rocco reached for the yellow pages.

"What are you doing?"

"I'm ordering a security system that'll scream when a cat lights on your porch."

"Great. My neighbors will love that."

"Then I'm going home to get cleaned up." Rocco silenced me with a look. "This is Detective Rocco DeLuca of the Chicago Police Department. Who am I speaking to?"

I made a face. Rocco always pushes his way to the front of a line.

"Marcy, I want your very best alarm system and I need it installed today."

"You're getting crazy, Rocco."

"And you're still not staying here tonight," he mouthed.

I was too tired to argue. "I'm going to bed."

My hair and clothes reeked like a bad night in Baghdad. I showered and splashed my skin with lavender, tugged a soft cotton night shirt over my head, and fell into bed. Then I reached for the phone and called my mechanic.

"Jack. This is Cat."

"Speak up, Cat. I can hardly hear you."

"That's cuz I'm whispering. I'm calling about your car."

"You mean Dorothy."

"OK. Dorothy."

"I love that car."

"Does your car…"

"Dorothy."

"Does Dorothy have insurance, Jack?"

"What do you mean?"

"I mean does she have *lots* of insurance."

"Why would she need insurance," he said guardedly. "What are you trying to say?"

The seven dwarves were back with sledgehammers. I cradled my head.

"I'm saying Dorothy's gone to be with your dad. Let her go, Jack. She had a good life."

◇◇◇

A loud bang shook the walls. I jolted from a troubled sleep. My heart slammed wildly in my chest. I listened. There it was again. An intruder outside my bedroom door. Eddie had sent someone to finish the job they botched last night.

Fear gripped my throat. My eyes swept the room for my vicious guard dog. I groaned. Inga was at Mama's. I was home alone with Freddie Kruger.

I crept from my bed and tiptoed across the room to my dresser, opened a drawer, slid my hand beneath silk panties, and whipped out the pistol. The cool steel steadied my hands and my breathing came easier. Somebody better start talking. I wasn't calling the cops.

I flung the door open. A man, his sandy hair cropped short strutted toward the living room. I blew the hair from my eyes and did my best Dirty Harry impression.

"Make my Day, Bucko. I have a bullet with your name on it."

The man screamed like a little girl. His hands shot in the air. "Don't shoot!"

"Turn around."

"I can't. You made me have an accident."

I released the safety and he spun around like a top.

"Lady, you scared the piss out of me. Your brother let me in."

My eyes froze on the lake expanding in his pants.

"Are you *still* going?"

"Hey, I drank a pot of coffee this morning."

I checked him out. His standard company uniform had been tailored for a perfect fit and his nails manicured. I put the gun away. If this guy wanted to kill me I'd take him out with my bare hands.

"Sorry about the Dirty Harry thing," I said. "Can I wash your pants?"

"Never mind," he sniffed. "I have a dry pair in the van."

"Go already," I said.

He went. I slipped on black jeans and a soft tiger print sweater and matching peep toe wedges. I was pouring myself a cup of coffee when he returned.

"Love the shoes!" he said.

He eyed my coffee and I hugged my cup closer. I figured he'd had enough.

"I'm Eric. You were smart to order our premium platinum package."

"I didn't. My brother did."

"Oh?" Eric's eyes sparked interest. "I just love a man in uniform."

I laughed. "Rocco's straight as an arrow and too much of a slob to be gay."

"Unfortunately that's just a stereotype. I've had boyfriends who were pigs. Like my purpose in life was picking up after them."

"You're preaching to the choir, honey. Like we have nothing better to do."

I poured him a cup of coffee.

Eric twisted a kitchen chair around and straddled it, resting his arms on the back. "Most people make the mistake of compromising on our added safety features because they're so pricey."

I massaged my temples. "How pricey?"

"When you think of it," he soothed, "what's money compared to your personal safety? Will we be billing your brother today?"

"No. I'll take care of it." Infidelity is a booming business.

I tromped to the bedroom for a check and muttered under my breath. To think Rocco wanted me to be a dispatcher.

◇◇◇

With my premium platinum alarm system fully installed I asked Eric to drop me off at Tino's Deli.

"Sure," he said.

I grabbed my house keys and a voice squawked behind me.

"I got your ride, girlfriend."

Eric screamed.

I whirled around with a groan. I'd recognize that grating voice anywhere.

Cleo waved her Flaming Flamingo fingertips from the doorway. Her soft dark curls were gathered in a clump on top of her head and big silver bangles jangled from her wrists and ears. The last time I spoke to Cleo she was going to kill her husband and I was going into an exploding building.

"Your door was unlocked," she said. "Not smart."

"Not again," I said.

I turned to my home security guy and he groaned

Eric ran out the front door to his van. Cleo waved and I set the lock behind him.

Cleo threw herself on the couch. Her short lavender sundress showed off a lot of leg and a double whammy from a generous boob goddess. She leaned against the sofa cushions and grinned.

"Boyfriend?"

I threw her a look. The guy was a screamer and a pee-er. "That was my home security guy."

Cleo scoffed. "Home security my ass. He left the door unlocked."

"Try the doorbell," I said pointedly. "Why are you here?"

"I'm in deep shit, Cat. I need your help."

"You didn't kill your husband, did you?"

"Of course not."

"Did you run over your sister?"

Cleo snorted. "She's such a drama queen. You shoulda heard her holler when I pumped buckshot in his cheating ass. Not that it was easy, that man can run."

"You *shot* your husband?"

"It was self-defense."

"The man was running away. I don't think that qualifies for self-defense."

"Believe me. That wasn't the side I was aiming for."

I cradled the sides of my head. A Cleo size headache was coming on. "Are the cops looking for you?"

"My husband cooked the books at work. He knows if he calls the cops I'll sing like a bird."

"You're not going to shoot him again, are you?"

"That coward ran," she spat. "He can't even take it like a man." She covered her face with her hands and the shrill left her voice like all the helium gone from a balloon. "The bastard cleaned me out. I'm bare bones broke. I can't pay my bills."

"We'll try to get your money back, Cleo, but it'll take some time."

"I hope his butt hurts like hell."

Cleo shadowed me to the kitchen. I threw a couple aspirin in my mouth, chased them down with water, and turned to face her.

"Forget the cheater and your ho sister. Sell your weapons. Get a job. Find what you love to do and do it."

"That's why I'm here." Her face broke a smile. "I want to be a detective like you. I want to partner up."

"No!" I squawked like Cleo.

"I'll work off my bill."

"Consider it paid in full."

Cleo's face puckered. She blinked her big brown eyes hard. She worked up something that might have been tears.

"I can't pay my rent," she sniffed. "I need this job, Cat. I got the talent. I'm smart. I'm good with guns."

"I'm not hiring. I already have a partner."

"Your *dog?*"

"She's vicious."

"You haven't seen my buckshot."

I sighed.

Cleo looked around and smacked her lips. "Maybe I could move in until I get a job."

A wave of panic crashed over me. "Don't you have family?"

"No."

"Take mine."

"My mom's siding with my sister. She was always her favorite. I just got you, Cat."

"We just met, Cleo. You're a client."

Her lip puckered.

I buckled. "Can you type?"

"Partner!" she squeeled.

"This is a *temporary* arrangement. Just until you get on your feet."

"Whoo-hoo!"

"Don't even think about moving in. I'm writing you an advance for your rent."

"I'm a detective," Cleo danced around the room.

"No, you're not a detective. You're here to ASSIST me. No shooting allowed."

"Right," she winked.

"You can start next week," I said and slung my bag over my shoulder. "Drop me at Tino's."

◇◇◇

Since Jack blamed me for the demise of Dorothy he hadn't returned my car. He was holding the Silver Bullet hostage. My plan was to schmooze Jack with lunch delivered to his shop so he'd bring my car back. I've seen Tino's putenesca bring grown men to their knees.

I sailed into the deli and Tino shook his fists. "Sweet Caterina, almost blown to bloody pieces. Good you should come to me." He lowered his voice. "I will get you out of town safe."

I hugged him. "Thanks, Tino, but I'm not leaving town. I'm here because Jack won't give me my car back. That and Rocco ate Inga's sausages."

"What? You want his legs broken?"

"I'll just buy more sausages."

"Not Rocco. Jack."

"Tempting but I'll try schmoozing him first. A good mechanic is hard to find."

"OK. We save his legs for now."

"I want you to deliver lunch to Jack and his crew. Knock yourself out. And send a note. 'Sorry about Dorothy.'"

"Does Jack's wife know about this Dorothy?" Tino leaned close and his eyes gleamed. "Do you have pictures?"

I laughed. "Can you do it tomorrow?"

"The legs I could do today."

"It'll wait 'til tomorrow. Thanks, Tino. You're a good friend."

He grunted. "If you won't leave town you need protection."

"Rocco had the security company at my house all morning. It's a fortress. What I need is a car. I need a ride to Hertz."

"You need a body guard. I'll make a call."

I hugged him. "I'll be fine."

Tino pulled a ring of keys from his pocket. "Take my Buick. It's parked in back."

"I can't..."

He pressed the keys in my hand. "It has some extra safety features."

Thanks to Tino I had wheels and was back in the game. I zoomed across town to Eddie's house and parked down the street with my sights on the gate. Eddie probably wouldn't be home. He'd be out doing whatever it is gangsters do. With any luck he took the beefy door guy with him. I set my stun gun on max and tucked it in my belt.

Across the street the front gate began to glide to the left on the track. A frosty pink Lincoln drove out and rolled to a stop at the street. The third Mrs. Harr applied lipstick in the back seat. She leaned forward and said something to the beefy guy behind the wheel. He smiled and merged with the traffic.

I smiled bigger, shot out of the Buick, and barely skidded through the gate before it clinked shut behind me. I looked around. No one was on the grounds. Two economy cars were parked in the rear. I was alone with the hired help.

I dodged around the corner of the house pressing my back against the ivy. The balcony above me had a cozy table for two and a shot of the moon on clear nights. It overlooked the fountains and likely led to the master bedroom. I craned my neck and peered through a window that looked into a formal dining room. A young blonde in a starchy French maid uniform polished a small mountain of silver. With any luck she'd stay downstairs. I tested my weight on the trellis, hailed a couple Marys, and hiked up the ivy by hoisting one foot up and then another. I didn't look down or breathe until my legs kicked over the iron railing. I am the Pants on Fire Detective Agency and this is what I do. I pick locks and scale balconies. I'm a professional stalker.

Walking through the French doors into Eddie and Michelle Harr's bedroom was a little like stepping into a Laura Ashley catalogue. A dreamy canopy bed, lots of soft prints, and a stuffed Teddy propped on a pillow. The bear would be from the third Mrs. Harr's very recent childhood. It was a little creepy to picture Eddie there.

I didn't find what I was looking for so I poked my head in the hallway. No French maids with feather dusters. The room across the hall was a guest room. Little guest soaps, shampoos, and pretty new toothbrushes in the bathroom. Not finding it here. I slipped into the room next door and got a whiff of Old Spice and Cuban cigars. Oh yeah. I was in Eddie's study.

I zipped through drawers, flipped a Rolodex to R for Ross, rummaged through a closet, poked around the bathroom, and cracked the lock on an old trunk. I found a couple guns, chocolates, a cheesy Hustler magazine, and some little blue pills. I stuffed the chocolates in my pockets but I didn't find what I came for. I was two steps from the door when Eddie's voice bellowed from the stairs.

"Where the hell is Michelle?"

A jolt slammed my gut. I dived under the desk scuttling around a round file I'd missed earlier. Inside the basket was what I came for. It was my camera smashed to bits.

This French maid had a Spanish accent. And her voice was older than the polisher. "Mrs. Harr is having lunch with a friend."

"Hmmph," he snarled. What a control freak.

"Will there be anything else, sir?"

"Find Barney. There's a black car parked across the street. Tell him to check it out."

Holy shit. I fumbled for the tazer.

"Barney drove Mrs. Harr to the luncheon."

"What?" Eddie roared. "Where's my wife's driver?"

"Sick, sir."

"He'll come in or he's fired."

From under the desk I watched Eddie's shiny shoes stomp into the room. The maid's sensible Oxfords shuffled behind him, a blond Pomeranian hot on her tail. The dog's ears shot up. He smelled me or maybe it was the chocolate, but he crouched on his haunches and yapped bloody hell.

Eddie plopped down at the desk. I fixed the stun gun on his knees.

"What the hell is wrong with that mutt?"

The telephone rang on Eddie's desk.

"He sees something, sir," the maid said.

"He'll see the barrel of my shotgun if you don't get him out of here."

The maid scooped the dog up in her arms. "You can play outside, Frodo," she sniffed and they disappeared down the hall.

Eddie answered the phone. "Eddie Harr… It's about time you called me back. Spare me the excuses. We have a problem…A dame was snooping around the warehouse yesterday taking pictures. What the hell is that about?…I took care of this mess a week ago…You assured me she was working alone…Talk to Charlie and *handle* this. What d'ya think I'm paying you for?"

Click.

Eddie kicked back his chair and schlepped off to the bathroom. I heard a zip and psssss and before the shake I was onto the balcony and over the side. I hit the ground running. The Pomeranian was waiting. He yapped at my heels until I scaled the wall and vanished in a poof of burning rubber.

I swallowed my heart back in my chest, sank my teeth in a piece of chocolate, and cut across town to North Chicago. Thanks to Eddie and his Rolodex, it was time to stalk Charlie the Ratman. I rolled down my windows and jammed to Coldplay. When my booty vibrated I plucked my cell phone from my back pocket and took the call.

"Pants on Fire Detective Agency," I said. "We expose liars and cheats."

"Ms. DeLuca. This is Special Agent Harding from the FBI."

"Larry," I said. "Hi. How are you?"

His voice got stiffer. "I just had an interesting conversation with Captain Maxfield about an imaginary arms shipment and the lawsuit Eddie Harr may well file against the city."

"It wasn't my imagination, Larry. Eddie removed the evidence before we got there."

"Mr. Harr is a respected member of this community. You don't realize how confused you are as a result of your concussion."

"And you don't realize what a crook Eddie Harr is."

The agent sighed deeply. "There are a few things I'd like to discuss with you. I can stop by your house later or meet you for coffee."

"What things?"

"First of all when you were in my office you didn't mention your connection to a reporter who was killed in her apartment last week."

"What does that have to do with a gas leak?"

"Captain Maxfield tells me you have in your possession a laptop that belonged to the victim. Is that true?"

"Why do you ask?"

"The FBI is interested in Ms. Polansky's computer as part of an on-going investigation. I can swing by for the laptop today and get it back to you next week."

"Do you have a warrant?"

"I didn't think that would be necessary."

"But you're admitting the explosion wasn't a gas leak."

"Not at all. Now about that laptop—"

"Get a warrant."

Click.

Chapter Fifteen

The first thing I did when I got to the hospital was go to the gift shop. I thought it might be a good idea to buy a little something for Tommy since the last time I saw him he was getting blown up with Dorothy.

Once I started buying, I couldn't quit. I had magazines, balloons, flowers, dime novels, and the entire candy rack piled on the counter before I spotted a five-foot stuffed teddy bear suspended from the ceiling.

"How much for Yogi?" I asked the woman behind the counter.

She had that sympathetic look of someone who's seen her share of freaked out hospital visitors. But the gleam in her eye suggested that I was one for tonight's dinner conversation. Somewhere between the Clark bars and the Butterfingers, I realized how totally freaked I really was. Buying out the gift shop was my try at holding back a whole shit load of self-recrimination. Why couldn't I let anything go? Why did I always have to keep pressing every point? Every lead? Every …? Because it wasn't just me that got put in danger. The living proof of that was a red haired, freckle faced rookie cheese-head in a hospital bed two floors up. Oh yeah. I bought the bear.

Gift shop lady ordered a gurney to haul the first load of soft fuzzy things and calories to Tommy's room. I poked my head around Yogi's polyester fluff and looked in at Tommy. He was wrapped in burn-dressings. His burns were on parts of his torso and legs.

Tommy certainly had his angels. The bulk of the explosion had initially shot up and out and there were enough cops on the ground to yank him away before Dorothy became the Fourth of July Wonder.

"Hey," I said.

"Hey, back at'cha," said Tommy. "You know the gorilla isn't necessary."

"It's not a gorilla. It's a bear."

"OK." Tommy's eyes had a morphine sheen. "Hey! Guess what? I've been promoted! Injury in the line of duty!"

I groaned. "This is my fault."

"Oh come on. This is so not your fault."

"They were out for me, Tommy. This wouldn't have happened if you hadn't tried to drive Dorothy."

"Dorothy?"

"Long story."

"Hey listen. I'm a cop. You know what that means. We put ourselves in the line of danger, not cuz we're so into the danger part, but cuz we have this thing about 'to serve and protect.' Remember? We serve. We protect. It's right there on the side of the squad car."

"Serve and protect. Right."

"Come on, Cat. You come from a long line of cops. It's in your DNA. You know how we're hard-wired. We do what we do because we believe that the bad guys have gotta be stopped. Bad guys hurt people. We put ourselves on the line to stop them. Because somebody's got to do it."

"I get it," I said.

"Oh, I know you do." He was beginning to yawn and I could see the morphine had clicked into overdrive.

I decided I wasn't going to remark on that statement. Tommy yawned again. "Isn't that why you do what you do? To serve and protect?"

"You know Tommy," I said. "You ain't so bad for a cheese head."

"Serve and protect," Tommy's head lobbed to the side. He was out for the count.

◇◇◇

A low voice breathed in my ear. "Wake up, DeLucky."

"Uh, uh."

I didn't want to. I was lost in a delicious dream. I saved a blue woman from a shark and I was sailing with a hot guy in a little red boat, rocking with the waves. *Rocking, rocking.* I wriggled deeper into the chair. I liked the way this dream was going.

A hand stroked my cheek. I cracked an eye. Cobalt blues smiled back.

I caught my breath. No heady smells of salt water. Just stark, hospital smells of disinfectant. My eyes skimmed the room.

Tommy, out for the count, snored softly.

"Geez," I sighed.

Chance laughed softly, pulled me to my feet and held me against him while he wrapped his coat around my shoulders. The fabric was warm and soft. Cashmere, I guess.

"Your patient's sleeping. Let's get you home." He hung an arm around my shoulder and led me into the hall.

"Have you eaten?"

"No." An idea came to me. "The Cop Shop's vending machine has a ham and cheese sandwich that's not totally horrible. We can drop by the station and introduce you to Captain Bob. He'll have to admit I'm not crazy."

"Tempting, but I'm not wild about packaged ham and cheese. I know this Thai restaurant, a little hole in the wall, with…"

"No witnesses?"

"It's got great Pad Thai."

"You can't hide forever."

I spotted a starchy white collar down the hall and my heart soared. Who could doubt a priest?

"Father Timothy!" I called. "You're my witness!"

I rushed toward him.

"Caterina!"

"Tell mama to cancel the exorcism. Chance Savino is alive and here he…"

I swept my arm dramatically behind me. Savino was gone, poof, vanished like hot smoke.

"Coward!" I yelled.

Father Timothy stroked his cross.

"Surely you saw him," I said.

"Who?"

"Wait! I have proof." I whirled the cashmere coat from my shoulders and thrust it out with two hands.

"Proof?"

"This is *not* the coat of a dead man."

"I see," Father Timothy said.

Clearly he didn't.

I groaned inwardly and checked the pockets. No paper, no surprise. Just three hundred-sixty seven dollars in a money clip. I stuffed the cash back in the pocket, and placed the coat in the priest's arms.

"I saw a homeless man outside the hospital today. Would you give him this coat?"

"That's very generous."

"I'd rather give him a Porsche."

"I was going to call you, Caterina."

"If this is about the exorcism-"

He hid a smile. "I wanted to talk to you about Jack. You blew up his car."

"Jack wants to kill me."

"I think I talked him out of it."

"Wait. You're not sure?"

He waffled a hand back and forth. "Grief is so unpredictable."

I blew a sigh. "He'll have to get in line. Somebody's way ahead of him. Poor Tommy got caught in the crossfire."

His head tipped slightly.

"And Dorothy, of course," I added with due respect to my mechanic. "Jack loved her in a really sick way."

"Does this bomb have anything to do with pornography?"

"Maybe. I mean *no*! I'm a licensed investigator, Father. I don't do porn."

He eyed me with intense scrutiny.

I sighed. "The cops believe the explosion is connected to one of my cases. They have my list of cheaters."

"Do your cheaters bomb you often?"

This time I waffled my hand. "They're more likely to egg my car."

"A much more civilized response. You might want to send Jack a dozen."

"I may do that."

Father Timothy put a hand on my shoulder. "Jack has suffered a significant loss. He loved Dorothy."

"We're talking about a *car*," I reminded him.

"Jack's father died in that Mustang. There was a tragic accident."

"A gun went off in his mouth. How does that happen?"

"Dorothy was Jack's last connection to his father. He said when he drove the Mustang, he knew his father was right there beside him. He could smell his cigar."

I swallowed a huge gulp of Catholic guilt. I had been irritated with Jack because he didn't care about Tommy's injuries or the bulls-eye target on my own keister. I had minimized Jack's grief. I was ashamed of myself.

"Great. I killed a dead man."

"Jack needs to know you understand how he feels."

"I get it. What can I do?"

"Go talk to him."

"Does he still have his father's gun?"

"You've been friends a long time. Make this right."

"How am I supposed to do that? I can't bring Dorothy back. God knows I can't bring his papa back."

"You'll think of something."

I felt myself make a face. "I don't do miracles. Isn't that your department?"

"You might surprise yourself," he said with a smile. "I'll help in anyway I can. Call the parish if you need me."

"I'll call Mama. She has your cell phone on her Friends and Family Plan."

The elevator door opened and an older woman in a purple hat and doused in lilac cologne stepped out. Father Timothy knew her. Maybe I would too if I made it to mass more regularly. He took her arm and they walked down the hall together.

I stepped inside the elevator, waved off the lilac, and jabbed the L button. How on earth was I supposed to fix this with Jack? The door closed. The elevator jerked and the unmistakable aroma of cigar filled my nostrils. I sucked a breath and coughed.

My heart walloped in my chest. Had I lost my mind? Was I trapped in a small box with my crazy mechanic's Insane Father? I didn't like either possibility. In the end I settled on curtain number three where lilac woman smokes a cigar between the first and fourth floors.

It could happen.

When the door opened again I had a plan. I shimmied into the lobby laughing. I knew how to make things right with Jack. I couldn't bring Dorothy back but I could give him his papa again.

I made a mental note for Father Timothy. Maybe you don't always need a miracle if you know someone who does magic.

Then I called my Uncle Joey.

◇◇◇

The sun was high outside my window when I awoke the next morning. I padded to the kitchen in my bunny slippers. My brother had left a note on the table. *If you go out, take someone with you.*

Inga was at Mama's. For one crazy split second I considered calling Cleo. Just as quickly, I dashed the thought from my mind. Cleo had been under a lot of stress lately. I wasn't sure she could make it all day without shooting someone. I had a nagging headache already.

I made a pot of coffee and took extra care in dressing. I even shaved my legs in the shower. I was going to see Johnnie Rizzo, my womanizing, train-wreck of an ex-husband. I wanted to look smokin'.

It was more than a little bizarre, I had to admit, to consider Johnnie Rizzo as a mad bomber. The guy isn't a sociopath. He's commitment-challenged and an over-achieving cheater who can't keep his pants zipped.

I didn't dare tell Rocco Johnnie was on my suspect list. He'd be convinced I'd gone utterly mad. He'd say delusional, conspiracy theories are what concussions are made of. Rocco would remind me of the time Johnnie nursed a sick squirrel in a shoe box, or wept during *Schindler's List*. Still, a 300-grand insurance policy is a powerful motive. I felt compelled to confront Johnnie Rizzo and eliminate him as a suspect. At least that's what I told myself. Chances are, I just wanted an excuse to see my ex again.

The last time Johnnie Rizzo and I exchanged words was on the courthouse steps after the judge granted our divorce. Johnnie was angry because the judge made him pay back the money I'd invested in his restaurant as part of the settlement. I told Johnnie he's a big fat liar. He said something that sounded like duck poo. There weren't a lot of ducks in Chicago that day but there was a whole lot of traffic. I may have heard him wrong.

Since then I've seen Johnnie on the street a few times, always with a different woman. Maybe I'm getting older but the girls seem to be getting younger.

Johnnie Rizzo owns the Bridgeport Café on Morgan. That's where we met. A friend of mine used to work there. I covered for her the week her grandmother died in Montana. She fell in love with a rich rancher who looks like Tim McGraw. I wouldn't have come back either.

Meanwhile, back at the restaurant, I fell head over heels in love with Johnnie Rizzo. It happened in the walk-in cooler, thrust against a frigid wall, somewhere between a case of ranch dressing and a hanging slab of beef. Johnnie Rizzo is a great kisser with magic fingers. We were married a few months later.

My friend and Tim McGraw are expecting another baby in September. I'm done with Johnnie Rizzo. I haven't been back to the café since the divorce but I still miss the Friday night catfish special.

I made a call to the Bridgeport Bank and asked for Melanie. We've been friends since the third grade. She had warned me not to marry Johnnie Rizzo. There was no love lost between them.

"Hey girlfriend," I said.

Melanie lowered her voice to a whisper. "We shouldn't be talking. Jack said he won't fix my car unless I promise to hate you."

"It's OK. I know someone you can take your car to. Where is it now?"

"Jack has it."

"Melanie!"

"So I lied. Do you have any idea how hard it is to find a good mechanic?"

I massaged my temples. "I need a favor. I need to know about Johnnie Rizzo's financial status."

I heard her fingers fly across the keys. "You know I can't do that."

"You just did."

"Rizzo's two months behind on the restaurant mortgage. He has three overdrafts on his checking account." She cackled with undisguised satisfaction.

"Not good."

"Apparently Rizzo met with the bank manager last week. He's expecting some sort of windfall. He intends to pay the mortgage off next month."

A chill went through me. "That's a lot of wind."

"What's up, Cat?"

"I'll let you know. I want to talk to Johnnie first."

"Don't let him drag you to the cooler."

"I'll beat him senseless with a side of beef."

I called my Insurance Company and asked them to mail a change of beneficiary form. If I drown in the bathtub or cash in my chips on a hit and run, the three-hundred grand will go to Rocco. That's enough wind to hire a hit-man for Johnnie Rizzo and still take the family to Disneyworld.

◇◇◇

I parked the black Buick a block from The Bridgeport Café. I wanted to scope out the lay of the land first.

Johnnie's office faced the back alley and it wasn't too hard to get a gander through his window. How do you think I caught the lying cheat in the first place? All I had to do was press myself close against the brick building so he wouldn't see me coming and then, once under the window, stand up on tiptoe. Perfect. I could hardly be seen. Only the top of my head and eyes and only if you were really looking out the window. But Johnnie never looked out the window anyway. A Bridgeport back alley does not inspire scenic contemplation.

Fighting back a hatch of heroic thistle that had sprung up at the crack between the restaurant wall and blacktop, I let my head rise silently and got on tippy-toes.

The first thing I saw was a man's fly. Johnnie's fly.

What the hell is that doing here, I thought in my confusion. I'd know that fly anywhere and it certainly didn't belong in the back window of his office.

My eyes slowly traveled up the length of a navy silk shirt, softly hanging to hug a hard, lean torso, a column of smooth brown neck. They flitted past firm lips set into a smirk and landed on warm, brown, amused eyes. Johnnie's eyes.

Shit!

Johnnie slid the window open, still standing full erect.

"Well, isn't this a pleasant surprise?"

"Hello, Johnnie. I thought I'd drop by."

"Really? An interesting way to do it, Kitten. Most people use the front entrance."

"Well. I'll just go around and do that right now."

"Oh, no. This is fine. Really. In fact, I prefer it. It brings back fond memories."

There was only about seven inches of wall between my face and Johnnie's fly.

Despite myself and my sore tippy-toes, I felt that little thrill tumble in my stomach. Johnnie and I had always had good chemistry together. He had always been an intuitive and generous lover. I had responded in kind. What we had lacked in our marriage, we'd always made up for in bed. I had to make myself remember what it was that we actually *did* lack in our marriage.

Oh yeah! That little thing. What is it called? Fidelity?

"So what are you doing here, Kitten?" Johnnie asked. "Still stalking me?"

I saw his eyes flit to the left and I turned to look. Some cooks and wait-staff had come out to the alley for a cigarette break.

"Oh great," I moaned. "We have an audience."

"Oh yes," Johnnie grinned viciously, putting his hands on his hips as he let them slowly drift forward. He was loving this. Johnnie looked down from his superior height and practically purred. "To what do I owe this pleasure."

I could hear snickering behind me.

For once words failed me. I could think of nothing to say. What was I doing in this back alley anyway, stretched on my tiptoes like a schoolgirl. Why didn't I scuttle through the front door, march back to his office and say—

"So are you trying to kill me, Johnnie Rizzo, or what?"

I groaned. The words gushed from my mouth. I didn't mean to blurt them out loud.

The kitchen crew inched closer.

Johnnie's eyes softened. "My god, Kitten, it's been almost three years. You gotta get over me."

"Arrrrrgh!" My throat made the sound of a rabid seal.

"I can't help you, babe. I won't go down that road again. The problem is your meddling family. They ruined our marriage."

I choked on a mouthful of righteous indignation. "The *problem* was your—"

He put up a hand. "I'm not saying I wouldn't give us another shot. This isn't a good time for me. My sister's husband is buying half the business. We're expanding, putting in a sports bar. You won't recognize the place in a few months."

I groaned to myself. Windfall.

His magic fingers stroked my cheek. The delicious, heady smell of Johnnie Rizzo filled my nostrils. I could make out the ghost of a smile.

"Drop by anytime, Kitten. I'll make you catfish."

"I cut you off, Johnnie Rizzo," I said. "You're not my beneficiary anymore."

The confusion on his face was genuine. "What are you talking about?"

I knew at that moment Johnnie Rizzo was not the mad bomber. He doesn't keep secrets. He's like a goofy kid. He wears everything out there on his sleeve. How else could I always catch the cheater?

Oops.

"I, uh, I took your name off my life insurance policy."

"Just now?" Johnnie shook his head pityingly. "My god, Kitten. You've been hanging out in this alley stalking me for three years."

"No, no! I haven't."

"Move on, for chrissake. This isn't healthy. In fact, it's a little creepy."

He dropped the window, locked it from the inside, and stomped away. I stretched tall on my tippy toes, the top of my hair and eyes visible to an empty room.

"Come back, Johnnie Rizzo," I called. "It's not what you think!"

The kitchen crew bowled over in stitches. They gripped their guts in laughing. I shuffled to the car, slumped on the seat and bonked my head on the steering wheel.

Hank blared "Your Cheating Heart." I dragged out my cell.

"Pants on Fire Detective Agency."

"Call them off."

"Who is this?"

"You know who this is."

"I'll take a hint."

"David Reichert."

I racked my brain. "I'll go for a bigger hint."

"Minneapolis. The Annual Midwest Mortician Convention."

"Gotcha. So Dave, how much does it cost to get a hooker to lie perfectly still and play dead like that?"

"Not as much as the divorce, thank you very much," he said snippily.

"So why are you calling me?"

"The cops have gone bonkers. They hauled about a dozen of us in here. The thing is, we didn't do anything wrong."

"I have the photos."

"So maybe we chipped around a little. Are they charging us for that? I mean, is cheating a crime?"

"It isn't nice, Dave."

"This is about the flaming dog poop on your porch, isn't it?"

"*You* did that?"

"You gotta talk to them, lady. They're searching my house for plastic explosives. I mean, are you kidding me? I don't know how to build a bomb. I couldn't put my kid's bicycle together last Christmas."

"Answer their questions and you'll be fine. Good-bye, Dave."

"Wait! You gotta get me outta here. This is my one phone call. They think I'm talking to my lawyer."

"Gee, Dave. Looks like you dialed the wrong number."

◇◇◇

I stared at the phone in my hand a long time. I could take Johnnie Rizzo off my mad bomber list. I scratched Dave Reichert's name too. Maybe the whole cheating dozen had nothing to do with the fireworks at Mickey's. What if the link wasn't a cheater, but a client. Say, Rita Polansky.

I called the FBI. The voice was stiff.

"Special Agent Harding."

"Larry. This is Caterina DeLuca. I need a favor."

He groaned. Give the man some fiber.

"I need to know if the chemical signature in the two Bridgeport bombings is the same. I have a hunch one person is responsible for both."

Larry sighed deeply. "The first explosion was a gas leak. I can give you a copy of my report."

"I thought we were making progress, Larry. Why do you lie to me?"

"Secondly, the FBI isn't involved in the Bridgeport car bombing. Captain Maxfield of Chicago PD is leading that investigation."

"Bob won't listen to me. He's chasing a red herring."

Larry laughed derisively.

"Please make the call. I'll get back to you."

Click

◇◇◇

I drove past Swedish Covenant Hospital and North Park University, turned onto Christiana Street and read off house numbers. The house I wanted was several blocks down on the right, a smoky gray with white shutters, and frilly lace curtains. It wasn't the sort of rat hole I expected to find Charlie in.

The Dodge Charger wasn't in front of the house so I was pretty sure Charlie wasn't home. I marched to the door like I was expected, knocked, and waited thirty seconds before inserting my pick in the lock. The door swung away from me and my tools fell to the porch. I dived after them.

"I dropped a quarter," I said lamely.

"You're here to see Charlie," the old woman said. I know who you are."

"You do?"

The crows feet deepened and her eyes smiled. "You're my grandson's girlfriend. I've seen your pictures in his room."

My stomach lurched and I felt sick.

"Don't tell him I said that. Charlie doesn't like me snooping in his things."

"I won't. And please don't tell him I stopped by. He… uh… hasn't called lately. I don't want him to think I was checking up on him."

"I check on Charlie too. He got into that awful trouble when he was younger and I worry he'll get with the wrong crowd again. He's so unsuspecting and sweet."

My jaw dropped and the word slipped out. "Charlie?"

"He's a hunk, isn't he? Like his grandpa."

"Uh, would you mind if I looked in Charlie's room for just a minute. Our one month anniversary is coming up and I haven't a clue what to get him."

"Go right ahead, dear. Down the hall on the right. Don't mind the mess though. You know how he is with those candy wrappers."

I had a bad feeling in the pit of my stomach as I opened the door to Charlie's bedroom. The room was small with just enough room to squeeze a twin bed, dresser, computer desk, and night stand. The wall next to his bed was splattered with photos of me outside the hospital, in Tino's Deli, and through my parents' window during my intervention.

I did a mental head slap. I dragged my eyes away from the wall and searched for a clue.

There were little Starburst wrappers everywhere twisted in a bow. He hid a well-used crunchy porn stash in his underwear drawer. *Eeeuuw.* A fat bag of weed was stashed in a boot in his closet. And the top drawer in the nightstand held a lone photograph. Rita Polansky stood alone outside an abandoned building. I knew it well. I'd had an unfortunate encounter with the FOR LEASE sign in the photograph. A telephone number was scrawled on the back of the picture. I copied it quickly and scurried out the door.

Chapter Sixteen

I picked up the tail shortly after leaving Charlie's grandma's. He was tall or he sat on pillows. His mustache was fuzzy and his blond hair was cropped short in that Hollywood messy look. He was bronzed and buffed like a lifeguard but beach bums don't drive Hummers.

I led the parade to Oak Street and snagged a parking spot in front of a trendy boutique. The driver cruised past and made a U-turn at the end of the block and zoomed back to park across the street. I stood in front of the shop window and watched his reflection in the glass. He seemed more civilized than Charlie. He didn't look like he dealt in dead rats. I slung my purse over my shoulder and hightailed it inside the store. I had some digs to buy for a party.

The dress was a perfect fit with an outrageous price tag. On a normal day I wouldn't have tried it on but I had come close to my grand finale the other night. I had the clerk ring up the dress, killer four-inch stilettos, and a wonder bra for the plunging neckline.

I threw in a pair of designer jeans, a light White Sox jacket with big pockets, sunglasses, and a baseball cap. I changed into my new jeans, tied my hair in a ponytail, and pulled it through the cap. Then I grabbed my bags and slipped out the back.

I cut down the alley and back up to Oak, keeping my head low and blending with the crowd. I approached the Hummer from behind. The driver had stretched back in the seat behind a newspaper. He didn't see me coming. I wrapped my fingers around the 9mm in my pocket, zipped behind his bumper, and in three quick steps tapped the barrel of my gun on his door.

He glanced over and rolled down the window.

He had golden brown eyes and an intriguing cleft in his chin. He flashed an easy smile. "Nice hat. I'm a Cubs fan myself."

"I have a gun."

"I noticed."

"Why are you following me?"

"Tino said I should keep an eye on you."

"Liar, liar. You don't know Tino."

He jerked his head at the passenger seat. "I have your sausages. You left them at the store."

"Oh." I felt stupid. "I don't need a body guard. I can take care of myself."

"Maybe, but let's get you out of the street. If something happens on my watch I'll never hear the end of it."

We locked the packages in Tino's Buick and followed the aroma of sauerkraut to a cozy Bavarian café. He nudged me past the dinner crowd to a quiet table in the bar.

Without asking he ordered drinks and waved the waiter away.

"You're bossy," I said.

"Women don't usually notice until the third date."

"I'm surprised you get a second."

"You'll be crazy about me before dessert."

I made a face.

"I'm Max. Suppose you tell me why someone wants to kill you."

I lifted a shoulder. "I wish I knew."

"Maybe we'll figure it out. Until then you're stuck with me."

"Bossy, bossy," I said, but I didn't argue. "How do you know Tino?"

"We did covert ops together overseas."

I gaped. "You were *spies*?"

"Nothing so dramatic. It was a long time ago, before Tino retired to the serious business of cold cuts."

I smiled broadly. "I always suspected Tino was a government agent or a crook or both."

We ate weinerschnizel and drank pilsner beer. I told Max everything from the day Rita tearfully called Pants on Fire. Well, almost everything. I skipped over my encounter with Johnnie's fly and talked about some of my cases. The cops, hot on the trail of a near-cop-killer, would be drilling cheaters as we spoke. I finished with finding photos of me hanging like trophies on Charlie's freak-wall.

Max's warm eyes filled with compassion for my plight and he listened without interrupting. When I finished he leaned close, holding my eyes in his gaze.

"I have a few questions to fill in the blanks."

"Yes?" I said softly.

He took a drink of Pilsner and filled both our glasses.

"What the hell were you thinking? Is the concussion making you act this recklessly or do you navigate on self destruct."

"What?"

"You antagonized this whack job Charlie and his boss Harr at every turn. Harr knows you were stalking his house."

"Does not."

Max threw up his hands. "I can't protect a woman with a death wish."

"I didn't ask for your protection and I don't have a death wish. *Waiter*!"

"Yes, ma'am?"

"Check please."

"Cancel that. Bring two glasses of Pernod and your dessert tray."

I stood in a huff.

He flashed a dazzling smile meant to quash further protest. "Sit down, please."

Aware that people were watching I plunked down on my chair again. "OK. But I'm only staying for the apple strudel."

"As I see it you have two choices. First, and this is the choice I recommend, *leave town*. Give this Harr character time to forget you. I have a vacation house in Saint Thomas. It's safe, it's right on the beach, and you can stay as long as you like."

"I won't be bullied from my home."

"I thought you'd say that."

"But I'll take a rain check on the beach house."

He laughed. "OK, maybe you don't have a death wish. Second option. We do it my way and take down this dirt bag before he gets us."

"Us?"

"I'm in for the ride. You're stuck with me."

"I guess there's no changing your mind then." I checked the relief from my voice.

We shared the strudel and settled the tab.

"I always wanted to drive a Hummer," I said.

"Later." Max nudged me toward the door. "Today we take Tino's Buick. It's bulletproof."

"You're joking."

"Even a sausage maker acquires enemies."

I called Rocco from the car. "I have a phone number. Can you get me a name?"

I heard a rustling of paper. "Go ahead," he said and I rattled off the number on Rita's picture.

"I'll call it in tomorrow," Rocco said. "Where are you? Are you home?"

"We're getting close."

"We?"

"I have some good news. You get to sleep with your wife tonight. Tino got me a body guard *and* a bullet proof car. Did you know our deli-maestro was a government spy?

"No kidding? Who's the muscle?"

"Max, a friend from Tino's secret past."

"Well, Max had better not sleepwalk into your room tonight."

Maria snagged the phone. "Don't listen to your nosy brother. Are you sure you're all right? I wish you'd stay with us until this is over."

"Thanks, Maria, but I have a bodyguard."

"Does he look like Kevin Costner."

"He's taller." I glanced over and our eyes made contact. I looked quickly away. "And a lot bossier."

"Bossy will not work with you, girlfriend."

"Try telling him that. How's your sister?"

"Boinking some married fool. I want you to go to Nevada and take some dirty pictures. If my sister's lucky his wife will shoot him."

"We'll go together when this is over. We can do Vegas."

"Deal. Rocco can stay with the kids."

"*What?*" Rocco demanded in the background.

Max circled the neighborhood before pulling into the driveway. Max checked out my premium platinum alarm system and said it was worth every penny. I felt a little better about the check I wrote. Inside, I gave my new roomie an abbreviated tour of the important stuff. Guest bedroom, bathroom, and my stash of Ben and Jerry's.

I was heading for bed when the doorbell rang, freezing me in my tracks. Max waved me back, a Colt 45 suddenly in his hand. He moved to the door, his trained eye pressed to the peephole. He jerked his head and I joined him.

"Do you know this dangerous woman?"

A huge brown eye stared back at me through the peephole. I jumped.

"Cat, are you in there?" Mama shouted.

"She looks harmless enough."

"Don't be fooled."

I punched the alarm and opened the door and Mama's eyes widened on Max. "I didn't know you had company. And so *late*."

Max shot out a hand. "I'm Max, Mrs. DeLuca, a friend of Tino's. I'll be here a few days keeping your daughter safe."

"Such a nice boy." Mama ignored the right hand and grabbed his left. "And single."

"Guilty as charged."

"Italian?"

"Danish."

Mama pulled her hand away. "What a pity."

She pinned her attention on me. "People are talking, Caterina Deluca. Jack said you blew up his poor Papa's Dorothy."

"What kind of man names his car Dorothy," Max said.

Mama fixed a practiced eye of Catholic guilt on me. "Jack's sainted father died in that car. A terrible accident." Mama crossed herself. "The gun went off. Shot him right in the mouth."

"And they say guns don't kill people," Max said.

Mama pulled a tissue from her bra and dabbed an eye. "At least Jack's Papa and Dorothy are together again."

Bingo. My plan grew legs.

Inga had followed Mama through the door. She jumped all over Max, slapping his leg with her tail and licking his hands.

"Who's this?"

"This is Inga."

"She had a sleepover at Grandma's."

I squinted. "Is that cake around her mouth?"

"Apple Cake and ice cream for dessert," Mama said.

Inga ran to the kitchen and returned with her leash. I scooped it up and Max folded his arms.

"Where do you think you're going?"

"We run every night before bed."

"Not without me you don't. Care to walk with us, Mrs. DeLuca?"

"You kids go ahead. I brought eggplant parmesan to put in the fridge. I'll let myself out."

"I'll show you how to work the alarm system," I said.

"All this because my daughter takes dirty pictures." Mama clicked her teeth disapprovingly. "She's a dispatcher, you know."

"Really?"

"Don't encourage her," I said and kissed Mama on the cheek. "Thanks for taking Inga."

"She's my favorite grand-dog," Mama smiled, "but don't tell the others."

Chapter Seventeen

Max did a quick perimeter check before we left the safety of the house. As an extra precaution we slipped out the back door and cut across the alley through a neighbor's yard to a parallel street and the Catholic high school. We ran at an easy jog and I lengthened my strides to match his. The sound of our feet on the pavement struck a strong rhythmic cadence. I pounded the long stretch until the tension drained from my body, then walked the final stretch home.

Max went to bed with a bottle of water and I closed down the house. I nuked a cup of cold coffee, smothered chocolate syrup over two scoops of Ben and Jerry's Cherry Garcia, and padded to my bedroom. Inga was at the door. Her tail wagged wildly.

I balanced the dishes and twisted the knob, kicked the door open and booted it closed with my bum. I set my sugar and caffeine fix on the dresser and shuffled off to the bathroom. I brushed my teeth, washed my face, stripped my clothes off; and grabbed my oversized Chicago Bears jersey off the hook on the door. I came out tugging the jersey over my head and stopped at the dresser.

Ben, Jerry, and Juan Valdez were gone. In their place was a card. It read *Chance Savino* and a telephone number.

"Hello, DeLucky," Chance grinned. He stretched across my bed with his fingers locked behind his head and tell-tale chocolate around his mouth. Damn he was fine. Inga lay on the bed beside him with a hint of ice cream on her mouth, too.

My breath caught. I yanked down my nightshirt.

"No need to do that on my account."

"How the hell did you get in here," I demanded. "And Inga, you traitor!"

The beagle stretched out on her back beside him. She slurped a wet kiss on his face.

"Yuck," I said.

He rubbed her belly. "We bonded in your car."

Inga sighed shamelessly.

So did I. Chance Savino was a world of trouble. Buildings explode around him, bodies pile up, and he likes to play dead. But right now I was imagining him naked.

"To answer your question, your mother let me in."

"She didn't."

"I told her I worked for the alarm company and was doing a follow up to make sure everything was functioning correctly." He sipped my coffee. "So, who's the boyfriend?"

"None of your business."

"I bet I've seen more of you than he has."

"You don't know that."

"And they're spectacular."

My cheeks flushed hot.

"Your mother said he's your bodyguard. I can't help but notice he's sleeping in the other room."

"The FBI said you're dead. You can't believe everything someone tells you."

A smile tugged the side of his mouth. "I'm not sure that makes sense."

"Everyone thinks I imagine you. They're saying I'm crazy."

"I can't believe it didn't occur to them sooner."

"I know! I'll take your picture and when they see it they'll…" I collapsed on the side of the bed.

"Is this the part where I say 'Cheese'?"

"No, dammit. Eddie Harr stole my camera."

"Harr?" He expelled a breath. "Dammit, Delucky, you have no idea what you're getting yourself into."

"You were there. You saw what they did to Rita. They butchered her."

His tone softened. "Leave it to the professionals. They'll figure it out."

I stared at the ceiling and contemplated how I got into this mess.

"I suppose you came by for your coat."

He shrugged. "I saw a guy wearing it today. He looked good."

"Then what are you doing here?"

"I may have dropped something in your car the other day. I came back for it."

"Let me get this straight. You didn't come to see me?"

"Should I have?"

"You came here because you want to break in my car and steal something?"

"Not steal. Retrieve. So where is it?"

"Where is what?"

"Your car. It's not in your garage."

"Why don't you tell me what you're looking for?"

"Why don't I spend the night and see if you can get it out of me."

"I don't need to know *that* badly."

He rolled across the bed toward me. I stopped breathing. He laughed softly and his eyes crinkled at the edges.

"Get your car back and I'll show you." He touched a fingertip to my nose. "We'll talk tomorrow."

I bounced off the bed. "Stay here! I need a witness."

"Max!" I flew down the hall.

Max staggered from his room in red plaid boxers, wrestling a gun in his hand. It had been too long since there was a gorgeous man in my bedroom and now I had two in one night. Despite death threats, dead bodies, and a throbbing concussion, things were definitely looking up.

"What happened?" Max waved the weapon around.

"There's someone I want you to meet."

He pushed me aside and kicked my bedroom door open.

"Max," I announced. "This is..."

I blinked. Chance was gone.

"Damn! I told him not to leave."

I saw a glint of temper in his eyes. "You opened the door without calling me."

"He was in my room when I went to bed."

"Who?"

"Chance Savino."

"And Inga didn't bark?"

"I guess they bonded in my car."

"You're not making sense. The alarm was set. There's no way he could leave without setting it off."

I felt a headache coming on. "He must've seen Mama punch in the code."

"Your mother saw him?"

"Of course she saw him," I said impatiently. "She let him in."

"And she'll verify that?"

"Great. I need a credible witness and Mama's all I got."

"This should be entertaining. Call her and put her on speaker."

I punched her number.

"Hello."

"Hi, Mama. It's Cat."

"Yes, dear."

"I'm calling about the man you let in the house tonight."

"He's Italian you know."

"So was Al Capone."

"Ah, but Capone was married."

Max smirked.

"You can't be letting strangers in my house, Mama. That defeats the whole purpose of the alarm."

"You don't think I'd let just anyone in. He has a good job with the alarm company. What more do you want?"

"Mama, he's the guy I've been telling you about."

"Who?"

"You know, the guy I followed into the building before the bomb went off."

She gasped. I imaged her clutching her heart. "The man who died in the explosion?"

"Yes! Yes! That's him!"

"Don't be *matto*. I know a dead man when I see one."

Click.

"You want to call her back?" Max grinned.

I blew a sigh. "She's talking to Father Timothy. She has him on speed dial."

Max threw an arm around my shoulder. "You're not crazy, Cat."

"Thank you."

"It's just a glitz in your genes."

Max ducked down the hall and didn't flinch when I nailed him with a pillow.

I was torn from my dreams the next morning by the aroma of sizzling bacon and hot coffee. Showering quickly, I pulled my hair up in a clippie thing, threw on a cotton cami and baggy sweats, and raced Inga to the kitchen. Max stood at the stove in black Levis and a white tee stretched tight across his muscled chest. I began working on a fantasy that involved Max, my silk sheets, and a revolving breakfast buffet table.

"One egg or two?"

"Huh? Oh, two Over easy. I'll make toast."

"Too late." I heard a pop and toast appeared.

"I'll get butter and jam."

"Sit." Max placed his hands firmly on my shoulders and twisted me around to the table. Jam, honey, butter, and a pile of newspaper stared back. He had finished the paper and completed the crossword puzzle. In ink, smarty pants. It was almost seven.

Max placed a steaming mug of coffee in front of me. "The DeLuca men would starve if they had to make breakfast," I said.

"I'm guessing your husband didn't make breakfast either."

"My husband made a lot of things. My best friend and a couple waitresses at his restaurant. Never breakfast at home."

"And now you catch cheaters. Ironic, don't you think?"

I smeared jam on my toast. "Such is life."

Pat Benetar blared from my cell phone. "Call Me."

I put the call on speaker. "Talk to me," I said.

The voice was stiff. "Caterina, this is Jack."

"Hey, Jack. Is my car ready?"

"Is Dorothy put back together?"

"Jack, I'm sorry about Dorothy. You'll have to settle the loss with your insurance company."

"You're a cold woman to ask about your car when you killed Dorothy."

"It must be awful for you that someone is trying to kill me, Jack, but I need my car."

"So your boyfriend said."

"What boyfriend?"

"Don't play games with me, Cat. I caught him sniffing around my shop this morning. He said he left something in your car."

"A tall guy? Dark hair, blue eyes?"

"A thief."

"I'd know that description anywhere."

"You should also know I won't be going to your birthday party."

"Ah c'mon, Jack."

"And you can't marry my nephew Devin."

"*What?*"

"Your mother told me to bring Devin to the party. With your porno business and these terrorist connections she'll have to understand."

"Whoa, Jack. I don't want to marry Devin—"

"I refuse to expose Devin to your criminal ways."

"Didn't your nephew rob a bank a few years ago?"

"That was then. Devin's my top mechanic now."

"Can he fix my car?"

"You don't get it, Cat."

Click.

"He hung up."

"Cheer up," Max said. "Devin's not the only criminal in town. Tino wants to hook you up with his second cousin."

"Tino's cousin is a crook?"

Max grinned. "Yeah. He's a lawyer."

I stared glumly into my coffee. "I need a boyfriend for my party."

Max carried his plate of scrambled eggs to the table and sat across from me. "How about the boyfriend who showed up at Jack's."

"Chance Savino. He said he hid something in my car before the building blew."

His forehead puckered. "Really? I wonder what."

"I'll let you know. As soon as Jack locks up I'm going in."

"B&E?"

"I have the technology."

"And Jack thought your criminal ways were a bad thing."

I stabbed a slice of bacon. "But I still need a date for tomorrow night. Someone to pose as my boyfriend and call off the matchmaking hounds. Someone like…" my eyes fell on Max and my face brightened. "Hello, lover."

Max raised his hands defensive mode. "Don't even think about it."

"C'mon, Max, it's just one night."

"Uh uh."

"Give me one good reason."

"I'll give you four. Tino and I go way back, you and I just met yesterday, no one will buy it, and I met your mother. She doesn't like me."

"You had to tell her you're Danish."

"Take my advice, Cat. If you ever want a serious relationship again, move far away from your family."

Inga growled softly. Max gripped my arm and silenced me with a look. He pulled a gun from the back of his jeans.

"Ouch," I mouthed.

I heard it too; a muffled scraping noise coming from the side of the house.

We followed the sound to my office. Max leaned back and nudged the curtain with a finger. A round ruddy faced man shuffled his feet on the porch. I squinted harder. He sort of looked like my last blind date. But this guy appeared smarter. With his wild hair and mustache he looked like a chubby Einstein. My date had been an idiot. Not the same guy.

I shrugged a shoulder.

Max flashed his palm. "Stay."

I pinned my ear against the door. Max punched off the alarm, cut to the kitchen, and out the patio door that leads to the backyard. I didn't want fireworks. If this guy was one of Eddie's goons I hoped he was man enough to pack a pistol and leave the explosives at home.

Einstein rapped his knuckles on the door. I held my breath.

He pounded the door with his fists.

"Open this door, Ms. DeLuca. I hear you in there and I won't leave until—OH!" The muffled voice now screamed. "Help! Help!"

I jerked the door open. Einstein sprawled mustache down, eating porch. Max's knee dug in his back and he swung his arms wildly behind him, missing Max and hitting air.

"Ms. Deluca, look out!" the man wailed. "Close the door and call the police. I'll hold this maniac off."

"This maniac is my friend."

He gasped. "You're gonna run off clients with friends like that."

"You were acting strange. You were doing something with your feet." I checked out the shoes. Ferragamo Oxfords, nice.

"I was cleaning the dog shit off my shoes." He stared accusingly at my beagle.

Inga wagged her tail.

Max appeared comfortable enough. "He's not packing any weapons."

"Okay, Max, let him up."

Einstein scrambled to his feet swatting his mustache and shirt.

"Who are you and what are you doing here?" Max said.

He turned his back to Max and faced me. "I want to hire you. You helped my brother George. I'm Roger King."

I eyed him suspiciously. "George King is a foot taller and hot as a smoking pistol."

"So I lost a bet with God. I called but your answering machine said you'll be back next week."

"So call me next week. I'm sort of into something right now."

"Please help me. I think my wife wants to leave me."

"Big surprise," Max said.

Roger made a blubbering sound that I thought only sea life could make. I softened, just a little.

I turned to Max. "Roger can come inside if he takes his shoes off. Stay with him while I call George. I wanna know if Einstein is his brother."

Chapter Eighteen

Max's eyes didn't leave Roger until I returned to the room.

"Did you talk to my brother?"

"I did."

George King hired me a few months ago to check out his partner. Our friendship lasted longer than his roommate and we still catch a movie from time to time.

"George told Roger to call me."

"I told you my brother gave me your card."

"My address isn't on the card, Roger."

Roger scuffed a sock on the carpet. "George told me where you live. I was supposed to call for an appointment."

"Good advice. Your brother is worried about you."

"Hah. George never liked my wife. He refused to give her a chance. She's my soul mate."

"According to George you met your soul mate at a strip club in Vegas. You tucked five C notes in her G-string for a lap dance and married her a week later."

Max blinked. "Your soul mate's a Vegas stripper?"

"*Was*," Roger said. "That was a long time ago."

"Last year," I said. "She's half your age. George said she—"

Roger bristled. "Her name is Bambi."

"Of course it is. Your brother says Bambi married you for your money. She pressured you to change your will and take out several large life insurance policies."

"She worries about me."

"Your brother worries about you. I'm not so sure about Bambi."

"Incredible." Max shook his head.

"According to George you were hospitalized last week. The doctors said you somehow ingested anti-freeze. He thinks Bambi is trying to kill you."

"Bambi is no gourmet cook, but she wouldn't poison me on purpose."

Max threw his hands in the air. "How'd you make your money?"

"George and Roger launched a software company in the early eighties," I said. "They can dial Bill Gates' private number."

"No shit."

"You said you thought your wife wants to leave you. Why don't you tell me about it."

"She's seeing someone," Roger moaned.

"Who?"

"I don't know but she's not the same. She's gone all the time, preoccupied, and she hasn't given me a lap dance since—"

"Too much information," Max cut in.

"George said you have a prenup."

Roger nodded. "If I file for divorce Bambi gets $250,000 and her jewelry. If she files or cheats she gets nothing."

"And if you die she gets it all."

"I want her back." George said. "Find out who she's seeing and get rid of him. Pay him off, threaten him, sic Max on him."

"If I agree to help you, you'll have to do everything I say. I haven't time for explanations."

Roger's face broke in a smile. "George said you'd fix everything."

"Call Bambi from your cell phone and tell her you've been called out of town on business."

"I've never lied to Bambi."

"Well that makes one of you. Check into a hotel. You can't see or speak with her until I say."

"Gee, Cat, I—"

"Go to the bank and withdraw all the cash you'll need. Do not use a credit card or anything she can trace to find you."

"I don't know if—"

I tugged his mustache to get his attention. "You came to me for help. Now trust me." I wrote my personal number on a card. "Call me if you absolutely have to. Like if there's a lot of blood. I'll call you when I have something."

Roger's brow furrowed while he mulled it over. "I just want to be happy," he said bleakly.

"You will. Don't forget your shoes."

I shooed him out the door and Max grinned.

"What?"

"He'll be happy as a monk. Short and fat with no booty on his lap."

"Don't underestimate Roger. He's smart. And he's faithful."

"He's irritating."

"He's rich. Lots of women want a guy like Roger. Someday I'll introduce him to my cousin Ginny. She's a computer geek too."

"Does Ginny lap dance?"

"Every good woman does," I smiled.

I tromped to the office closet and pulled out my little black bag of tricks. Binoculars, video and audio recorders, and a GPS tracking systems.

"I need a new camera before we check out Bambi. Come on, Inga."

"Whoa. Tino doesn't allow dogs in his car."

The beagle wagged her tail. "Inga is part of my team."

"Good luck explaining that to Tino." He glowered at Inga. "No drooling."

Max waited outside the photo shop and sucked down two red-hots while I picked out my camera. I slipped out the door behind him and snagged the third from his hand as he opened his mouth.

"Hey!"

I wiped the mustard from his lip. "Mmm. Thanks."

We cruised north to Roger's home in Glenview and parked across the street. Three elegant stories of river rock and green tinted glass.

Max whistled low. "I can't believe that dumb shit lives *here*."

A Las Vegas lap dancer whipped a pearl-colored Escalade into the driveway, Metallica blaring from the speakers. She kicked the door open and swung her long bare legs outside.

Max caught his breath. "I can't believe—"

I nudged him. "You're drooling in Tino's car."

The legs skipped up the steps, arms loaded with packages. A Bloomingdale's bag slipped from her hand and she leaned over to recover. The painfully short mini skirt rolled up her thighs and bared all.

"Yaowsa," I said.

Max caught his breath. "Commando."

"Nope, thong. I can see the dental floss."

Bambi disappeared behind the front door and Max breathed again.

"Does your cousin look like that?"

"No, but her boobs don't deflate when you poke a pin in them."

Max snagged the binoculars and caught glimpses of the bleached head through the windows. I got the play by play. Salad for lunch, one hundred crunches and various contortions to stretch every muscle in her body, and a steam shower.

"Roger should invest in some curtains," I said.

"Not on my account."

An hour and a half later Bambi emerged from the house and zoomed away in the Escalade. Max was hot on her tail.

Bambi's first stop was a salon where she had a manicure and a pedicure. I was guessing she also had a bikini wax because she eventually came out the door walking funny. She walked past the Escalade and across the parking lot to a sidewalk café where she was greeted by a biker dude who had obviously come into money. Designer jeans, eel skin cowboy boots, and a white silk shirt you could see through. I read the tattoo on his arm through my binoculars. A red heart with *Stacey January 17th 2006*, written in black italics.

The kiss was long and Bambi swallowed a lot of tongue.

"Say cheese." I snapped the picture.

Max turned on the recorder and aimed the mike toward the ogling couple.

"Damn. I'm not picking them up."

I dug into my bag of tricks. For $25 you can buy a wireless audio device that will transmit to your cell phone. I like to keep a few on hand.

"I'll take the smallest mike," I said. I dashed across the street and approached the table closest to Bambi and her mystery man.

"How is everything," I asked fluffing the flowers on the table. I moved to Bambi's table and did the same, dropping the audio device into the centerpiece. The waitress approached as I stepped away.

"May I help you?"

"These tables need fresh water."

The astonished server disappeared. I did too.

"You're good," Max laughed.

"How are the acoustics now?"

He put my phone on speaker. "Loud and clear."

Tattoo man leaned close and whispered into the flowers.

"I don't see why you got your tit in a wringer, Stace."

My eyes widened. "Stacey?"

"So the old man went on business a few days. So effin what. All them rich guys go on business."

"This is different, baby. It doesn't feel right. What if he's on to me?"

"They got nothin' to pin me to you."

"It's that stupid meddling brother. What if he convinced Roger to file for divorce?"

"I waited a year for this and I ain't settling on for allowance. We do this and we roll the rest of our lives."

"Don't cause a scene." She eyeballed the other tables. "We finish this now. Make it look like an accident."

Tattoo broke an ugly smile. "I'm looking forward to this one."

He caressed her leg and nibbled her ear. "We got time."

She pushed him away. "I gotta be home when Roger calls. I'll let you know where he is."

"You won't get off that easy in a few days. We'll have nothing but time."

"And money," she purred.

Bambi paid the check with a credit card and he followed her to the Escalade.

I dashed to their table heading the busboy off at the pass. I confiscated their glasses with a tissue, the mic off the flowers, and stuffed a fat bill in the busboy's hand. I was gone before he closed his mouth.

I hopped in the passenger seat beside Max.

"Follow?" he said.

I copied down biker dude's license plate.

"I'd rather ID these clowns. We should get these prints to Rocco. And a copy of the audio to Captain Bob."

"I suppose stopping a multi-millionaire's murder would put you back in the captain's good graces."

I made a face. "If Roger doesn't weaken and call the black widow first. I'll give him a call."

"You wanna get Roger's attention? Sit on him. It worked for me. And it definitely worked for Bambi."

Chapter Nineteen

It was after five by the time we got back to the Precinct and dropped the glasses off with my cousin in Forensics. Captain Bob refused to see me but I left a message and a copy of the tape. I called Roger and threatened his life if he spoke to Bambi. I figured he'd be dead anyway.

We parked around the corner from my mechanic's shop. The lights were on and Jack's bank-robbing nephew was working late. Before long a greasy looking teenager in a jumpsuit drove a late model Volvo through the bay entrance. He scanned the area for witnesses and quickly slammed the door down behind him. Almost immediately the sound of power tools revved to life. Fifteen minutes later the bay doors reopened. What appeared to be a U-Haul truck with a dozen cans of spray paint pulled out and headed for the Dan Ryan.

"I'll be damned," Max said. "Devin has turned his uncle's business into a chop shop."

"Looks that way."

"Do you want to call it in?"

I shook my head. "I'll stop by tomorrow and tell Devin the cops are on to him. That should shake him enough to straighten up or set up shop elsewhere."

My cell phone vibrated in my jean pocket. It was Rocco. I put the phone on speaker.

"So did you get a read on the glasses I dropped off?"

"I did, but it will cost you dinner. Maria took the kids to her mom's for a birthday party. I haven't met this bodyguard of yours and if you take care of him like you took care of me he's starving."

"He's supposed to take care of me, Rocco."

"Hey, I'm hungry," Max said.

"We're waiting for Devin to lock up so I can B&E Jack's shop. I need something out of my car."

"Eat first. You don't want to go to jail hungry. The food sucks."

"Good tip," Max said. "Where do we meet?"

"At Mama Stortini's on Morgan."

My tummy did a flip flop. Stortini's puts out a seafood linguini that rivals Tino's.

"I reserved a table by the window where we can keep an eye on the car and avoid more fireworks," my brother said.

The greasy teenager returned in a spanking new Beemer. A purple and gold tassel swung from the rear view mirror, somebody's graduation gift.

Max turned the key and jammed the car in drive. "We're on our way. Devin's going to be a while."

Rocco waited for us in front of Stortini's and pulled the cones from our parking spot when we approached.

"Sweet," Max said.

I chuckled. "Rocco gets the best parking places. He uses those cones all over Chicago."

I took care of the intros and the guys checked each other out. They were about the same height and in good shape but Max spent more time in the gym and he didn't need a woman to match his socks.

When the waiter brought our plates and a bottle of Chianti I turned to Rocco. "What did you find out about the number I found in Charlie's room?"

Rocco pulled a scrap of paper from his pocket and punched a number in his phone. He held it to my ear.

A monotone voice answered. "FBI. How may I direct your call?"

My eyes widened and Rocco clicked the phone shut and stuffed it back in his pocket.

"Eddie Harr has a mole in the FBI," he said. "This is a powerful and well connected organization. It's not too late..."

"Don't say it," I said.

Rocco grinned. "It's not too late to be a dispatcher."

I scrunched my face. "Is it too late to be an only child?"

Max changed the subject. "Did you get any prints off the glasses."

Rocco brought out a file. "Kenneth Turner and Stacey Pope were married five years ago in Reno. They both have rap sheets. Check fraud, identity theft, nothing real serious, and there's no record of a divorce."

"Good news for Roger," Max said.

"Nothing we tell Roger will sound like good news. The woman he loves wants him dead. She's a scammer, he's a fool. That's pretty tough to sugar coat."

"I'm going to introduce Roger to Ginny," I said.

"Good. Two computer nerds no one else wants. Sounds like a perfect match."

The linguini was the best, maybe even better than Tino's, and it was served with crusty rosemary bread and Italian salad. When the waiter cleared our plates he brought steaming mugs of coffee, a tray of biscotti, and spumoni ice cream.

"What did the captain say when he heard the tape?"

"He said, 'What a goddam idiot.'"

"Ken or Stacey?"

"The computer geek. He said the guy's beat with the ugly stick and thinks a twenty-five- year-old stripper is hot for him."

I stiffened. "Looks aren't everything. There are true Beauty and the Beast romances out there."

"Name one."

"Julia Roberts and Lyle Lovett."

"She looks like him without makeup."

"Ari and Jackie."

"That went well."

"Boris and Natasha."

"You got me. The problem is we have the tape but it's not admissible in court. We can probably get a search warrant for the house but we won't find anything. Even if there's Prestone anti-freeze in the garage there's no proof she spiked his iced tea with it."

"Damn."

"What I can do is call a buddy of mine who works for the Glenview P.D. I can meet him up there and bring them both in for questioning. We'll play the tape and show them what we've got. Bimbo's marriage to—"

"It's Bambi."

"Whatever. The marriage is a fraud. Threaten bigamy charges and if we're lucky Bambi will run back to Nevada and never return."

"And Roger's off the chopping block. He won't be good to them dead any more."

Max nodded. "It should work. But before you bring them in we'd like to tell Roger. He'll want to freeze her bank and credit card access or she'll clean him out."

"Talk to Roger in the morning. After he takes care of business we'll bring them in. It's the best we can do. At least the sucker will be safe."

"But someone else won't," I said. "She'll go back to Las Vegas, stick silver whirleys on her nipples and attach herself to a pole—"

"Go on." Their eyes glazed over.

I glared. "And Stacey will find some other poor schmuck."

"Rich schmuck," Max said.

"Poor rich schmuck to scam, hitch, and kill."

Max looked disappointed. "You skipped the part about the lap dance."

I threw a biscotti at him.

"I agree it sucks," Rocco said, "but without more evidence the best we can do is save this guy's ass. You did good on this one."

"It's not a wash yet. What if we get more evidence?"

"You mean enough proof to convict."

"Enough proof to send her away until her boobs droop."

"Does silicon droop?"

"I hope it melts," I said.

Rocco tipped the bottle and the last of the wine splashed in his glass. "Another dead soldier."

"It won't work, sis. The only way is to catch them taking a pot shot at Roger. Tempting but it's not gonna happen."

"Hmm," I said thoughtfully.

"I know that look and you can forget it, Cat," Rocco said.

"What?"

"Forget the heroics. We play this one by the book. The last thing you want to do is piss the captain off. He's still taking heat from upstairs."

"Eddie Harr is crooked as they come," I said. "I can't believe Captain Bob apologized."

"Like he had a choice."

Rocco walked outside with us. "No sign of Charlie today?"

I shook my head.

"They might think their little car bomb scared you off. Stay away and they could stop swinging."

"Like that's gonna happen," Max said.

I snorted. "The people who killed Rita should pay for it. She deserves that."

"It won't bring her back."

"Don't you think I know that?"

Rocco kissed my cheek. "Be careful, Cat. I'll see you tomorrow at the party."

"Just a heads up, Rocco. I'll be your sister's date for the party."

Rocco's eyes narrowed. "You sleeping with my sister?"

"That's none of your business," I said.

"I'm not," Max said and Rocco smiled. "Yet."

"Max is dodging bullets with me while we figure this thing out. I don't know how to thank him."

"I'll take that lap dance," Max said and Rocco frowned.

Chapter Twenty

This time the lights were out in Jack's garage when we cruised by. There were cars parked outside the shop, presumably repairs he intended to return. My faithful Silver Bullet was locked up tight inside.

We parked and turned off the lights. I pulled on my black hoodie sweatshirt, gathered my pick and tension wrench, hugged Inga, and told Max to wait for me.

"I'm going with you."

"You're the getaway driver and my lookout. If you see blue lights call my cell. I'll hit the back door and meet you on the cross street."

Max grinned. "God you're sexy when you're committing a felony. Anything else?"

I stepped outside, closed the door, and whispered through the window. "If I'm busted bail me out."

A light from the parking lot lit the door of Jack's Repair Shop like a spot light. An unknowing burglar would try the back but I knew Jack bolts the back door with a bar from the inside. The front entrance was the only way in. Luckily, there wasn't much traffic this time of night when the proprietors of the neighboring shops had gone home. I moved purposefully to the door and worked my magic holding the pick in my mouth. Setting the tension wrench in the lock, I pulled the pick from my teeth and opened the door. I stepped inside and the odor of wacky tobaccy lingered in the air. The shop was dark but a few small windows filtered light from the street. Establishing my escape route first, I located the back door and unhitched the bar to insure a clean break. Then I saw my car.

My shiny Honda Accord was pinned in the back of the shop, blocked by several cars. All tuned up and spanking clean. I couldn't wait get my car back.

A hand reached around and covered my mouth, smothering my shriek.

"Don't scream DeLucky. It's me."

The voice was smooth as silk. I was still and he let me go. I spun around and slugged him.

"Ouch."

"That's for scaring the crap out of me."

"Damn, you pack a punch girl." He rubbed his arm. "I wondered when you'd be back."

"You were here before?"

"I was watching you and the guy who's not your boyfriend."

"You don't know that."

"He's not right for you."

"He made me breakfast."

Chance snorted.

"Besides you told Jack you're my boyfriend. If I have all these boyfriends I should probably be getting something out of it."

"I'm always willing to oblige," he said, slipping his hands around my waist.

I felt my face flush and stepped back. "I was thinking more along the lines of jewelry."

"Let me know if you change your mind. What are you doing here? Breaking your car out?"

"For two to five in Joliet? No thanks. I want the package you left in my car."

His smile flashed white in the darkness. "Not if I get there first."

Chance turned on a run and I pushed him back and clawed past him, racing to reach my car first. He charged after me grabbing the back of my hoodie and towing me toward him. I fought back, propelling forward when my feet slipped in a small pool of oil. Chance caught me in his arms but then lost his footing on the slimy surface and crashed on the concrete floor. I fell on top of him, his muscled body cushioning my fall. I lay stunned for a moment my head on his chest. A giggle rose in my throat until I burst into hysterics. "Nice moves, Chance. Are you okay?"

No answer. I turned over to face him.

I touched his face. "Chance, are you hurt?" The panic rose in my voice.

Savino opened his eyes. "I like this. I figured you'd want to be on top some of the time…"

In one swift motion his hands diverted my fists while his legs rolled over and swung me beneath him.

I fought and kicked with a fury but with his powerful shoulders he was stronger and had me pinned. He moved close, his breath hot on my face. He smelled musky and his lips brushed my neck.

The combat in me poofed like smoke and I stopped struggling. His cheek felt slightly rough and my skin tingled with a heat that rushed through me and headed south.

I moaned slightly and Chance whispered something in my ear. I didn't catch what he said but I was thinking the answer was "yes."

"What did you say?"

His breath was hot in my ear. "I said I wonder if Jack knows one of his employees is running an after-hours chop shop."

"Ugh!" I heaved with disgust and pushed him off me.

I clambered to my feet and brushed myself off. Dirty disgusting oil covered my new jeans and I kicked him in the shin.

"What was that for?"

I finger combed my hair and tried to gather my composure. "Your shoe's untied."

Chance glanced down and I barreled past him sprinting to the car. I yanked the passenger door open. My fingers stroked the door, around and beneath the seat, searching for something out of place.

I heard a low chuckle behind me. "Let me in there and I'll show it to you."

Chance offered his hand. I pushed it away and stood on my own. Damn he was easy on the eyes.

"Fine, Savino."

He leaned into the car and emerged with a small black bag.

I gasped. "You tore my seat."

"A small hole with a jack knife. You never would have noticed."

He opened the bag and poured the contents into my cupped hands. A cluster of pink and red stones danced in the dark.

I caught my breath.

"Diamonds from Australia." His gaze held mine.

I tore my eyes away. "You're a thief." I poured the stones back and slid the black bag into my sweatshirt pouch.

He smiled. "So? You take dirty pictures. Your Mama told me."

I flounced toward the back door and the horrifying thud of metal on flesh jolted my senses. I spun around. Chance Savino lay in a crumpled heap on the cement floor.

A masked man stepped out of the shadows. My body began to shake. He stroked my face with the hard cold wrench and plucked the black bag from my pouch. The wrench clattered across the smooth floor and he disappeared out the back door.

I tore after him. "Stop!" I screamed. My phone vibrated in my pocket the moment I heard sirens wail. I ran back to Chance. "Wake up. The cops are coming."

"Cat!" Max called from the back door.

"Over here!"

He rushed to where I knelt beside Savino.

"We have to go. There isn't time."

Max hoisted me over his shoulder and hauled me through the door and into the Buick parked in the alley. He hit the gas, narrowly evading the blue neon posse skidding to a stop at Jack's Garage.

I breathed again. "Did you see the guy run out the back with the diamonds?"

"You found diamonds?"

"Pinks and reds." I pondered a moment. "Maybe it was Devin. He was tall but I can't be sure."

"Where does Devin live?"

I gave Max directions to Uncle Jack's house. "Devin isn't smart enough to move diamonds."

"Maybe it wasn't a planned hit. He returned to the shop for something and stumbled on…" he looked at me curiously.

"What?"

"You were in there a long time. What happened between you and the dead man?"

I felt my cheeks color. "I couldn't find the bag in the car and then Chance showed up. He found it right away and someone knocked him out cold and palmed the diamonds."

"Savino sounds like a dangerous man."

"You have no idea."

"This is where you thank me for keeping you out of lock up."

"Thanks, Max."

"And happy birthday." He reached in the back seat and handed me a single red rose.

"Huh?"

"It's after midnight. You're thirty."

"Ouch."

"For the next twenty four hours I'm officially your boyfriend."

I smelled the rose. "It's a three hour gig. And it starts at the party."

We parked in the shadows under a large maple tree and ten minutes later a rusted pick-up skidded to a stop in front of Jack's house. Devin crammed the last half of a burger in his mouth. The front door flew open. Uncle Jack stormed down the steps and yanked Devin from the truck by his ear.

"I wanted to do that," Max said.

"You're opening the shop in the morning and you reek like pot."

"You're killin' my ear."

"Smarten up. Hang around your loser friends and you'll be back in the pen."

Jack shoved Devin in the house and snuffed the porch light.

"Wait here." Max was out the car and across the street before I could respond. He returned to the car a few minutes later and threw a black ski mask in the back seat.

"He took the diamonds in the house with him. We'll have to get them later. Too bad his uncle won't let you marry the guy. You'd be rich."

"There aren't that many diamonds in the world."

"The pinks and reds are Australian. They're rare and exceptionally valuable."

"How do you know so much about diamonds?"

"I buy gifts for the women in my life. A new relationship, flowers and candy. Stage two, jewelry, silver or gold. Stage three, precious gems, including sapphire or ruby. Stage four, diamonds."

"How many stage fours have you hit?"

"Enough. But I never made it to the altar."

"You're terrified of intimacy. I saw it on Dr. Phil."

"You might be the cure." His fingers lightly caressed my cheek.

Oh boy. I pulled my gaze away. Max laughed softly and pulled on to the street. A light rain began to fall. I rested my head back and closed my eyes.

"Home, James," I said.

Chapter Twenty-one

I awoke on my birthday knowing I had thirty-year-old bags under my eyes. My solo B&E had been reduced to a party of thieves and I'd let a two-bit crook snatch a fortune from my hands. Devin's a klutz and he has sinus problems. I should've heard him coming a mile away.

I stared at the ceiling and imagined Chance Savino in the slammer. He was the reason I was in this whole stupid mess. I don't know why I still felt guilty for leaving him to get caught. And then, out of the blue the glorious truth hit me.

I hopped from my bed and did the happy dance with Inga barking at my heels. The illusive Chance Savino, a man deemed dead by the FBI, had been arrested, fingerprinted, and his fine mug was shot. It was now official, a matter of public record. Chance Savino was alive and Cat DeLuca wasn't so loopy after all.

Footsteps sprinted down the hall and Max burst through the door waving his gun.

"I heard a commotion. Are you OK?"

"I'm FAB-U-LOUS," I sang. "The truth is out!"

"What truth?"

"Chance Savino is alive and I am—" I snapped my fingers. "What's the word…?"

"Thirty?" Max said.

"No. Sane."

"Is that news?"

"Regretably, there were rumors."

I boogied my way into the shower and dressed quickly in a comfy lemon vee-neck tee and Levis. I found Max in the kitchen pouring two cups of coffee.

"Put the eggs away," I said. "Breakfast is on Roger."

I punched my client's number on my cell phone. For every gloriously happy life, someone else's was in the toilet. Right now that someone was Roger.

I pinched the smile from my lips. "Hey, Roger, how are you holding up."

"I miss Bambi," he whined. "Did you talk to her? Will she stay with me?"

"I want to talk to you about that. Where can we meet?"

"I'm downtown at the Chicago Hilton."

"Spendy."

"Bambi and I stay here when we go into town for a late dinner or play. We always request the same suite."

"And that's where you are now?"

"Uh huh."

I tried to keep the *you are such a sucker* sound out of my voice. "Do you think that was wise? Wouldn't that be the first place Bambi would look for you?"

"I just had to feel close to her. You're not mad, are you?"

"Roger," I said through gritted teeth. "You have to do what I say."

"I guess."

"Call the concierge and tell him you want a taxi to pick you up at a back entrance."

"I don't think there is a back door."

"He'll probably take you to the kitchen and you'll exit into the alley. Tell him you'll return tonight. Don't say anything more."

"This sounds very cloak and dagger."

"Take the taxi to the North Shore Inn and wait for me in the restaurant. Leave now and I'll be there as soon as I can."

"That won't work for me. I have a massage scheduled with Madame Butterfly at nine."

I knew that name. I photographed her once. "Well you're gonna have to cancel, Rog."

"Dammit, Cat. Do you have any idea how hard it is to schedule a full hour with Madam Butterfly?"

"Cancel but don't check out. We'll send for your things later."

"But you said to tell the concierge I'd be back."

"You'll lie."

Roger's voice was wary. "What's going on, Cat?"

"Nothing. It's my birthday, I'm famished, and you're buying me breakfast."

Roger laughed with relief. "Call me bonkers but for a minute I thought we had a problem."

I ended the call and stared at the phone in my hand. I hated this part of my job. Telling Roger what I knew about Bambi would break his heart. Breakfast wasn't going to be pretty.

My cell phone blared and I jumped. "Here's a quarter, call someone who cares."

Max grinned. "I changed your ring tone."

"It's Rocco. He wants to tell me a dead man is in custody and the Chicago Police Department wants to apologize for questioning my sanity."

"Put him on speaker."

"Talk to me, Rocco."

"You OK, Cat?"

"More than OK."

"You're slipping. Someone saw a prowler at Jack's last night and called it in. Would've been a helluva way to spend your birthday."

I giggled. "Too bad everyone wasn't so lucky."

"Did you find what you wanted in your car?"

"Some diamonds, but I'll tell you about that later."

"Diamonds?" Rocco's voice peaked with interest. "No shit."

I winked at Max. "Tell me why you really called, Rocco. I want to hear the best part."

"Uh, happy birthday?"

"Yeah, yeah. Did you talk to the officers?"

"No, but I read the report. You're cool, Cat. No one ID'ed you."

"You can't say it, can you? You hate to admit you were wrong."

"What are you talking about? I'm happily married because I admit I'm wrong whether I am or not."

"I'm talking about the guy they arrested. Chance Savino. You remember the dead man."

"There was no arrest at the shop last night. According to the report the back door was open and the intruder—that would be you—ran off."

"Don't jerk me around, Rocco."

"I'm not."

"Savino was there."

"What can I tell you? They didn't find him."

"Damn."

"Is Max there with you?"

"Yeah. He's laughing."

"Maybe he should take you to a doctor."

"Rocco?"

"Yeah?"

"Shut-up."

I tucked the phone away before I threw it at Max.

"Tough break," he said. "Your happy dance was a tad premature."

"Don't look so cocky. There's a simple explanation."

"Really? I'd love to hear it."

"It's obvious Chance Savino regained consciousness and escaped before the cops arrived."

"There wasn't much time. The sirens were closing in."

"The sirens must have acted like an alarm clock. You saw him lying there."

"No I didn't."

"I guess it was pretty dark," I conceded.

"I saw you."

"Savino's skin is darker. He's Mediterranean."

"So are you."

"He has a tan." I chewed my bottom lip.

"Let me get this straight. You're saying the FBI, Chicago Police Department, and a whole sea of your friends and family still think you are—"

I slapped my hand against his mouth and held it tight. "Let's just say an unfortunate misunderstanding persists."

I grabbed the leash, disarmed my premium platinum system, and the three of us were out the door and on the road in minutes.

"We'll drop by Jack's on our way to meet Roger."

"Better not let Jack see you."

"He won't if you distract him. I just need five minutes alone with Devin."

"What's your plan?"

"I'm taking the diamonds back."

"Flash a gun in front of witnesses?"

"Who's flashing? I'm telling Devin to hand the diamonds over."

"Good luck with that."

I smiled. "The summer we were in the seventh grade I played Texas Hold'em and bought a new bicycle with Devin's allowance. He didn't know how I did it."

"How did you?"

"Devin's left eye twitches when he lies. It's his tell."

"So what's your tell?" Max asked.

I grabbed my Dr. Pepper Lip Smacker and slathered it on. "You'll never know." I winked.

For me it's the lip smacker. My lips tingle when I lie. Ever since I was eleven I've been hooked on the stuff.

Max dropped me off at the back door and I waited until Jack's head disappeared under Tino's hood. I counted three mechanics elbow deep in engines and Devin flat on his back beneath a vintage VW bus. I'd know that wretched sinus sniff anywhere.

I kicked his leg with my Biala Mary Janes. He shot out from under the bus and hit his head on the bumper. Devin was, like I said, a klutz.

The guy Jack forbade me to marry bounded to his feet and his skin paled beneath the grease.

"Uh, Cat," he gulped. "It's you."

"Surprised to see me *so soon*?"

"Jack don't want you comin' around here."

"And Jack don't want you chopping cars. I have pictures if he's interested."

Devin's jaw clenched. "What do you want?"

"I want my diamonds back."

He snorted. Prison made him a more convincing liar. "I ain't got no diamonds," he spat, but then the left eye twitched.

"You're too smart for this," I said, telling the biggest lie of all.

"Oh yeah?"

"A few shiny rocks aren't worth going back to prison for. Don't make me call the cops on you."

"You can't. The diamonds were stolen long before you lost them. Am I right?"

"You're an ass, Devin. Where did you hide the diamonds?"

His sinuses wheezed and his gaze flickered almost imperceptibly to his tool box. Devin wasn't the same goofy kid I conned in seventh grade. He was harder and meaner now, but he wasn't any smarter.

"Get out," Devin said.

I leaned against the Volkswagen bus folding my arms in front of me. "I'm not leaving without the diamonds."

"We'll see about that." He turned on a heel and ran toward Tino's car.

"Jack!" he called.

I was in his tools before he hit the shop door. I jerked a greasy red rag from the bottom of the box. Voila the pouch. I stuffed it in my bra and the rag back in the box. With a little luck he wouldn't know the diamonds were missing until after work.

I bucked out the back door just as Tino's Buick screamed down the alley, slowing enough so I could jump in.

"Go go go!" I called, and Max laughed.

"I knew that stinkin' hairy dog was hers," Jack hollered. He waved a fist and Devin smirked behind him.

"You pissed Jack off," Max said. "You might need a lawyer to get your car back."

"I might."

"Did Devin admit stealing the diamonds?"

"No. He said you can't steal merchandise that's already stolen."

"Interesting defense. How's his left eye?"

"Twitching."

"You should've threatened him with your gun."

"I should've shot him."

I felt the soft velvet against my breast and I sighed happily. "Let's find Roger. I'm starved."

◇◇◇

The North Shore Inn is a quiet, luxurious hideaway on Lakeshore Drive and possibly the last place Bambi and her trigger-happy other half would look for Roger. The hotel has catered to movie stars and heads of state and the kitchen is ruled by one of America's top chefs. Ray Risho is an excitable man and is rumored to chase mediocre cooks with a butcher knife.

We elbowed our way into the restaurant and scanned the crowded room for Roger. The bold Hawaiian print shirt and Bermuda shorts were dead ringers. Roger jumped to his feet unnecessarily, and waved us to his table.

"Happy birthday, Cat." Roger tucked a small package in my hand. "Open it!"

I tore past pink ribbon and silver paper to a velvety black box. Rogers and Hollands Jewelers.

Max swore under his breath. "I'm looking like a cheap bastard."

"Why yes you are," I said.

Cascading emeralds were joined together by a delicate gold chain. I caught my breath.

"Emerald like your eyes," Roger said, enormously pleased with himself.

Roger was a big dopey guy with a huge heart. "This is the best present ever!" I dangled the brilliant green stones in the light. "Stage three," I noted for Max and he growled.

"Don't mind him," I said to Roger. "Max has intimacy issues."

"If Roger had a few we wouldn't be having this conversation."

I hugged Roger. "I'll wear this tonight at my party and I want you to come with us."

"You do?" Max frowned.

"It'll be fun. Besides I want you to meet my family."

"What should I wear?"

"Not that," Max said. "Can I give you some advice?"

"No," I said.

"You're a stage four guy, Roger," Max said.

"What's stage four?"

"You met and married Bambi in a week."

"Actually it was five days."

"Suicide."

"This is coming from the man who ground you into my step," I reminded him.

"Take it slow next time, get to know the girl."

Roger gaped like a goldfish. "I can't get to know a girl. I'm married."

I took a deep breath. "Well about that, Roger. You're not. Bambi was married when you met her. Your marriage is kaput."

"Kaput?"

"Null and void," Max said.

Roger smiled. "My brother put you up to this."

"He didn't," I said. "Bambi's real name is Stacey Pope. Her husband is a sleazy biker dude. He has a criminal record and a lot of tattoos. He fully intends to kill you."

Roger laughed indulgently. "You're mistaken."

Max slapped a disc on the table. "See for yourself. Cat wanted to spare you the video but you won't listen."

Roger waved it away. "I know what computers can do."

The waiter brought steaming mugs of coffee and a platter of scones and fruit. He took our order. When he left again, I pushed back my chair and hugged Roger tight.

"I know this is difficult for you. You have every reason to be upset."

"I'm not upset."

"Of course you're upset," I shook him. "Bambi wants to kill you."

"You're choking him," Max said. "I bet Roger wants his necklace back."

"I'm going home tomorrow," Roger coughed.

"Fair enough but I have you today." I sat down and pulled a folded paper from my bag. I slapped it on the table. "Is Bambi home now?"

"She's at the gym. She has a morning session with her trainer."

"I want you to call her."

"I can't reach her for an hour."

"Leave a message. Read exactly what I've written."

Roger skimmed over the page and glanced up hopefully. "I'll see Bambi today?"

"You will if she shows up."

"Can I drive my own car?"

"I'd rather you take Tino's. It has a few surprises."

Roger punched some numbers and got Bambi's voice mail. He read from the script.

"Bambi, this is Roger. I know you're cheating on me. I haven't told anyone yet. If you want to give this other guy up and start over meet me at one o'clock at Pederson Park. I'm driving a black Buick. If you don't come I'll call my lawyer in the morning and you'll need to be out of the house by the end of the week."

Roger was pale when he finished. "Bambi will be livid."

"Not as much as she will be after your next call."

I waved another sheet of paper and Roger's eyes widened.

"I can't freeze my assets."

"You're only freezing Bambi's access to your assets."

Roger sniffed. "My wife says she loves me."

"Your wife wants you dead," Max said. "She's cheating on you with her real husband."

"So make him go away."

"What?" Max said.

"Look what you did to me."

"And you're still here. Besides I don't think it would scare him. They do that shit in prison for entertainment."

"Can you kill him?"

"You're funny," I said.

"I'll pay you."

"How much?" Max asked.

"Negotiate with Roger tomorrow," I said. "He's my client today."

◇◇◇

It was almost one when Roger drove Tino's black Buick into Pederson Park. I crouched like a pretzel on the floor in the back.

"I hate a big black car," Roger said. "I feel like a funeral director."

"Why don't you pretend you're a gangster?"

Roger raised his collar. "Do I look like a gangster?"

"You look like a computer geek. Like my cousin Ginny. She's perfect for you."

"You forget I'm married."

"And you forget you're not."

"I'm sure Bambi will explain everything when she gets here."

I clapped my hands. "If you believe in fairies," I sang.

"I wish you'd sit up here with me. What will Bambi say when she sees you skulking in the back."

"In my business we skulk, Roger."

"I don't see her," Roger sighed deflated.

"We're early. Park where I told you along the boulevard and turn off the key. Did you bring your book?"

"Yeah, I started reading the final book in the *Green Martians From Lexor* trilogy last night. You see, the leader Tamadam escaped the evil overlord Leberdunly and—"

"Good," I stopped him. Roger so deserved my geeky cousin. It would take time to get over Bambi. My cousin Ginny is patient and a saint. She gives up chocolate for Lent.

"Sit back and pretend you're reading. Try not to talk."

"Should I tell you when Bambi drives in?"

"You're talking. Hide your mouth behind the book if you have to say something. Lock the doors and stay in the car. No matter what happens."

"Skulking makes you paranoid."

"Talk into the book, Roger."

Roger shoved his seat back.

"Ouch," I said.

"Sorry." I heard pages flip as Roger thumbed to his place in the story. He was soon absorbed in his book and I listened to the pages turning. Roger was a fast reader averaging three breaths per turn. I played with the emerald stones against my neck but I wouldn't get too attached to them. Roger would know soon enough that I set him up. He could want his rocks back.

The 9mm in the back of my jeans jammed against my flesh and my legs felt numb. I tried to wiggle the pins and needles from my limbs, keening my ears for cars that slowed and checking my watch every eternal five minutes.

Roger threw his book on the seat. "She's not coming, is she?"

I stiffened. A diesel engine cruised toward us, the third time in six minutes. I pulled the gun from my pants and spoke tersely to Roger.

"Look straight ahead and don't speak."

"Is Bambi here?" The wild Einstein hair whipped around and Roger froze on a tattooed hand.

"Gun!" Roger screamed and four chilling blasts sliced the air. Roger slumped over the steering wheel and the horn howled. The driver broke away in a blaze of screeching tires, the stench of scorched rubber burned my nostrils.

I crawled up the seat and fell out the door. My legs were jello and I clung to the car for support. Behind me the blare of a siren knocked me to my knees. The chase was on, Rocco, parked three cars over in an unmarked police car in hot pursuit and Max, his face grim and unrelenting, brought up the rear.

"Roger! Are you hit?" My voice, caught in a sob, was drowned by the horn. I yanked at Roger's door. It was locked and I reached through the back and jerked the door open. With all my strength I shoved Roger off the horn and rubbed my hands over his body searching for blood. His clothes felt dry and I slapped his face begging him to respond.

Tino's car of tricks scored four bullets, two frozen in the door, two cut short at the window. My god, Roger had a heart attack. I pressed my fingers to his neck and felt his pulse going strong as a horse. I knew it then. Roger had stared death in the face and passed out cold.

Chapter Twenty-two

I arrived at the Moose Lodge for my thirtieth birthday party on Max's arm wearing the outrageously priced dress, the plunging neckline, those four-inch metallic stilettos, and Roger's emerald necklace.

Max leaned down and kissed my cheek. "You look amazing."

"You look pretty amazing yourself."

We stepped through the door to shouts of "Happy Birthday, Cat!" Then they saw Max. Friends and family checked him out like a rack of beef. Everyone wanted to meet the mystery man and demanded to know where I'd been hiding him. Max was interviewed, interrogated, and drilled with questions concerning virility, children, and fiscal responsibility.

Mama raised her hand and the crowd hushed like she'd hit the mute button on a remote.

"Caterina's man is not Italian," she announced sorrowfully.

An audible gasp echoed around the room.

"But then Caterina is no spring chicken," my sister Sophie was quick to point out.

"We know she's been plucked a time or two," a fool shot from the back in range of my three brothers.

SMACK

"OW! Uh, sorry, Cat, I was just kidding."

Max grinned widely, enjoying the plucked chicken joke way too much.

"Sophie's right," Mama announced, muting the crowd again. "With Cat we can't be too choosy."

The crowd murmured sympathetically.

"We eat!" Mama shouted.

Everyone cheered and the music kicked in. Uncle Joey had made arrangements for an Elvis impersonator and the sequined King curled his lip and swiveled his hips.

Max was the bomb. He ate three generous servings of Mama's lasagna, topped her glass with champagne, and danced with her like she was twenty. Mama purred like a kitten and the warranty on my biological clock wasn't mentioned again all night.

"You're more than perfect," I told Max later on the dance floor. "Everyone's buying the charade but Tino. He just sits in the corner and chuckles."

"A couple more martinis and he'll fall off his chair laughing."

Rocco and Maria danced by and Maria gaped at Max. "Cuter than Kevin Costner," she sang. She batted her eyes as Rocco swept her away.

"Kevin Costner?" Max grinned.

"You're a chick magnet. The women are all over you."

"It's my raw sex appeal, Kitten."

"Well they can't have you. You're mine for the night."

His hot breath caressed my ear. "I thought this was a three hour gig."

He laid a long stemmed red rose across my lips before I could respond.

We tangoed and Max dragged me across the floor, spun me like a top, and dipped me low, his lips gently touching mine.

A pudgy finger tapped his shoulder and Max pulled me up and swung around.

I squealed and threw my arms around Roger. "I was afraid you wouldn't come!"

"The cops came by the house and arrested Bambi," he whined.

"I know. Rocco told me."

"The neighbors were over for coffee. I mean why today? They never came before."

"She needed an alibi," Max said and Roger's round shoulders deflated like he stuck a pin in them.

"Dance with me."

"Knock yourself out but I get to take her home."

Max made a run for the lasagna but my sister descended like a hawk and captured him in her claws. I winced.

"Who is she?" Roger said.

"I never saw that woman before in my life."

"You mean she's crashing your party?"

"She's crashing my life." I came clean. "OK, Roger, she's my sister Sophia, but I don't want you to think the DeLucas all need therapy."

"Do they?"

"Definitely."

Roger stepped on my foot. "Sorry. I'm not a very good dancer."

"It's OK," I squeaked. "Most women will take a slow hand over fast feet."

"It didn't work for Bambi."

"I don't know if it helps but Bambi played you. It was never about you."

"It doesn't help a damn."

Max cruised by swinging Sophia around on the dance floor, clearing people for three feet in every direction. I hardly recognized my sister without a baby attached to her nipple.

The music stopped and I hugged Roger quickly and straightened his tie. "Come with me. I want you to meet my brothers."

My cousin Ginny was at the buffet table with the twins. She's my mother's sister's second daughter. She wears thick glasses and is less striking than her four sisters. But she's kind and generous and smarter than the other four put together.

I made the introductions.

"You can't beat Mama's spaghetti," the twins said.

Roger stared into the brown doe eyes behind thick rimmed glasses and stammered like a school boy. I shoved them both on the dance floor.

Max escaped Sophia, leaping from the frying pan into the fire. Papa, in interrogation mode, cornered him beneath a bright white light. I grabbed a glass of wine and watched the entertainment. When the grilling was over, my commitment-phobic date made a beeline for the bar.

Papa hunted me down, smiled broadly, and hauled me out to the dance floor. I looked over his shoulder. Max had a drink in each hand.

"Max is a son to me already. I see the way he looks at you."

Oh boy.

"He's not a cop but he's hard working and his legs look strong. He'll breed strong boys."

Yikes.

"You both have my blessing."

I groaned inwardly. What had I done? I dragged Max to my birthday party so people wouldn't think my love life was in the toilet. I didn't count on my parents squeezing his name in the family Bible. Everyone was nuts about Max. They'll expect a wedding.

Papa eyed my necklace. "Gift from Max?"

"No. Roger gave it to me."

He frowned. "Who's Roger?"

I flicked my head. "The guy over there dancing with Ginny."

"Short, fat guy?"

"You know how they say married people start to look like each other. Roger and Ginny have a head start."

"Your Mama got my mustache." Papa held my face in his hands and he kissed both cheeks. His eyes leaked.

"Set a date with Father Timothy, Caterina. I've waited long enough for your sons."

Chapter Twenty-three

Melanie and I were best friends in grade school. We spoke pig latin on the playground and everyone thought we were speaking French. We were the coolest kids in school until our teacher took a baseball in the head at recess and we got a substitute. Ms. Channing was from Quebec and her English wasn't great. She was, however, a whiz at French.

Melanie and I are still friends and we never keep a juicy secret from each other. She cornered me at the party, steaming. I carved a chunky wedge of chocolate cake for emotional support.

"I thought we were friends," she said in a tiff. "I come to your party and what do I hear?"

Melanie does wounded like an Italian mother.

"I hear my best friend is engaged and she didn't even tell me. Eva Simpson told me and she's the last to know anything."

"I know it looks bad, Mel, but—"

"And who the hell is Max? I didn't even know you were seeing someone. How long has this been going on?"

"I, uh…"

Melanie's eyes froze on the emeralds around my neck.

"Max?" She said pettily.

"Roger."

"*Roger?* Who the hell is Roger?"

"A lot has happened. I'll fill you in later."

"I'll take the short version now."

Uncle Joey danced by with a bottle of champagne. I tossed the contents of my glass down my throat and held it out for a refill.

Joey whispered. "This isn't what it looks like with you and the bodyguard is it?"

"No it's not. Did you hear that, Melanie?"

"I heard nothing."

He flooded my glass with bubbles and chortled away.

"The short version," Mel demanded.

"OK. Rita Savino hired me to follow her husband but he wasn't her husband and after the explosion the FBI said he was dead but it was Rita who was dead."

Melanie frowned. "The shorter version. The part where you sleep with Hunka Hunka and don't leave the good stuff out."

"The bomb went off, Inga ate my pizza, and I got a concussion."

"Omigod, Cat. Is that where you met Max? He's a doctor?"

"He's a spy."

"Your mama said you were bonkers."

"I'll fit you in for the exorcism. Somebody blew up my car and nearly killed Tommy."

"Who the hell is Tommy?"

"So Tino loaned me his bullet-proof car and Max."

"So how is Hunka Hunka in bed?"

I tossed more champagne down my throat. "Did you catch the part about the murder, the car bombing, and some whack job wanting to kill me?"

"Work it, girlfriend. Max is a prize."

"Oh please, Rapher's a hunk."

"*Was*. Now all he does is drink beer and belch."

"Rapher drank beer and belched when you met him."

"It's not disgusting until you're married."

Mel took a bite of my cake and her eyes glossed over. "Fabulous."

"Have a piece," I said.

"Can't. I'm on a diet." She stabbed her fork in my cake and crammed another bite. "Seriously, Cat, I'm worried about you. You should see a doctor about this dead guy. My mother-in-law knows a good one."

"I have a doctor."

"This guy's a shrink."

"He can't be that good. Your mother-in-law is loony."

I got that sudden itchy feeling on the back of my neck like somebody watching my back. I spun around. Chance Savino's hard muscular physique leaned against the door. He gave the ghost of a smile. My stomach did flip flops.

"Bonkers, huh?" I twisted Melanie around. "So who is that?"

"Where?"

I looked again. "Damn!"

Savino was gone. I shoved the cake in her hand and wobbled to the door in my stilettos.

"I'll get the shrink's number for you," Melanie yelled finishing in French. "Ou-yae eed-nay elp-hay."

"Bite me."

"I'm eating your cake."

I pushed the door open and stormed out to the parking lot. It was deserted.

"Come on, Savino. I know you're out here."

No answer.

"Not funny. Quit playing around."

A blanket of darkness and a chilling gust of wind blew off the lake. I shivered. Something wasn't right. I caught a little movement in the corner of my eye. Yellow eyes blinked in the shadows. I ceased breathing. A primordial fear gripped me and my stomach twisted. I swung around and calculated the distance to the door. Forty feet, four-inch stilettos, and a terrifying urge to run for my life.

I couldn't run but I set my sights on the door and wobbled as fast as my shoes would carry me. Thirty feet, twenty feet. I counted down and behind me thundering footsteps pounded the pavement. I broke into a precarious run. My heart raced and I gulped small terrified sobs.

Perhaps with a fair start and a pair of flats I could have outrun him but he came at me full throttle. I felt the heat of his body behind me and his breath hot on my hair. A long snake-like arm reached around me and my heel caught a snag in the pavement, knocking me off balance. My arms flailed and I crashed to the ground, skinning my knees and catching the asphalt with my hands. He thrust his hands under my arms and dragged me into the shadows. My skin stung and I heard my dress rip. I couldn't make out the face of my assailant but he was taller and thinner than Charlie. I was thinking the rat sent someone else.

He jerked me to my feet and slammed me against the brick wall. I fought back savagely, hurling fists and pummeling his chest. I tried to jab his eye and shove a knee in his groin and he snorted.

I stopped like he slapped me and stared hard, willing my eyes to adjust to the darkness.

"Devin?" I blinked and stared again. "What the hell are you doing?" I shoved him. "You ruined my new dress." I looked down and my feet were bare. My four-inch stilettos had been abandoned in the parking lot.

"They were Italian," I moaned and kicked him in the shin.

"You know why I'm here," Devin said and his eye didn't twitch.

"I know you scared the bejesus out of me. I thought you were someone else they sent to kill me."

He didn't flinch and I saw it in his eyes. Devin had killed before. Maybe it happened in prison or maybe outside but it wasn't keeping him awake at night.

"Gimme the diamonds, Cat. I'm taking them back."

Some bodyguard. I wondered if Max was still attached to the bar. I could hear a flood of laughter and Elvis doing "Jailhouse Rock." I wanted to scream but it would do no good. No one would hear me inside.

Something silver flashed in his hand and he shoved me back against the brick again, this time pressing a knife to my throat.

"I'm meeting a fence tonight with the diamonds. He's not a guy you can screw around."

"I don't have them on me."

"We'll go to your house."

I took a ragged breath. My voice sounded hollow to my ears. "The diamonds are in my purse. I brought them to the party."

"You're lying." His other hand squeezed my throat.

"Devin, stop, you're choking me."

He smelled of whiskey and his unfocused eyes darted wildly. He sniffed and I suspected he was snorting more than sinuses.

"Here's an idea. Forget the diamonds, go to rehab and take your life back."

"I'll just take the rocks. Where are they?"

"I told you. In my purse."

"You're jackin' me." He tightened his grip, my eyes stung and I couldn't breathe.

"Help!" I choked barely audible to my own ears. A dark wave crossed my vision and I collapsed on the ground.

"Give up the diamonds or I'll cut that pretty face."

A chilling voice growled from the shadows. "That would be a very bad idea."

Devin spun around and Chance Savino kicked his legs from under him. He rolled to the ground with an astonished snort, and clambered quickly to his feet. Savino lowered his shoulder and charged like a bull. They crashed in a tangled blur of thumping fists. Devin collapsed on the blacktop, wrenching a gun from his jacket pocket. Chance kicked it away from his hand and hammered him unconscious with his own weapon.

Chance knelt beside me and hung his jacket around my shoulders.

"Did he hurt you, DeLucky?"

"Look at my dress. My heels are ruined." I threw a hand at my battered heels stranded on the asphalt.

Chance jogged across the parking lot and salvaged my shoes. The leather was scuffed, but he carefully put them on my feet and assessed the damage. I was a mess. My arms were scraped, my legs bloody, and I'd mopped the parking lot with my dress. I stared at my strappy metallics and blinked back the tears.

Chance studied Devin's face. "Isn't that Jack's nephew? The guy you can't marry?"

"Yep. Devin smashed your head last night and took your diamonds."

Chance studied me curiously. "Oh? I thought that was you."

"Me?" I flung my finger at Devin accusingly. "He's the one who schmucked your head with a crow bar and grabbed the stones. I thought the cops arrested you. I did the happy dance because I had proof you were alive."

"Happy dance? I heard what Devin said to you. He didn't have the diamonds. He was trying to get them from you. Maybe you and Devin are partners and you double-crossed him. I didn't figure you for a thief."

"That's the pot calling the kettle black."

"I want those diamonds, DeLucky."

"Screw you."

He gently pulled me by the lapels of his jacket and kissed me. His lips were soft and warm and a little groan escaped my throat. His tongue touched mine and a flame rushed through me.

The cobalt blue eyes crinkled the hint of a smile.

"Happy birthday, DeLucky."

"Shut up and kiss me."

The door flung open and music jammed the parking lot. My sister stepped outside. She caught us in the shadows, Savino's arms around me, his face close to mine. Sophie squawked triumphantly and raced inside.

"Great! Just peachy."

"Who was that?"

"My big-mouth sister."

Chance brushed his lips against my hair.

"Keep the diamonds warm for me. I'll be back."

The door exploded and the entire party rushed outside. Sophia always was a tattle tale.

"There they are!" My sister pointed an accusing finger and Uncle Joey swept a blinding flashlight on my torn dress and bruises. My friends cried out and rushed to my side. I turned to Savino but he had vanished behind the building. There was only me there, bruised and bleeding. Plus the guy who beat me up. It seems I'd knocked him senseless.

Papa hugged me and ground his shoe into Devin's fingers. My lip quivered and the dam broke. There was no stopping the tears. Mama fussed and promised cannoli. My sister glared and I winked at her. Max brought the car around and helped me inside.

"Did you get your purse," he said.

"I didn't bring one."

"Whose jacket are you wearing?" My sister snickered.

"I, uh, borrowed it before I ran outside."

"You didn't have..." Melanie began and I stopped her with a look. Her eyes widened and she bit her tongue.

"Take the coat and return it later," Mama said. "You need the warmth."

"Shouldn't someone call the cops?" someone said.

"We are the cops." Uncle Joey's eyes didn't match the smile.

"You'll call it in, won't you?" I said.

"Don't worry, baby." Papa rested a shoe on Devin's face. "Your Uncle Joey will take care of it."

Melanie wrung her hands. "How can such a terrible thing happen?"

"It's those damn dirty pictures," Mama said sorrowfully.

I waved.

Max cruised out of the parking lot onto the street. He glanced in the rear view mirror and jumped. Roger and Ginny sat in the back seat.

"How'd you two get here?"

"I need my family at a time like this," I said.

"Who was that terrible man?" Ginny said. "Why did he want to hurt you?"

"Devin is on drugs. He needs treatment."

Max glanced sideways. "Did he say anything about the diamonds?"

"Devin didn't mention them," I said.

"Diamonds?" Roger's voice perked.

"You're a stage four guy," Max said. "Step away from the jewels." He glared at me.

"You took a big chance leaving the party alone. I'm your bodyguard for chrissake."

"I was after Savino. He was standing by the door."

"Of course, the dead man." Max shook his head. "Tonight I had a date with a beautiful woman. This isn't how I hoped it would end."

"We had fun. You got to meet my family, didn't you?"

"Don't ever leave me alone with your sister."

"The twins liked you."

"How do you know? They never left the buffet."

"And papa gave us his blessing."

Max shuddered. "I thought he was showing me his scar. I never want to be that close to a man's naked butt again."

Chapter Twenty-four

Ginny and I awoke at nine to a gentle knock on the door. I was sore and my skin hurt when the sheets rubbed against it but for the most part my birthday had been a success. Bambi and her tattooed husband were in the slammer, I got the diamonds back, and Elvis rocked. On the down side Melanie ate my cake and I got my butt kicked. Again. My fabulous dress was trashed but the aroma of hot coffee and bacon wafted in from the kitchen. It was a brand new day.

Inga lay flat on her back between Ginny and me, paws up, wagging her tail.

"Anyone hungry?"

Max opened the door wearing dark wash, low rise Levis and a dazzling white tee-shirt. You could see every muscle ripple and the affect, I noticed, wasn't lost on Ginny. Her eyes were saucer-size, glued to his six packs.

Ginny sat up and tucked the covers under her chin. "Is Roger awake?"

Max made a face. "Bambi's been calling all night. Can you believe it? She wants him to bail her out of jail."

Ginny gnawed a lip. "He isn't doing it, is he?"

Max shook his head once, sharply. "He made waffles."

"Good. I love waffles," I said.

Ginny and Roger had sat by the fire late into the night. They talked about computers and time travel and Bambi. Roger's eyes busted a faucet and Ginny held his hand and listened. They were two big geeks with enormous hearts. Roger's was broken.

"How is he?" Ginny said.

Max grinned. "Ask him yourself." He ducked out of the room.

We tugged on robes and slippers and tromped off to the kitchen. Roger slumped at the table over the newspaper. I doubted he'd slept much. His eyes were puffy but they lit up when he saw Ginny.

She brushed back a strand of her long black hair. "Good morning, Roger," she said shyly.

Roger kicked his feet self-consciously. "Thanks for listening, last night."

I poured juice and coffee. Max pulled bacon and a platter of waffles from the oven and set them on the table.

Roger slapped the paper in front of my cousin. "There's a Star Trek Convention in Cleveland next October. Can you believe it?"

She caught her breath. "We were talking about Star Trek last night."

"Trekkies," Max said. "Who would've guessed?"

"Maybe William Shatner will autograph your Captain Kirk doll," Roger said.

Ginny's doe eyes widened. "What are you saying?"

Roger stared at his shoes. "If you'd like to go to the Star Trek Convention with me, I'll reserve a couple rooms."

Ginny hugged her arms and giggled. "Cleveland! Wow!"

Ginny doesn't get to travel much.

We ate breakfast and Roger told Ginny about Cleveland.

"It's an extraordinary city," he said.

"Would that be the same Cleveland that's in Ohio?" I said.

A loud smack thumped the door. "What's that?"

Max pulled his gun from its shoulder holster. "Sounds like someone clobbering the front door with his foot."

"Wait here," Roger said boldly and followed Max to the living room.

Ginny shuddered. "Do people always want to kill you?"

"It's been a busy week," I said, licking blueberry syrup off the knife.

We listened. Loud voices, accusations, tense conversation, and familiar snorting. I dropped my fork. Suddenly I wasn't hungry anymore.

Roger led the way to the kitchen and Max pushed Devin ahead of him. He was a mess. His hands were bandaged, fingers smashed, an arm in a sling, and I gathered from his posture some ribs were broken. I was cheered considerably.

"I can see why you knocked with your shoe," I said.

Max smacked him in the head. "Jack is waiting outside for Devin. Your Accord is back."

"The Silver Bullet? Wow."

"Jack said you won't get a bill. He's all worked up over what happened last night."

"Who told him?"

"Your Uncle Joey brought Devin home."

"After he was hit by a truck," I noted.

"I wanna talk to Cat alone," Devin said.

"Over my dead—"

"It's OK," I said, and Max smacked him again.

"I'm right outside this door."

"Me, too," Roger growled and Ginny kicked Devin's shin on her way out.

I tugged the sleeves of my robe to cover my bruises. "What do you want, Devin."

"About last night," Devin began. "I was—"

"You were an ass. If you ever touch me again I'll shoot you."

"Your uncle worked me over good."

"I'm surprised you made it home."

"He and Jack go way back."

"Lucky you."

"Joey found a pipe in my car. He gave me a choice. Six months in drug rehab or go back to prison."

"Bye bye."

Devin shrugged. "I can't hang around here. Some guy wants those diamonds."

"Sucks to be you."

Devin looked hideous with a black and blue eye and a fresh cut on his cheek. I almost felt sorry for him.

"Damn shame, Cat, those diamonds were sweet." His swollen eyes swept the room.

I stiffened. "The diamonds are gone. I turned them in."

"Yeah? Joey didn't know nothing about diamonds."

"It's FBI. They were smuggled from Australia."

Devin stared hard trying to decide whether to believe me.

"I don't care if you kept the diamonds, Cat. I ain't coming back for them."

The left eye twitched.

"Max!" I called. "We're finished here."

◇◇◇

Ginny took Inga for a walk around the neighborhood in my pink Liz Claiborne sweats. They were a bit snug, but in all the right places. Roger's eyes glazed over when he saw her and I had to pinch my lips to keep from smiling. It would take time before Roger could feel whole again, but there would be life after Bambi.

"Your mama dropped by with your cannoli," Roger said.

"She came early."

"She peeked in your room."

"She was checking on the sleeping arrangements. Ginny's mama would be in the car."

"She said Father Timothy would be stopping by. Something about reserving the church."

I blew a sigh.

"Max is a great guy."

"I *am* a great guy," Max appeared in the doorway with Rita's laptop under his arm. He placed it between Roger and me on the couch.

"Is this the laptop that belonged to the reporter who got whacked?" Roger said.

My head snapped a double take.

Max laughed. "We had a lot of time to talk this morning. We thought you'd never wake up."

"I wanted to bring you breakfast in bed," Roger said.

I hugged him. "Bambi is an idiot."

Roger flashed a crooked smile. "So, do you think this Eddie Harr is behind Rita's murder?"

Max stretched out in the leather easy chair and locked his hands behind his head. "A guy named Charlie pulled the trigger but he's just one of Eddie's dirt workers. He left a trail of Starburst candy wrappers twisted in little bows."

"They follow Charlie wherever he goes," I said.

"Then it shouldn't be too hard to pin the murder on him," Roger said.

"It would help if forensics bagged the bows," Max shrugged. "They went out with the trash."

I knocked on the laptop lid. "There should be something here to link Harr to Rita."

"How so?"

"Rita had Eddie Harr pegged for the low life scum he is. But you'd think she was writing a fluff piece on him."

"Can a computer geek take a look?"

Geek Joey Jr. was still out of town. I shoved the laptop over.

Roger is built like a teddy bear with a round belly and not much leg for a laptop. I watched him scootch, roll, then finally prop up a sofa pillow to even out his stomach-to-lap ratio.

"Let's sit at the table," I said. "I'll make fresh coffee and tempt you with Mama's cannoli."

Roger shoved himself off the couch. "Keep the temptation coming. If your client was hiding anything in here, I'll find it."

I ground beans and brewed coffee and Max pulled Mama's Tupperware from the fridge. We dragged chairs on either side of Roger. His fat fingers flew at a furious pace.

When the coffee was ready I filled three cups and left one empty by the pot for Ginny. A deep chuckle gurgled in Roger's throat. Max jerked forward and I wiggled between them.

"What did you find?"

"Rita's cache," Roger said with satisfaction. "Your client was a smart cookie. She gave away just enough to make you think there wasn't more. No one could have known."

"Harry Kaplan knew," I said bitterly. "He was going to let them get away with it."

"Harry?"

"Rita's boss," Max explained. "Harry's letting her killers get away because his wife is too voluptuous."

Roger looked more confused than ever.

I plopped a cannoli on Roger's plate. He took a bite and his eyes melted.

"Ginny has Mama's recipe," I whispered in his ear.

Max scrolled down the page. "Maybe your client wasn't so smart after all. She was squeezing some punk who works for Eddie, a guy she calls AJ. Rita knew this AJ was involved in a hit and run where two children died. She threatened to turn him in if he didn't roll over on his boss."

"Did this AJ give her anything on Eddie?"

"Maybe. There's some numbers and banking info here, I don't know what it means. Also something about a national charity financed with government and private funds. Rita claims large amounts of cash were diverted from the fund and funneled to dummy accounts. She also believed weapons and contraband were loaded in trucks and shipped south of the border."

I slapped Max's shoulder. "See!"

"Where can we find this AJ character?" Roger said.

"We got a phone number," Max said. "I'll call Rocco for an address."

Roger commandeered the computer again and punched some keys. "Here is Rita's calendar. And this is her final week, the last days before her murder."

Max leaned close reviewing Rita's appointments the last days of her life.

"Monday. FBI. WPP?" he read.

"Witness Protection Program," I said. "AJ wanted out."

"Maybe. Or WPP could be something else."

"What? A sandwich order? White bread, pastrami w/ pickles." I threw Max a look. "AJ agrees to testify against Eddie. Rita goes to the FBI Monday. Thursday she's dead."

Max grunted. "You could be right. Tino says there's a leak in the FBI."

Roger tapped the screen. "The day before Rita died she met E.H. at 10 a.m."

"That's Eddie Harr unless Max can make a sandwich out of it." I checked the address and sucked a breath.

Max looked at me sharply. "Do you know the place?"

"I was there that afternoon. The fireworks knocked me out of my shoes."

"Max said they found Rita's husband in there."

I smacked Max. "No. This guy had a snake tattooed around his neck."

Roger shuddered. "Gross, Rita."

Max drove Ginny and Roger to their cars at the Lodge. I showered quickly and dropped my towel on the bed. The lump under my blanket sighed.

"Cleo wants to replace you with buckshot," I said.

I blow dried my hair and slipped into a red-ribbed, scoop-necked tee, straight leg linen pants, and beaded flip flops. I slathered on Dr. Pepper Lip Smacker and a few strokes of mascara before trotting to the kitchen for a snack.

A clatter froze me in my tracks and I slapped my mouth to squelch a scream. The refrigerator door was open, two new suede shoes visible beneath the door. My intruder's head was buried in my food stash. He was perilously close to Mama's cannoli.

My heart hammered in my throat. I flew down the hallway, snagged my baseball bat from the coat closet, and raced back to the kitchen. My heart raced in my throat. I tiptoed to the refrigerator, turning the bat ever so carefully so as not to bloody the autograph. I growled to myself. I bet nobody messes with Ken Griffey's refrigerator.

I swung the bat over my head and was going for a home run when the fridge spoke.

"Don't you ever go shopping?"

I dropped the bat behind me. The refrigerator door closed and Uncle Joey appeared noshing on a cannoli.

"You scared me. Doesn't *anybody* knock? How'd you get past my premium platinum system?"

"I stopped by to see how you were doing. Inga said you were in the shower."

"She can operate the alarm?"

"You know your Mama can't keep a secret."

Inga trotted through the door, tail wagging.

"Slacker," I said.

Uncle Joey smiled. "Did Devin apologize?"

"I got my car back. And Devin's going to treatment."

"He got off easy."

"You beat the shit out of him."

"Next time he won't be so lucky."

He grabbed a cannoli for the road and I followed him to the door.

"Thanks," I said.

"What for?"

"For last night. For taking care of Devin. For taking care of everything."

"You have no idea." He smiled and kissed my cheek. "Lock the door and reset that alarm."

I poured a big glass of chocolate milk and was reading the paper when Max showed up bearing sausages and pasta salad. I let him in.

"How's Tino?" I said.

"Hung over. He hardly noticed the bullet damage to the car. He asked how the wedding plans were coming."

"Tino's a funny guy."

Max pulled a bowl of grapes from the refrigerator and put the sausage and pasta salad on two small plates. He slammed two beers on the table.

"I love it when you feed me," I said.

"You still haven't told me what Devin did with the diamonds."

I don't know why I didn't tell Max I had the diamonds. Maybe I've worked too long on my own. Maybe it comes down to trusting someone else. I've never been very good at it.

I blew out a sigh. "The guy is a hustler and a druggie. He tried to deal with the big boys and lost his shorts."

Max groaned. "Devin lost the diamonds?"

"They were in his shorts."

"You're *certain* the—"

"Zip, kaput, nada."

"And we can't get them back?"

"Maybe if you're a psychic or magician."

"Damn, Cat. You held a fortune and it fell from your fingers."

"More like ripped from my hands."

Max was still for a moment, then he rallied and raised his beer. "To the women I've loved and the diamonds I've lost," he said.

I clinked my frosty bottle against his. "To a girl's best friend."

Chapter Twenty-five

Max rang Rocco and got a name and address that went with AJ's phone number. The name was Natalie Crane and the address was an apartment in Archer Heights. Natalie didn't have a rap sheet, I was guessing AJ did. Then I made my call.

"Harry Kaplan," the voice said.

"Hey, Harry. It's Caterina. Did I catch you at work?"

"If I was at home with my delicious wife I wouldn't answer the phone. I'm glad you called."

"What's up?"

"The wife and I made reservations for our anniversary next month. I'm hoping you can take the kids for three days."

I crossed my fingers. "Is Harry Jr. over that pyromaniac phase yet?"

"The boy hasn't set a fire in weeks."

"Glad to hear it."

"I wouldn't leave matches around though."

"Good tip. Does he still stick Jaime's toys in the blender to watch her cry?"

Harry laughed. "Kids outgrow these things, Cat."

"Gotcha."

"I wouldn't give him a puppy for Christmas though. Jaime's four and she's a handful. She puts her brother to shame. Remember *The Exorcist*?"

I groaned. Three days with Satan and I'll never have kids.

"Thanks a lot. Actually I'm calling about Rita's laptop."

Silence.

"I'm in."

"I told you to leave it alone."

"You got a phone call and someone threatened you."

"I can't get involved. I have a wife to protect."

"You had to know there's stuff in there that connected her to Eddie's organization. Rita saw Eddie the day she was murdered."

"You don't want to go there."

"Rita was getting information from one of Eddie's goons. Did she mention a guy named AJ? I'm on my way to talk to him now."

"You're a dead woman, Caterina."

"I don't get it, Harry. You're the one person who knew what Rita was into but you didn't turn the laptop over to the cops. Why is that?"

Harry huffed defensively. "I didn't have a chance. I heard Rita choked on a tofu burger."

"Nice try Harry. You had every opportunity."

"You're the one who charged into the office—"

"That electric blue eyeliner was my easiest disguise ever-"

"And you hitched Rita's laptop. If anyone should've called the cops, it was you."

"Don't you dare lay this guilt trip on me, Harry Kaplan. I can't believe you're going to let them get away with this."

"They already have." Harry's voice was strained.

"You think they'll leave you alone after this? You've been at the *Tribune* for thirty years. How many stories have you written that had happy endings?"

Click.

◇◇◇

A woman with cascading auburn curls and a baby on her hip answered the door.

"Natalie Crane?" Max said.

"Who wants to know?"

Natalie had clear, astute eyes that only a fool would lie to.

I stepped in front of Max and flashed both the sharp stilettos I'd changed into and the kind of pearly whites you get with a humiliating adolescence of orthodontry and the nickname Train Tracks.

"I'm Cat DeLuca and this is Max Pedersen. We're hoping to talk to AJ."

The eyes drilled me. "Are you cops?"

"No. AJ was working with a friend of ours, Rita Polansky. Did he ever mention her?"

"AJ doesn't talk about his job."

Just as well, I thought.

"Rita was killed a few days ago," Max said and Natalie stiffened.

"My husband doesn't kill people," she said shortly and swung the door but Max stopped it with his foot.

"That's not why we want to talk to him," he said.

We waited a few beats while Natalie's frank eyes shot through us.

"I'm looking for AJ too." She turned on her heel and we followed her inside.

The apartment building was a converted warehouse renovated into spacious living spaces. The living room walls were lined with framed prints of rock legends. Two black leather armchairs and an expensive looking couch flanked a brick fireplace.

"When did you see AJ last?" I said.

"He went to work Wednesday and I haven't heard from him since."

"Is that usual?"

"AJ always calls." Natalie chewed her lip worriedly. "I'll put the baby down and make tea."

"I'll help." Max cued me with the bug eyes and trotted after her.

I prowled through an old desk, going through drawers and thumbing through papers, crayons, play dough, stationary, stamps, and letters. I stuck my head in the coat closet and rummaged through pockets. Nothing. Nada.

I closed the closet door and a photograph across the room caught my eye. It was a family portrait, possibly a K-Mart special. Mama, Papa, and baby.

I shuffled to the mantle for a closer look. It was the snake that stopped my heart like a dagger. The tattooed reptile twisted around daddy's neck and a skull-shaped rattler edged his ear. My stomach twisted. I knew it then. The guy Natalie was waiting for wasn't coming home. He and I were both at the explosion, but he'd had no chance to survive. He already had a bullet in his head.

"Tea water's on," Natalie announced and joined me at the mantle.

Max looked at the family photo. "A mini-AJ," he grinned. "The baby's a spitting image of his dad."

"Without the tattoo," I said pointedly.

Max peered closer. "Oh shit," he said and glanced at the baby.

"What?" Natalie said.

"Nothing," I said brightly. "He thought he heard the tea whistle."

We talked weather and baseball and when we drained every drop of tea we stood to leave.

Natalie blinked back tears. "AJ isn't coming home is he?"

"I, uh, I don't..." I stammered.

Her intelligent eyes wouldn't be lied to.

"It was something in the picture," Natalie said. "I don't know what but after that you didn't ask about AJ again. You stopped trying to find him."

"We uh...uh, we..." I stuttered.

"What?"

Max held her hand. "We're sorry," he said.

I left Natalie's apartment with more questions than answers and a sick heart.

Max hung a loose arm around me and beeped the Buick, unlocking the doors.

"You OK?"

I nodded. "Thanks, Max."

"What for?"

I looked into his dark gray eyes and leaned against the passenger door. "Everything. You're a good friend."

"I got your back, babe." He leaned his hard body against mine and searched my eyes, his lips lowered slowly teasing mine.

I was getting way over my head. Avoidance was the answer here.

"We could do Thai for supper." My voice was about an octave higher than usual.

Max chuckled. "Take out?"

"I know a place that delivers."

The sound of an engine mixed with images of Pad Thai and hot steamy sex. I turned around, glanced at the driver, and caught a gasp. I jerked back for a double take.

"Holy shit!"

Time slowed to a crawl. I watched in horror. Charlie wrestled a 350 Magnum from his lap. Words strangled in my throat and I squawked like a chicken. Max in one cool unfettered motion made Charlie in the green BMW, pulled his Colt 45, threw me on the ground and landed on top of me, his body shielding mine as he fired.

Gunfire echoed and I went rigid with fear. The engine roared and Charlie bolted. Max dashed to his feet.

"He's a dead man."

Max quickly hoisted me in his arms, threw me in the car, and climbed over me. The Buick leapt to life and flipped a Uwee, tires screaming in hot pursuit. We were off to the races.

I hung on for dear life and made my peace with God.

"I lost him," Max said finally, turning down yet another street.

"We got too close, when we found AJ's house. Eddie won't stop now."

"They must have had this place staked out waiting for us," Max said angrily. "No one knew where we were going."

I stared at my shoes and grabbed my Dr. Pepper Lip Smacker from my purse.

Max swore. He slammed the brake, slashing fifty to ten mph in seconds. "Who did you tell, Cat?"

"Uh, maybe Harry."

"Harry. Rita's boss, Harry?"

"Yep."

"Harry *is* dead."

Harry was still at the Trib when we pulled into the employee's parking lot. We parked next to his Suburban and waited an agonizing forty-four minutes for him to exit the building. It took Max forty-one minutes to cool down and put his gun away.

Harry unlocked the Suburban's door with the remote while tugging at his tie. Max and I split. Max followed behind Harry while I came around the front. He whipped his head and his thyroid eyes widened freakishly. He knew he was trapped.

"Surprise, Harry. I'm still alive."

Max's muscle mass swelled under his shirt and Harry appeared to shrink in his suit. "Who's that?"

"Max is my bodyguard. He kills with his bare hands."

Max shoved him against the SUV and slammed him in the gut. Harry dropped to his knees.

"A little late to pray," Max kidney punched him and Harry collapsed on the ground. Max's size thirteen's crunched down on Harry's ear, digging his face into the asphalt.

Harry gasped. "They said they only wanted to talk to you."

"I want their number."

"Okay but it's a tracfone. It won't help you. C'mon Cat. Lighten up. They didn't hurt you."

"Only because they missed," I snapped. "They *shot* at me. They tried to kill me."

"Well that was rude."

"Rude?"

"What choice did I have? My wife, my children…" Harry shuddered.

"If anything happens to Cat, the safety of your wife and kids will be the least of your problems. Do you understand what I am saying, Harry?"

The employee door opened and three women strolled to their cars. Max yanked Harry to his feet and he brushed himself off.

"You ruined my suit." This guy was unbelievable. Did he not get it?

Max grabbed Harry by his tie and pushed him behind the wheel. I moved into the passenger seat and Max sat directly behind Harry.

"I don't deserve this," Harry mumbled. "I told Rita to drop it but would she listen to me? One girl from Oregon can't change the world."

Max growled. "If you compromise Cat's safety again I'll…"

"Yeah, yeah, I got it. I'm dead either way." Harry said.

"Oh no, Harry, I have something much worse. Max will seduce your voluptuous wife with red roses and chocolates and make mad passionate love to her."

"I will?" Max blinked.

"He wouldn't!" Harry choked.

"Max is a hard-bodied love machine." I fanned myself. "Just look at him. He's a Viking god. Your wife will fall head over heels and," I snapped my fingers, "just like that, out you go."

"Stop it!" Harry cried.

We stepped out of the car and Harry peeled out, tires screaming.

Max growled.

"Harry's not so bad really. He's just," words failed me, "Harry."

"He's spineless."

"Did I mention he punched a priest?"

"Good. He's going to hell."

"Harry thought the priest was hitting on his wife."

Max cocked a brow. "The wife must be gorgeous."

"Only to Harry."

Max grinned. "And to you I'm a Viking god."

"I may have embellished." I kissed his cheek.

"What's that for?"

"For throwing yourself on top of me when the bullets started flying. Really, you were very brave."

Max hung a loose arm around my shoulder. "I can do that even without flying bullets."

"Now you're just showing off."

Chapter Twenty-six

It was after seven and the shadows stretched long as Max turned onto North Michigan Avenue. I was tired, stiff, and wondering if this Viking god does massage.

"Let's go home," I said.

Max's brow furrowed.

"What is it?"

"You're not safe at home until we finish this. Eddie's not going to let this ride."

I knew Max was right. Eddie gave me a breather. He figured I learned my lesson until I showed up at AJ's door. Obviously he didn't know me very well.

"This is what I'm trained for. I'm sure the FBI will be more than happy to make a deal with Charlie to indict Harr."

"Charlie killed Rita," I protested.

Max shrugged. "God will sort it out. Or you can let Charlie make a deal with the Feds, then have your Uncle Joey be judge, jury, and executioner."

I balanced my hands like a scale. "God or Uncle Joey, it's a tough choice."

"I'll take my chance with God."

We drove on silently, until my curiosity about where we were going kicked in.

"I take it we're not doing Thai."

"What do you say we get a couple cheeseburgers, greasy fries, and shakes to go?"

I made a face. "I say this had better *not* be my last supper."

It was dark when we reached Charlie's house. We circled the block, checking for his wheels.

"Charlie lives in this back bedroom?"

"It's the one with my pictures plastered on the wall."

"You go to the door and keep granny talking. I'll climb through lover boy's window and search his room."

Grandma turned the porch light on when I rang the bell. I saw her watery eye peer through the keyhole.

"Cat, is that you?"

I tasted a sour mouthful of guilt. There are a few absolutes in my life. Not deceiving little old women is one of them.

Grandma swung the door with a force that shook the hinges. "You have some nerve traipsing over here, little lady."

My mouth tasted better already.

"What's wrong, Grandma?"

"Don't you 'Grandma' me, you trollop. Charlie told me everything. I know what you did to him."

"Let me guess. I forced him to shoot at me."

"You broke his heart. Charlie saw you with that sailor."

"That was my brother, Mrs. Ross." I gave her my best *how could you think such a thing* look.

"And the two musicians from Georgia?"

"Cousins," I smiled brightly. "I come from a *really* big family."

Grandma's liquidy eyes stared deep into mine. I widened mine and thought about puppies.

"Perhaps Charlie misjudged you," Grandma said.

"Your grandson is insanely jealous."

"Charlie's been hurt before."

She took a long hard gaze south from my red-scoop necked tee to my crimson red toenail polish. "Perhaps if you dressed differently Charlie wouldn't call you a tramp."

"Perhaps Charlie will have to get over it."

She chuckled softly. "Why don't you come back in the morning. Charlie's working late tonight."

I blinked back the tears. "Gee, Grandma, I don't want to lose a great guy like Charlie. I really need to talk to him tonight."

She hedged. "Charlie doesn't tell me where he goes."

"But you know," I said encouragingly. "Help me find him so we can get things straight between us."

"You didn't hear this from me."

I zipped my lips and threw away the key.

She whispered. "Charlie had a telephone call this afternoon and I listened in. Sounds like a security job. My Charlie moonlights a lot."

"What did the guy say?"

She thought hard. "Something about a truck and needing some extra back up."

"Where?"

"I don't remember exactly. Maybe it started with a C."

"Kids First?"

"That's it."

Bingo.

I threw my arms around her shoulders and squeezed. "You may have saved our very special relationship."

She looked small and vulnerable in the porch light. "Charlie is one in a million."

"Thank God."

I ran down the steps, guilt gnawing on me. Charlie's grandmother had built a fragile happiness around her piece-of-shit grandson. It was about to crumble around her.

I waved one more time to Grandma from the car and pulled into the street.

"Okay Max, you can come up and join the party."

He scrambled over the seat with a lumpy yellow pillowcase. "I found a few treasures in Charlie's room."

I pulled over beneath the closest street light and Max emptied the bag on the seat between us. A string of pearls, a diamond brooch, assorted other jewelry, a scattering of precious stones, and nine Rolex watches sparkled in the light.

"Charlie's one in a million," I said.

Max thrust a fist in his pocket and pulled out a wrinkled wad of paper. "This was in the garbage with a hundred Starburst wrappers."

"Poor Charlie. There's no Starburst in the clink."

"The note says 9:30 W. That could be Wednesday."

"As in today..."

Max sighed. "It's not enough. It means nothing."

The clock on the dash read nine twenty-five.

"It means we're nailing Eddie Harr but we'll have to hurry. You drive and I'll hail the troops. The cops won't wanna miss this one."

"You're insane," Max said.

I kissed Max on the cheek as I climbed over him and commandeered the passenger seat. "Admit it, I grow on you."

"Like a fungus," Max smiled. "Where to?"

"Eddie's warehouse. They're sending out a shipment."

Rocco didn't pick up the phone the first time I called. Or the second. I punched redial and my brother answered. He was short of breath and out of sorts.

"This better be important."

"Maria's gotta be knocked up by now, bro."

"Good-bye."

"Wait! I need your help."

"Are you hurt, Caterina? Is your life in danger?"

"No, but—"

"Later."

"Don't hang up, Rocco! Charlie tried to kill me today."

He expelled a breath. "Dammit, Cat, are you okay?"

"I think so. Charlie's at the Kids First Project warehouse and they're loading assault rifles. Call the captain. Eddie's goin' down this time."

"Get out of there. Where's Max."

"Uh—he can't talk right now."

Rocco muttered something to Maria and she took the phone. "Rocco's getting dressed. He's calling the captain."

"Gotcha!" I tossed my cell phone on the dash and grunted with satisfaction. "Backup is on the way."

Max raced across town toward the warehouse. My phone blasted. "Here's A Quarter, Call Someone Who Cares."

"That'll be Rocco. I'll put the phone on speaker. Bro, are you on your way?"

The rigid voice on the other end was happy as a heart attack.

"Caterina, this is Captain Maxfield."

"Bob! We got Eddie dead to rights this time."

"What we got, Caterina, is to get you to a doctor."

"I'm a little beat up but don't worry. I'm healing just fine."

"A head doctor."

Max snickered.

"That's cold, Bob."

"We're still dodging a lawsuit after your last hot tip. The city of Chicago's lips are firmly attached to Eddie Harr's ass. I want you to leave him alone."

"Eddie Harr killed my dear friend."

"Polansky? You met that woman once."

"We hit it off. We were practically sisters."

"Listen to me. Forget Eddie. I don't care if he wheels a nuclear tomahawk down Main Street. Walk away and call your shrink."

I crammed the phone in my pocket and slapped a hand on Max's mouth to muffle the gales of laughter.

"Now *that* was rude. Who needs the Chicago PD anyway? We'll bring Eddie and Charlie in ourselves."

Max choked.

"You're the super spy, aren't you? You can kill with your bare hands."

"You do need therapy."

"I thought you were good."

"I'm the best but I'm doing the math. We're way outnumbered and the bad guys have a hell of a lot more weapons. I'm not opposed to back-up."

I hauled out my phone and searched for a number.

Max hid a smile.

"I'm calling Special Agent Larry Harding of the FBI. We're buddies."

"FBI? You didn't mention him before."

"He's a schmuck."

Special Agent Harding's telephone went directly to voicemail and I left a message. "Hey, Larry, this is Cat. Cat DeLuca," I added to be clear.

"Yep, you're buddies alright," Max said.

"Eddie Harr is shipping arms tonight. I'm on my way to the Kids First warehouse. I need back-up. Please hurry."

I listened through the delivery options and marked it Urgent.

"Does your buddy like you enough to drag his team out in the middle of the night to save your admittedly fine ass?"

"Harding is…uh…"

"He doesn't like you at all, does he?"

"Nope. Not even a little bit."

"Then he won't be coming."

"Probably not."

"We're running short on back-up. Shot down by your brother, Chicago's finest, and the Feds." Max hauled out his phone.

"Who are you calling?"

Max winked. "Babe, I've got friends in low places."

Chapter Twenty-seven

Max drove slowly past the Kids First Project warehouse. At the back of the building the loading dock was lit up like Wrigley Field. A big ass black and silver semi was parked in the distribution bay. I counted four beefy guys covering the truck. One, I was guessing, was Charlie.

Max parked Tino's Buick down the street and cut the lights. He reloaded the Colt 45 in his shoulder holster and tucked a backup around his ankle. I pulled the 9mm from my gold Chanel shoulder bag and checked the safety before jamming it in the back of my pants.

"I counted eight vehicles," I said.

"One guard smoking in front."

I missed the smoker. "Can you take him down?"

"With my bare hands."

Max reached over and pinned his hand on my knee. "I'm going in alone."

I flung his hand off me. "The hell you are Max. We're a team."

"Wrong, Cat. I'm your bodyguard and you're staying here."

I saw a glint of shiny silver handcuffs in his left hand. "Then you'll want to keep an eye on this body." I kicked open my door and escaped outside.

Max swore and clambered out after me. "Okay, fine, but this is just recon, not an attack. Stick with me."

"I'm on you like paper on taffy."

We darted across the parking lot and weaved though a scattering of cars to a green BMW with a fresh bullet hole in the back window.

"Nice shootin' Tex," I mouthed.

Max pressed an index finger to his lips, cueing me to silence.

I punched his arm. The hired gun leaned against the BMW's hood a few yards away. I wasn't blind or stupid.

Max motioned for me to wait. Before I could mouth a protest he edged around the Beemer. I slid around the other side and hunkered down behind the front tire and peered cautiously over the hood. The muscle had a large flat face and an unlit cigarette hung from his mouth. He struck a match and thick lips and a honking huge schnozzola flickered in the firelight. It wasn't pretty.

A shadow caught the corner of my eye. Max charged from behind, hooking an iron arm around the thick beefy neck, locking him in a choke hold. Schnozzola gasped, kicking his feet as his air shut off. I rocketed in as he went down and sucker punched him with the butt of my pistol.

"You know he was already out cold."

I blew on my pistol. "It was a team effort."

Max made a face. "So much for the recon mission."

We dragged the dead weight around the side of the building. Max grabbed my hand and we ran to the front entrance. I fumbled in my pockets and for a few nail-biting moments a spotlight above the door lit us up like the Fourth of July.

I set the tension wrench in the lock, pulled the pick, and hauled Max through the door.

"Impressive."

"Stick with me, babe," I said. "I'll show you my magic."

Max snatched a peppermint candy from a bowl on the counter and popped it in his mouth. His eyes followed a trail of framed pictures on the wall. Eddie Harr grinned at us in a dozen.

Max whistled softly. "Damn. How does somebody get in the White Sox dugout?"

I tugged his sleeve. "What do you care? You're a Cubs fan."

We passed through the reception area and moved quickly through the corridor to the two doors at the end of the hall. There were voices behind the door leading to the warehouse and a forklift whined at full throttle.

Max listened. "There's at least three guys plus one on the forklift and four outside back."

"We can take them down."

Max grabbed my neck and knuckle-rubbed the top of my head. "Recon, sister. We're after something that'll force Captain Bob to reconsider."

I jiggled the knob to the volunteer's workshop and a bell on the other side of the warehouse wall screamed. I jumped.

"Nerves of steel," Max grinned.

The sound of heavy work boots plonked our way and a voice growled into the telephone.

"This is Burt."

The message from the other end was brief.

"Dammit," Burt swore and slammed the phone down. He whistled and hollered and the machines turned off.

"We got company," Burt bellowed. "That damn woman is back and she brought her boyfriend. *Find them!*"

Max cocked his head. "They know you?"

"Oh shit," I said.

"And move this rig outta here," Burt roared.

The giant diesel rumbled to life, gears gnashing in a rush to exit with Eddie's cache.

"We may need more bullets," I said.

Max grabbed my hand and we ran back through the twisted corridor, my ragged breath barely audible above the loud clacking of my shoes.

Behind us the door to the warehouse blasted open. "They're here!" Burt's voice shouted.

A stampede of rushing feet pounded the hallway and my feet flew faster.

"You know that magic you promised to show me," Max shouted.

"Yeah?" I gasped.

"*Now* would be a good time."

We skidded into the lobby and I kicked the front door open, grabbed a shoe in my hand, and launched it across the asphalt. I grabbed Max and we ducked behind the counter. Eddie's punks slid into the lobby and stormed out the door brandishing guns. For a moment they hesitated under the spotlight searching the shadows. There was a wild cry, someone snared my shoe, and they plunged into the night.

When they were gone Max brushed himself off. Giving a low throaty chuckle he pulled me to my feet and into his arms. "That was magic, Babe."

"Oh yeah," I said all cocky. "They think we got away."

He looked at his watch. "Until they find the car. I give them three minutes. Maybe four."

"Dammit Max." I pushed him away. "Now what?"

He smiled. "That should put a couple hoodlums around the Buick about the same time Tino screams in with his team. Tino hates it when people mess with his car."

My face broke in a giddy grin. "You mean Tino's coming?"

"That's what I call reinforcements."

The farthest distance from the loading docks was a waiting room. We steered clear of the windows and waited for our back up. I hate to wait.

"What time is it?" I said.

"Two minutes since you asked last."

"Call Tino."

"He'll be here."

I sighed. "I'm getting a soda. D'ya want one?"

"Gimme Mr. Pibb."

"Tough guy."

I held out a hand. "I threw away a hundred dollar shoe," I said.

"Anytime, gimpy." Max burrowed deep in his pocket and emptied a fistful of change in my palm.

The vending machines were located in a small alcove down the hall. I limped there and pressed my face against the glass. I spun the sugar and carbs around. Cherry pies, Ho Hos, peanuts, candies, chips, corn dogs, pretzels, and Almond Joy. A veritable feast.

"What to choose?" I mumbled.

"Starburst," a soft voice growled. I twisted around and almost gagged on the heart in my throat.

"Hey, Charlie," I said to the gun in his hand.

"I didn't want to have to do this," he said. "I don't like hurting girls."

"Then don't."

He shrugged, unconvinced.

I tore my eyes from the gun and took in his dirty blond hair, bug eyes, and pocked face. Charlie wasn't pretty. There was toad somewhere in his genealogy.

I managed a sour smile. "So, big guy, why did you kill Rita?"

He shrugged. "Polansky had a death wish. Apparently so do you."

I was quick to set the record straight. "See, that's where you're wrong Charlie. I want to live a good long life like your Grandma."

Charlie growled. "You got no business talking about my Grandma."

"And you got no business telling her I'm a hootchie. Your Grandma likes me. She thinks we're engaged."

Charlie sneered. "Girls like you don't go out with me."

"Did ya ask me, Charlie?" I inched closer.

He tightened his grip on the gun. "No tricks. Stay where you are."

"Whatever." I counted the change in my hand. "We'll share a Starburst. I like the little bows you make with the wrappers."

Charlie didn't hide his pleasure. "You noticed?"

"I noticed other things about you too. You have a really hot car."

"General Lee."

"Take me for a spin in the General, Charlie. But lose the gun. Girls don't like guns."

Charlie mulled what I said in his thick delusional head.

"The boss wouldn't like that," he decided.

"He wouldn't have to know." I winked and moved a little closer, the Starburst in my open hand.

Charlie's eyes widened. "You joking? The boss always knows."

Maybe Charlie wasn't as dumb as he seemed.

Where the hell was Max anyway? AKA my bodyguard. It might occur to him I could use some help here. I mean how long does it take to get a soda?

I stretched my neck in a big circle, snuck a peek behind me, and swallowed a scream. A big honker filled the doorway and the bulging eyes were pissed.

"Have a nice nap?" I said.

"You!" He tapped the red bruise on his cheek. The butt of my pistol was all over it.

"You did this, bitch."

"Did not," I lied and smacked my lips. They stuck. It was a hell of a night. No Dr. Pepper Lip Smacker, no Max. And me wearing one miserable shoe.

Schnozzola reached into his jacket pocket. I caught a glimmer of metal.

"A knife?" My voice rose in disbelief and a shudder sliced through me like a blade. "You've got to be kidding me."

"You can't kill her," Charlie said to my surprise. "It's the boss' call."

I hooked two fingers. "Eddie and I are like this."

He ran his finger along the blade, drew blood, and smiled.

"Sicko," I said.

"I'll hurt her just a little," he said and Charlie, a team player, nodded.

Schnozzola lunged for me and I dove low. I rolled on the floor striking him in the knees. He went down hard and I clipped his arm with the side of my hand. The knife dropped and I swung my lone shoe and sent it skittering across the floor. I jumped on his big belly and pummeled him with my fists. He laughed and whacked me on the side of my head, tossing me off him like a salad. I jerked to my knees and plucked the 9mm from my jeans but Charlie punted the gun from my hand.

"You can't bring a gun to a knife fight," Charlie said and flung a Starburst bow on the floor. As if *he* ever followed any rules.

I hurtled to my feet and stomped Schnozzola in the groin. He recoiled in a ball on the floor.

I blasted to the closest big metal box and tugged it off-kilter with all my might. The vending machine crashed to the floor, pinning Schnozzola and splaying broken plastic and junk food across his chest.

"Damn, girl!" Charlie said.

"Three brothers," I gasped, out of breath.

"Caterina!" a voice down the hall thundered. Relief rushed through me and I felt my legs go.

Charlie snatched a Starburst package off the floor. "Later." He vanished down the hall.

"Papa?" I squawked.

The echo of running feet charged the hallway. Rocco finished first through the door waving a gun. Papa, Uncle Joey, and the twins were close behind.

I gave a crooked smile from my perch on the vending machine.

"Nice trophy," Uncle Joey said.

"Get her off me," Schnozzola rasped.

"Did he hurt you?" Papa demanded.

I waggled a stocking foot. "I lost another hundred dollar shoe."

"Sick bastard," Papa said, and the twins kicked the goon.

"Owwwee!"

Rocco helped me down. "Tino's guys are mopping up outside. They beat the crap outta a couple guys. Bloody noses, a few broken teeth."

"This one could go to the hospital," the twins said with admiration.

I held my breath. "Did you find Eddie's guns?"

Uncle Joey shook his head. "Max said somebody tipped them off."

I groaned. "We got nothing?"

Max flashed a smile from the doorway. "Did somebody mention my name?"

"Where the hell were you?" I sputtered. "I had two guys on me. I dodged a gun *and* a knife."

"Babe," he smiled. "You had it handled."

"*Two* guys?" the twins frowned. "You let a guy get away?"

Max ambled to the soda machine, slid a dollar in the slot, and pushed a button. He raised his Mr. Pibb to the guy on the floor.

Joey scooped the knife from the corner and kneeled beside the vending machine. The blade glinted against Schnozzola's throat.

"Eddie's shitty equipment collapsed and crushed your bad ass. Sue your boss if you like. But if you mention my niece's name I'll cut your heart out."

"Damn straight," the twins snarled, stuffing their pockets with candy.

Max plucked my gun from a corner and tucked it in my pants.

Papa growled and Rocco pushed Max aside. "C'mon, sis. You don't want to be here when Captain Bob arrives."

"Wait!" the guy wearing the vending machine cried. "You can't leave me like this."

"Bye bye," I sang, and forged down the hall.

"Owwee!"

I looked back startled. "What the…"

Rocco gripped my shoulders, turned me around and steered me toward the exit.

"The twins are a little pissed about that shoe."

Chapter Twenty-eight

We stepped outside into the parking lot and I took a big gulp of fresh air.

Tino rushed to squeeze me in a bear hug. "Caterina!" He felt soft and warm and smelled of sweet wine and oregano.

He stepped back and swept his arm across the parking lot.

"He's showing off his carnage," Max murmured. Eddie's guys littered the ground, the shit beat out of them.

"My men did this for you," Tino said, "and still they don't tell me where you are."

I worked my throbbing temples with my fingers. "They didn't know."

Tino shrugged. "Max took a couple guys down himself."

Max smiled. "I saved your life, Babe. You can thank me later."

Papa growled. "Save your own and get the car."

Max winked and jogged off to the Buick.

Tino gathered his army and disappeared into the night.

"Tino knows this isn't Afghanistan, doesn't he?" I said.

Joey grinned. "He knows enough to retreat before Captain Bob rides in."

Captain Bob. The name sent chills down my spine. I staved off a wave of panic and assessed the damage. There was no truck, no illegal weapons. No evidence of a crime. What we had was a B&E felony, a man struck down by a potato chip machine, and some do-good charity workers ambushed at work. There was only one left thing to do.

"I'm moving to Mexico," I announced. "Tonight."

Brakes screeched and a car careened into the parking lot. Busted. If Bob was behind those blinding headlights I'd race like hell for the border.

Eddie's guys staggered to their cars and the speeding vehicle skirted around them like cones on an obstacle course. I put it in reverse and ducked behind the DeLuca offensive line.

The car screamed to a halt at Papa's feet, tires smoking. I copped a peek from behind the twins and Chance Savino sprang from the driver's seat. I blinked, shook my head, and looked again. What the hell is *he* doing here, I thought.

Savino didn't waste words. He shoved his way through a barrage of Italians and when he reached the end of the huddle the tightness left his jaw and relief flooded his face. He threw out his arms and for one crazy moment I thought he would wrap them around me.

Instead he planted his hands firmly on my shoulders and shook me fiercely.

"Are you out of your mind, DeLucky?"

My voice quavered with the jostling. "Nice to see you too, Savino."

Papa frowned. "*Savino?*"

"Chance Savino's dead," the twins said, smacking down Skittles.

He let go of my shoulders and it came to me then. *Chance Savino was alive and I had witnesses.* Five of Chicago's finest and one hot bodyguard who disappears every time someone tries to kill me.

A drum roll would be nice but I threw out a hand for flair. "Papa, Uncle Joey, Rocco, Vinnie, and Michael," I announced, "*this* is Chance Savino."

The twins were unconvinced. They dropped Skittles in my outstretched hand.

Max blazed to the curb in the Buick.

"One car left," Papa said with satisfaction. "Must belong to the guy trapped under the vending machine."

"What guy?" Chance said.

I popped some Skittles in his mouth. "You don't want to know."

Chance moved closer, lifted my chin, and searched my face in the street light. Papa growled.

His gaze froze on the bruise Schnozzola left when he cuffed the side of my head.

"Who did this to you?"

Savino touched the side of my face and I winced. "Where's your bodyguard?"

As if on cue Max appeared. "I got the car, Babe. Let's blow."

Chance nailed Max with his fist. Max staggered backwards and crashed on the asphalt. He shook the cobwebs from his head and dabbed his bloody lip with the back of his hand.

"Who the hell are you?" Max said stroking his jaw.

"That's for letting Cat come here tonight."

"Letting me?" I said hotly.

Max reeled to his feet and rolled up his sleeves. "I'm gonna kick your ass, you son of a bitch."

I whipped the 9mm from my pants. "Enough already or I'll shoot you both."

Savino's passenger door shot open and Special Agent in Charge Larry Harding scrambled out. I groaned inwardly.

"Everything OK here, Agent Savino?"

I gasped. "*Agent* Savino?"

"We're good."

Harding cleared his throat. "Did you notice a woman with a head injury is waving a gun."

"You've met Agent Harding, I believe."

"Took your sweet time getting here," Max growled.

"Agent Savino?" I pushed him. "Shut up."

He grinned. "So I'm not a crook. You're not going to hold that against me."

I gritted my teeth and lowered my voice. "You're a crook all right. I know all about your miserable diamond scheme. The good old boys at the FBI think the diamonds were lost in the explosion. But you kept them for yourself."

"Would those be the diamonds you lifted from me? Who's the real crook here?"

I stomped on his foot and twirled around to face Savino's partner. "I have something for you, Larry."

I pounced to the Buick, whipped the passenger door open, yanked out my leather Zac tote, and emptied it on the hood. Squealing triumphantly I snapped up the little black bag and plopped it in Agent Larry Harding's palm.

He looked confused. "What..."

"Diamonds," I said crisply. "A small fortune I imagine."

Max shot me a look of betrayal. "*You* had the diamonds?"

"Madre Santa!" Papa breathed and the DeLuca men locked their eyes on the small sack in Harding's trembling fingers. The Agent caught his breath and peered in the bag greedily. I whipped around to face Savino squarely. His face was a mask.

Special Agent Larry Harding's voice was tight. "I don't know what game you're playing, Ms. DeLuca."

He held the bag in his right hand and tipped the contents into his cupped left. What he got was air. He tossed the bag on the ground.

I scooped it up in my hand and jammed my fingers inside. The diamonds were gone.

A twisted smile played around the edges of Chance Savino's mouth.

"Perhaps you should accompany me downtown, Ms. DeLuca." Agent Larry Harding faced me squarely. "Is it true you dreamed up these diamonds?"

Who got to the diamonds? And how? I closed my eyes and replayed my steps since snatching the diamonds from Devin's toolbox. My purse was with me everywhere but the shower. I opened them again and Uncle Joey winked.

"Ms. DeLuca," Harding repeated, "did you or did you not imagine these diamonds?"

The twins flicked Sugar Babies in the air and caught them with their tongues. Max scowled at me, and Chance Savino mouthed *liar, liar.* I pretended not to read lips.

I turned my head around to meet Special Agent in Charge Larry Harding's level gaze.

"I see dead people," I said. "Diamonds, I'm not so sure about."

Chapter Twenty-nine

The day Dorothy was to be interred, I arrived at Mickey's as the tow truck pulled up and dumped her charred remains alongside a spanking new fire-hydrant. The video in my head hit replay and for one awful moment I relived the fiery blast and Tommy's deafening scream. I squeezed my eyes shut and when I opened them again Uncle Joey stood beside me. He pressed a warm cup in my hand.

"Coffee," he said, "with something to put the color back in your cheeks."

I wrapped my fingers around the cup gratefully and followed him inside.

Mickey's was abuzz with preparation for Dorothy's funeral. The women from the Moose Lodge, dressed in Sunday best, set tables for a funeral brunch.

The twins, hanging out with the food, sampled the seven-layer dip.

"Caterina is here," Mama said with the relief of someone ready to hand off the show. "She knew Dorothy better than any of us."

The Lodge ladies nodded somberly. "She was the last to see Dorothy alive."

"And the first to kill her," my sister Sophie snickered.

Mama held up a fistful of napkins. "Would Dorothy prefer yellow or white?"

"She liked blue."

"Of course!" Mama smacked her forehead. "Dorothy *was* blue!" Mama hauled a hankie from her bra and dabbed her eyes.

"I'll run to the Jewel for the blue," I said seizing my escape.

Papa raced me to the door. "Got it!"

There was a flash and he was gone.

"This is a good thing you're doing, Cat," Mickey hollered from the rafters. "We're expecting a big crowd."

He was hanging a long streamer emblazoned *Dorothy's High*.

"Dorothy's High?" I said.

"The printer got it wrong. It was supposed to say *Dorothy's Riding High*," Mickey shrugged. "I think Jack will get the message."

"What message is that?"

Father Timothy walked through the door flanked by two nuns, Uncle Joey, and Elvis.

"I booked music for the funeral," Uncle Joey announced.

Elvis stood shaking his hips.

"Do 'Honky Tonk Angel,'" Father Timothy said. "It's my favorite."

"You're such a priest," I said.

"How do you like my sign?" Mickey said.

Uncle Joey frowned.

"He doesn't get it either," I said.

Rocco strolled through the door blowing dust off a running-horse emblem he retrieved from the rubble outside Mickey's door. "Jack will want to keep this. I found it in the wreckage."

"That used to be a fender," the twins said, sampling the antipasto.

"There's not much left of Dorothy to see," Rocco sighed regretfully.

"That's OK." Sister Margaret crossed herself. "People are coming to see the woman who killed her."

I groaned.

"Tough crowd," Uncle Joey said.

Father Timothy checked his watch. "It's show time. Take your places. We start when Jack arrives."

"Are you sure he doesn't know?" Mickey said.

"Totally clueless as always," I said. "Tino and Max are bringing him in."

"Jack can be stubborn," Mama said. "What if he refuses to leave the shop?"

"The guys will handle it. Tino wasn't always a sausage maker, you know. He was a spy like James Bond."

"Really?" Father Timothy said.

"She's delusional!" Sophie sang.

"Just watch," I said. "They always get their man."

◇◇◇

The black Buick screeched to a halt beside Dorothy. Max jolted from the back seat, seized Jack's greased and lubed coveralls and deposited him unceremoniously on the sidewalk. Jack swung a bloodied fist and slammed air. His eyes fixed on Dorothy. A tortured sound escaped his throat.

As Tino told it later, he had wheeled the bullet ridden black Buick to Jack's garage. Max hopped in the backseat and Tino waved him over.

Jack was drinking again. His face showed a dark stubble and a bloody bandage swathed a hand. The mechanic dropped another finger in an engine.

"I saw Cat DeLuca drivin' your car last week," Jack said.

Tino nodded.

"You heard what she did to Dorothy."

"Cat didn't blow up your car."

Jack leaned back and his bloodshot eyes scanned the full length of the peppered Buick. Ridicule gurgled in his throat.

Tino ignored him. "Hop in. There's a noise in my engine when I drive."

"You still friends with Cat DeLuca?"

"I am."

Jack spat. "Take your business elsewhere."

Max then leaped from the back, grabbed Jack's shoulders, and dragged him inside. Jack kicked his legs out the window and sputtered curses all the way to Mickey's Bar and Grill.

Jack's jaw dropped. He looked around the crowd. Elvis sang "She's A Machine." Rocco presented Jack with the running-horse emblem.

"That's your fender," the twins called from the crowd.

Father Timothy cleared his throat.

"We have gathered here today to remember Dorothy."

A few sniffles sounded from the crowd. I wondered if everyone understood Dorothy was a car.

Father Timothy's voice resonated with feeling. "Dorothy's service on earth has ended. We recognize how faithful she was to both Jack and to his father, Bernie."

"Amen, brother," a voice called out. I twisted my head around. It was a Baptist.

"Dorothy was loyal, true, and reliable," the priest continued.

"She required very little maintenance," Jack choked.

"Dorothy is no longer here with us. She has gone on to be with Bernie. The roads they travel are paved with gold."

A voice sniggered. "If I know Bernie, he's chippin' gold and playing poker."

"Potholes in heaven," someone laughed.

The priest lifted his hands. "In the midst of this company we trust Dorothy to God's care. Her ravaged body we commit to the ground." He made a sign with his hand.

"Iron to ore."

"Glass to sand."

"Rubber to recycle."

Father Timothy ended with a prayer.

The band started up and Elvis belted out "Swing Low, Sweet Chariot." Pale in his dress whites, Tommy the rookie came forward. He clutched a single long-stemmed red rose in his hand. A hush rippled through the crowd.

Tommy stood silently a long moment. He made his peace, knelt, and placed a rose on the pile of rubble. The men and women of the precinct fell in line behind him, each offering a blood red rose to the fallen Mustang. When they had finished, the residents of Bridgeport followed. One by one we tossed a flower on the remains, until Dorothy, smothered with splashes of green and velvety red petals, glimmered in the sun.

My heart swelled in my chest. Jack had his miracle. He'd lost Dorothy but the community rallied around him. The people of Bridgeport weren't about to let the sky fall on his house alone. They didn't care that he was totally nutso. He belongs here. He's one of us. That has to count for something.

Papa pressed a blue napkin in my hand, and smushed another to his face.

Mama yanked a dinner bell from her bra. "We eat!" The twins led the stampede to Mickey's door.

Jack lingered outside. He hunkered down on the spanking new fire hydrant beside Dorothy. I approached him uncertainly. He hadn't shaved and he smelled like booze. He looked older than I remembered.

"Thanks, Cat," he said without turning his head.

"I never meant for anything bad to happen to Dorothy."

"I know. But it don't bring my dad back."

I smiled. "Maybe this will."

A horn blared and Jack did a double take. A smoking red 1953 Bel-Air Convertible barreled down the street and jerked to a stop beside Dorothy. Jack did a double take.

Uncle Joey grinned goofily from behind the wheel. "Bernie knew a sweet ride."

"Olivia?"

Jack raced to the rear bumper and dropped to his knees. His fingers felt for three notches etched in the chrome. His dad carved them the night he took Clarabelle and a bottle of his papa's whiskey into the backseat. It was the night Jack was conceived.

Jack felt the scratches with his fingers. "How did you find her?" he said incredulously.

Uncle Joey pitched the keys to Jack. "Maybe she found you."

I gave Uncle Joey a squeeze and sniffed the shoulder of his jacket. An aroma I'd smelled before filled my nostrils. My eyes widened knowingly.

"You smoked a cigar in Olivia," I said.

"Don Diego. I asked around. It was Bernie's brand."

"I met a woman who smokes them in elevators."

Jack hopped in the driver's seat. He sat frozen for a moment. Then he threw back his head and laughed.

"Now that's magic," I said.

Uncle Joey smiled. "I thought it was a nice touch."

Chapter Thirty

I had a glass of wine at Mickey's and made a date with Tommy to do Chicago. I couldn't face another buffet and luckily, Mama didn't notice. She was busy heaping cake and ice cream on plates for the twins.

Uncle Joey drove me home in his car. "You shouldn't be alone until we get the guy who got Tommy."

"Any leads?"

"None that panned out. We're all over your case files."

"At least you solved the case of the flaming dog poop."

"What can I say? We're Chicago's finest."

I hesitated. "Eddie did it."

"The poop?"

"Dorothy."

He mulled the possibility over in his mind. "You could be right. But you won't convince the captain to go after Harr. He's retiring next year. He's going to need his pension."

At the house, I punched in the code and opened the door and Inga charged full speed, howling. She bounced off the porch, zagged circles in the grass and galloped full-speed back inside.

"Some watchdog," Joey said. "She's leading the way to the silver."

I reset my premium platinum alarm system and trotted after her to the kitchen.

Max and Tino were at the table, hunched over a game of chess.

"Who's winning?" I said.

"I am," Max said.

"I got fifty bucks on Tino," Uncle Joey said. "Any takers?"

Dead silence.

"Thanks a lot, Cat," Max said. "I saved your life last night."

"And I'll buy you dinner with the fifty bucks I just saved. I'm starved."

Tino picked off Max's queen. "Checkmate."

Uncle Joey tucked his fifty away. "Nobody beats Tino at chess."

"Dammit," Max said.

Uncle Joey chuckled. "Put in your order. I'm buying. I've got Happiness Chinese Restaurant on my cell."

"Cat still owes me dinner," Max said.

Thirty minutes later we sat at the table around open cartons of Kung Po and Dim Sum. I stabbed giant prawns with my chop sticks but broke down and used a fork for the fried rice.

"Cheater," Tino said.

I made a face. "I know you were a spy."

"You were hit in the head by an exploding building."

"It was a sign. It said FOR LEASE."

The door bell rang followed by a commanding knock. Max stuffed a scallop in his mouth, pulled the .45 from his shoulder holster, and beat Uncle Joey to the door.

"What the hell, Cat," Joey called. "You rob a bank or something?"

There was a shuffling of feet on the hardwood floor.

"You have company," Tino said. We ditched the squid and padded to the living room.

Captain Bob positioned himself by the fireplace, arms folded across his chest. Two uniforms anchored stiffly beside him. My stomach roiled in a knot. This couldn't be good. I was reasonably sure it wasn't about my unpaid parking tickets. Uncle Joey takes care of them.

Bob's face was red and a jutting blue vein pulsed on the side of his neck. The facial twitch was new.

"There was a break-in last night at the Kids First warehouse," Bob said.

"Oh?" Minnie Mouse took over my voice.

"Eddie Harr believes members of the Chicago Police Department were involved and he's citing police harassment and brutality. Several employees required medical attention."

"Wimps," I squeaked.

"I assured Mr. Harr this was an unfortunate and random act by completely insane individuals with no connection to the department."

Bob glared at me. His jaw worked savagely.

"Can I get you something?" I said. "Coffee? Tea? Valium?"

He snarled.

"Cut to the chase, Bob," Uncle Joey said.

"At five a.m. this morning a man named Charles Ross was found dead in his car."

I caught my breath. "Ratman?"

Bob referred to his notes. "A suicide note was on the dash."

I flopped next to Tino on the sofa. "Somebody murdered Charlie. I can't believe it."

"Suicide," Captain Bob barked like I was deaf. "In his note, Ross confessed to killing Rita Polansky."

"Charlie could write?" Max said.

"He typed the note," Bob said, "but he signed his name."

"Oh Puh-leeze!"

Bob ignored me. "Ross claimed responsibility for the two bombings. It was a crime spree. He's responsible for the deaths of three persons and for using the Kids First Project to smuggle arms out of the country. Ross said he couldn't live with the guilt."

"Guilt wasn't a big problem for Charlie," I said.

"We expect to close the case within a few days," Bob said. "Pending autopsy and handwriting results."

"How convenient," I said. "Charlie confessed everything but Eddie's traffic tickets."

"The hit you took from that brick has you imagining things."

"It was a FOR LEASE sign," Max said.

"Well there's a VACANCY sign up there now." Captain Bob tapped his finger on my forehead.

Tino snickered.

"I'm delivering a message from the Chief," Bob said. "Leave Harr alone."

"C'mon, Bob. Charlie didn't kill himself. He took the fall for his boss. Rita Polansky connected Eddie Harr to organized crime. I can show you her laptop."

"Polansky was crackers too."

"Too?" I squawked.

"For godsake, Cat, see a doctor."

Captain Bob stomped to the door. The two stiff uniforms followed him out and slammed it shut.

"They're closing the case," Max said.

"But the autopsy results—"

Joey cut me off.

"Don't count on it, kid. Everything is neatly wrapped up now. The brass hates wrinkles."

"It's over," Tino said. "Max can go home. Harr is off the hook and he won't make waves. He knows if anything happens to you he'll be under the spotlight again."

Joey nodded. "You're safe now."

I dropped on a chair. "You're leaving?"

"I should feed my fish," Max said. "I have plants."

"But what about slick Eddie? He's getting away with murder."

"Give it time," Tino said. "The scales of justice balance themselves. Eddie will slip up one day and make a mistake."

"You have my phone numbers, fax, and email," Max said. "If anything changes I'll be here in an hour."

Max walked down the hall to his bedroom and I shuffled after him. His duffle bag was on the bed and he was already packed.

"You knew about Charlie."

"Tino told me this morning."

Of course he did. "When we met you said I could drive your Hummer."

"That was when you had a gun on me." He wrapped his arms around me. "Now that you are no longer my security detail, I have a cabin in Wisconsin outside Baraboo. We can go next weekend."

For one delicious moment his lips caressed mine. His fingers danced across the nape of my neck and down my spine. Tino canceling Max was actually turning out to be a good thing.

He pulled away and smiled. "And you can drive."

I hugged two retired spies and a crooked cop at the door and they left in a parade. I pasted a smiled on my face and waved from the porch. They drove away and I felt terribly alone.

I loaded the dishwasher and cleaned the room. I hadn't had a decent night sleep in over a week. My cook was gone but at least Mama's cannoli was on ice. I poured a huge glass of chianti and wondered what schmuck Eddie paid to pull the trigger on Charlie. My life looked a little better at the bottom of the glass.

Inga trotted to the back door and dropped the leash in my lap.

"Well Inga, we're free. Let's blow this gin joint."

Chapter Thirty-one

I scooted to my bedroom, smushed my hair in a pony tail, and grabbed the brightest thing in my closet, a fuschia pull-over hoodie, and my favorite pair of Rock and Republic pants. I stuffed a bottle of water, apple, and a sausage for Inga in my front pouch. Inga chased me to the porch. I swung the door closed behind us and broke into a slow jog.

We took the side streets to the Catholic high school and ran the track. The sun was warm on my skin and it felt good to sweat.

Inga and I shared a snack on the school lawn and walked home. I exchanged gossip with neighbors, helped Mrs. Betrolli carry in her groceries. When I rounded the corner to my house a shrill voice nailed me.

"Yoo hoo! Caterina!"

I took a deep, groaning breath. It was Gladys Pickins, Bridgeport's self-appointed neighborhood watchdog. Mrs. Pickins is quick to point out an unmowed lawn but her specialty is moral insensibilities. Sam and Harvey who live across the street are her top priority. I'm a close second.

"Sic her, girl," I whispered. Inga wagged her tail.

"Hello, Gladys."

My neighbor narrowed her eyes to small slits. It was her mean look. I stepped back.

"I read your name in the paper. It said you're a terrorist."

"I read the paper too. It said the explosion was caused by a gas leak."

"I don't believe it."

"Neither do I."

"I'm watching you, Caterina. I've seen the trail of men coming and going."

"I have clients, Gladys. I own a respectable business."

"That's a hoot! Hot Pants Detective Agency."

"It's Pants on Fire."

"Same difference."

"The difference is whether you're taking pictures or posing for them." I reached into my pouch to get my keys and unlock the door.

Gladys is a mean-spirited old witch without a friend in the world. No one visits her, not even her kids. For one brief moment I felt sorry for her. I heard my voice say something crazy.

"Why don't you come inside and have a cannoli with me. It'll be fun."

"With one of your *clients* waiting for you?"

My heart stopped dead in my chest. I stared at my front door. "You mean…"

"You don't fool me, Caterina DeLuca." She turned on a heel and tromped away.

I froze at the edge of the sidewalk trying to remember if I had set the alarm. I was more emotionally exhausted than I thought. And my gun was in my top dresser drawer. Victoria's Secret was safe.

I forced myself to breathe. I considered the facts. One. Gladys Pickins is crazy and she wasn't even slammed in the head. Two. Nobody wants to kill me anymore. Except maybe two hundred of Tommy's closest friends and family. But they're good people. The kind who would drop arsenic in my punch. Not the kind who would break in just to murder me. And three. There wasn't a strange car on the street. Did I mention Gladys is crazy?

Besides I wasn't alone. My vicious sidekick was with me. As if on cue Inga rolled over and scratched her back on the soft grass.

"Oh yeah, girl," I said. "We're going in."

I unlocked the door and Inga bounded to her water dish. No sniffing the air, no hair up on her back. I made a fist and yanked my elbow back hard. "Whoo hoo!" Just as I suspected. Gladys Pickins was a whack job and Inga and I were alone.

I hit the radio button and shimmied to my bedroom.

I got my mo-jo workin' but it just won't work on you.

I pulled my ponytail, opened my dresser drawer, and dropped the hair tie inside. My stomach flipped. I did a double take and looked again. My fingers ferreted futilely through satin and lace. The 9mm was gone. And Victoria's Secret, gathered in a sorry muddled hump, was far from safe.

Chapter Thirty-two

Gladys Pickins, it would seem, isn't quite as crazy as the woman who didn't call for backup. I strained my ears for a sound. A creak on the stair or the metal scrape of a sharpening axe. I got nothing but my head hammering with a vengeance.

I closed the drawer and calculated a beeline to the front door. Zero to sixty in three seconds. With any luck my intruder ran off while Gladys zoomed her binoculars on Sam and Harvey.

"Inga, come!" I called and made a dash for the door. Inga bounded from the kitchen and I smelled Tino's Deli. I stopped in my tracks. A big fat sausage hung from Inga's mouth. Her new best friend trotted behind her clutching the bag of Tino's smoked sausages. Special Agent in Charge Larry Harding's other hand gripped my gun.

I grabbed the edge of the couch for support.

"Traitor," I said. Inga licked his greasy sausage fingers.

"She's a nice dog."

"I'm trading her in for a pit bull. What the hell are you doing here?"

"I think you know."

"Not even a clue. You scared the shit out of me."

"Where's the laptop?"

"Are you kidding me?" My voice rose incredulously. "You're here for the laptop? You couldn't get a warrant? Knock on the door and ask nice or tell Chance to pick it up..."

I stopped cold and looked hard into the steel-gray eyes. I got it then.

"Chance doesn't know you're here."

Larry gave a crooked smile.

Without meaning to I spoke the words aloud.

"It was your number Charlie wrote on Rita's picture," I said, sealing my own fate.

"I'll take that laptop now."

"You're not in it, asshole. Rita said she suspected a leak in the FBI."

He appeared surprised. "That's it?"

"That's all she wrote. What happened? Did Rita catch you that morning with Eddie Harr? Cuz she didn't enter her notes about that meeting in her laptop. Maybe she ran out of time."

He barked an evil laugh. "Couldn't be late to her own funeral."

"Go to hell."

"I'm afraid you'll win that race." He pulled a pair of plastic gloves from his pocket and stuffed his hands inside. "For what it's worth, I'm sorry."

"You're *sorry?* You can't kill somebody and say *sorry*. You'll never get away with this."

"I don't have to. But you will. You killed yourself. The headaches, the concussion, the madness drove you to it."

My throat constricted. I felt like I couldn't breathe. I had to keep talking.

"What made you crack, Larry? Did your boss pass you over for a promotion? A messy divorce? A meltdown? Why would a federal agent team up with Eddie Harr? Was it money?"

"And the early retirement plan."

"You'll spend it in Joliet."

"I'll take that laptop now, Cat."

Harding tossed the bag on the floor and Inga charged the sausages. She whaled over the recliner and whacked his arm in flight. Diverting his attention for one brief moment was all I needed. I whirled at him with all my might, my flying weight propelling him backwards. I grappled his wrist with both hands, my nails clawing his skin.

The 9mm went off wildly. The bullet chipped the fireplace and the smoking gun dropped to the floor. I kicked my foot and the gun skirted across the hardwood, spun under the couch, and ricocheted off the wall. Harding howled with rage. He nailed my cheek and a sharp pain pierced my head. His big hands clawed at my neck and I jammed my knee up into his groin. He screamed. His legs gave way and I twisted sideways and broke free.

I hurdled over the couch and landed on the gun. I rolled on my back. He rocketed after me, bounding onto the couch cushion, reeling above me wild eyed, his breath ragged. I flexed my hands around the hard steel and aimed the pistol over my head. Right between his eyes.

I fired. He flew back and he went down hard. I flinched at the sound of his head crashing the coffee table. My Chihuly vase shattered to tinkling bits of priceless glass. Inga crawled behind the couch and trembled beside me on the floor.

I had killed a man. The adrenaline crashed. I could barely breathe. I was too numb and shaky to think. The gun burned my hand and I dropped it. I hugged my knees a long time until the shaking stopped. When my legs would hold me I pulled myself up and stumbled to the kitchen. First I called Rocco. My brother was on his way when I called Chance.

◇◇◇

Captain Bob was not a happy man standing in front of my fireplace for the second time that day. This time he brought half a dozen reinforcements. Not to be outdone Rocco brought seven DeLucas.

"Merda!" Papa muttered. He held my hand, too worried to show off his scar. My crazy cousin Frank brandished his gun and practiced his quick draw on the porch. Rocco spoke quietly with the captain and the twins finished the forgotten bag of smoked sausages. Uncle Joey manipulated the crime scene. He spoke on his cell and whispered instructions to my cousins. The FBI's

golden boy draped spread-eagle across the broken coffee table, head dropped back to the floor. An Adam's apple protruded from the stretched turkey neck. Special Agent in Charge Larry Harding's steel eyes gaped open, surprised by death.

I felt numb. I answered Captain Bob's questions. He asked the same ones a hundred times. My answers didn't change.

Bob shook his head gravely. "I don't think I can help you with this one. But I can put in a word with the DA."

I frowned. "What word?"

"Insanity."

"It was self-defense," Rocco countered. "A witness saw Larry Harding let himself into her house."

"That same witness believed he had a key. She claims Harding was a john keeping a date."

Uncle Joey lowered his voice. "I made some calls, Bob. We can say the guy fell off the pier and drowned."

"There's a bullet in his head."

"I know a guy," Joey said.

There was a rap at the door and Chicago's finest parted like the Red Sea. Chance Savino blazed into the room. Two stiffs in suits scurried after him.

"Feds." Uncle Joey made a face.

Chance Savino glanced at his partner laid out on the table like Mama's buffet. He took in the hole between the eyes, the lips drawn back in a horrific grimace. Savino's jaw tightened and something hard grew behind his eyes. He crossed the room in three long strides and knelt in front of me. The DeLuca men closed in.

His finger brushed the scratches on my neck. "Are you OK, DeLucky?"

I nodded and jammed my hand in my pocket. Where the hell was my Dr. Pepper Lip Smacker.

"Liar, liar," he said. He went to the kitchen, found me a glass of red wine, and pulled up a chair. "Tell me what happened."

"Your partner had an accident," Uncle Joey said. "He drowned."

Savino raised a brow. "There's a bullet in his head."

"Not a problem," Rocco said. "Joey knows a guy."

I told the story again starting at the beginning. When I was finished, Captain Bob folded his arms across his chest.

"We're going for insanity," Captain Bob said.

Chance stood and leveled his gaze at the captain. "Dead men can't plea."

"Huh?" I said.

"Eddie Harr is under investigation by the FBI. His connections to Organized Crime made him the target of an FBI undercover operation that blew to hell last week when Harr killed our informant. The operation was top secret. We've had leaks at the Chicago office and suspected a mole. Somehow Larry found out and blew my cover. The Bridgeport bomb was a big clue."

"Tell Mama to call off the exorcism," I said. "Savino's not dead and I'm not crazy."

Captain Bob snorted, unconvinced.

Savino shook Captain Bob's hand. "The FBI is taking over this investigation, Captain Maxfield. You and your men are free to go."

For once Bob didn't argue jurisdiction. He signaled retreat and wagged a finger at me. "Stay away from Eddie Harr," he said and shuffled his men out the door.

"I'm guessing the dead guy on my sister's table was on Eddie's payroll," Rocco said.

Savino nodded grimly. "Agent Harding came under suspicion after the bombing. I asked him to work with me so I could keep my eye on him."

"Puh-leeze." I exaggerated an eye roll. "Where were you when he broke into my home?"

He winced. "I didn't know he'd come after you."

The DeLuca men growled.

"The FBI will launch a full investigation into Harding's death, of course, but there won't be any charges."

"Damn straight," Uncle Joey said. "This is a PR nightmare. The FBI hopes to sweep it under the media's radar."

"What about Harr?" I demanded. "He killed three people this week."

"He eliminated our witnesses. It'll be tough to build a case but we're not giving up."

Rocco hung an arm around my shoulder. "Pack your toothbrush, sis. I'm taking you home."

"Your sister needs to accompany me downtown for a formal statement," Savino said. "She can't stay here tonight, but the FBI will put her up in a hotel until she's able to come home."

Rocco narrowed his eyes.

"What about the damages?" I thrust my hands on my hips. "What about my Chihuly vase? My busted coffee table? My camera?"

"Itemize a bill," Chance said.

"Cha-ching," Uncle Joey smiled. "I'll make the list."

The FBI forensics team clamored through the door. I hugged the DeLucas and sent them away. Then I told the Feds to clean up the mess on the coffee table and disappeared into my bedroom with Inga.

My face was pale in the full length mirror. I stepped out of my pants and dropped my hoodie on the floor. I wouldn't wear them again. Joey could add them to his list.

I took a long hot shower. The hot water pulsed down my back, pummeling the tension from my neck and shoulders. When I stepped out again I was steamy and pink.

I toweled my hair, packed my toothbrush and an overnight bag. It was going to be a long night and I dressed quickly in a pair of jeans and a sweat shirt. I was tired and hungry and dreaded another splash at the FBI building where everyone gets to have a gun but me.

When Savino knocked I slung my purse over my shoulder and opened the door, bag and beagle in hand.

"Inga wants to ride in a Porsche Boxster."

"So would I. My car's in front."

The eerie zip of a body bag sent shivers down my spine.

"Let's get you out of here," Savino said.

"When do I get my 9mm back?"

"This is a complex case and it's hard to say how long the investigation will take. If I were you…"

"Yeah?"

"I'd find another gun."

"I'll put Uncle Joey on it."

I lowered my eyes and marched through the hall, past the living room, and out the front door. A large boat waited by the curb.

My face fell. "The Boxster?"

"Gone," Chance said. "It was part of my cover. This is my car. A 1959 Cadillac Eldorado Biarritz with a 'Q' engine with three dual barrel carburetors. She purrs like a kitten."

"You drive an Eldorado?"

"I'm restoring it. It's a classic."

"An *Eldorado?*" I repeated like he didn't hear me. The rusty, dented machine needed more than a paint job. It screamed Demolition Derby.

"What was that you said about my Porsche? Midlife crisis? A need to compensate?"

My face felt hot.

He flashed a smile. "I don't."

Savino opened the passenger door and Inga jumped inside and into the back. I slipped into the passenger seat. Chance leaned in, his lips lightly brushed my hair.

A gasp sounded from the bushes.

Savino glanced over his shoulder. "The witness?"

"It's my very own Gladys Kravitz. You're steaming up her binoculars."

A soft laugh escaped his throat. He closed my door, moseyed around to the driver's side, and slid in beside me.

The new leather seats and interior had a dreamy new car smell. "You can wow blind women with this car," I said.

"I'm wowing you." Savino cranked the key. "Listen to that engine purr. She's not finished yet but she's…"

"A boat."

"A dream," he laughed and pulled away from the curb. I waved to Gladys and wriggled down into the lush cushy seat. It was a delicious ride.

"I knew you'd like it."

"That's what they said about the Titanic."

Savino chucked a fist to his chest.

"Tell me about Harding," I said. "When did you know he was the leak?"

"A bunch of FBI guys were at the morgue after the explosion. We had a corpse, no ID. The body was on the table, a biker dude with tattoos and piercings. Some in incredibly painful places."

I made a face.

"Anyway, Larry said any dude who tattoos a woman holding a snake to his head has serious issues. I got to thinking about it and I went back to the morgue alone. Larry was right. The tattooed woman was drawn down his back, but it wasn't visible lying on the table. I asked around. No one mentioned the tattoo."

"Larry knew AJ. They were on the same retirement plan."

Chance shook his head. "How does a guy like Larry get sucked in with slime like Eddie?"

"What about you? You let the FBI think those shiny diamonds were lost in the explosion. Planning an early retirement?"

"No."

"You didn't turn them in."

"I hadn't really thought about it. I wasn't going to hand them over to pad a bureaucrat's pocket or fund a lousy war."

I studied his face. "So what were you going to do with them?"

Savino shrugged. "I don't know. There are a lot of good causes out there. Maybe a research hospital."

"Not stash a few away for yourself?"

"I wouldn't want to cross that line."

We were approaching downtown, not far from the FBI office. I poofed my hair and smeared Dr. Pepper Lip Smacker on my lips.

"What were you doing at that vacant building that day?" I said. "You were waiting for someone."

"I got a call from a guy who wanted to meet there. Said a reporter told him to call. Something about a witness protection program."

I felt sick. AJ wanted to get out with his family. Rita went to the FBI to ask for witness protection for AJ. She talked to Larry. It was AJ's death sentence.

Savino set his jaw grimly. "AJ was dead when I arrived. The fireworks were for me."

"In her last email Rita said she'd been 'duped.' I hope she put it all together before she died. I mean Turncoat Larry, the guns, the diamonds, and the cheating husband who smells like Red Door."

"It's a story worthy of a Pulitzer."

"The rat in my bed was a little overkill. I didn't see anything."

Whack, whack, whack. The hammers belted my skull and a glimpse of light slipped through a crack.

"Footsteps," I murmured with amazement. "Somebody running before the explosion." I smiled shakily. "I remember."

"Maybe you saw his face."

I closed my eyes. "Nothing."

"It could have been Harding or one of Eddie's goons. But even if it comes, it probably wouldn't be enough."

"Where was Harr at the time?"

"Slick Eddie? He was having lunch with the mayor."

Savino stopped the car and I looked around the parking lot. We weren't at the FBI office at all. We were at the Palmer House Hilton.

"Liar, liar," I said.

He slid me a look. "I said I would take you in for a statement. I didn't say when."

I plucked my cell phone from my jeans and punched some numbers. "If this is your cheesy way of getting me to a hotel room alone it won't work."

Savino closed his hand over my phone. "I only need a few hours alone with you away from your trigger-happy family."

Something in his voice stopped me. I tucked the phone away. "Why?"

He stared miserably into the parking lot, his jaw clenched tight. "Because something awful could have happened to you and I…"

"Nothing happened," I said.

"And I never told you…"

I caught my breath. "What?"

"You are the most stubborn, exasperating woman I've met."

"That's it?"

He smiled. "And incredibly sexy."

His lips were supple when he found mine. To my credit I pulled away.

The deep cobalt blues searched my face. "I could have lost you today."

For once I could think of nothing to say. A warm glow spread over me like melted butter.

"We'll have dinner at the hotel restaurant. I'll come back in the morning and take you in for a statement. I've reserved a room for you and Inga. I told them she's your service dog."

"What's my disability?"

He gave a lopsided grin. "Mental. You called my Eldorado a boat."

"Hey sailor."

He laughed softly and brought my fingers to his lips. I studied his reflection in the street light. God was just showing off when he made Chance Savino. He wasn't the hot guy in a Porsche Boxster. Dammit. He had a government salary and scruples. Well, some.

I grimaced inwardly and took a chance.

"Come upstairs with me," I said. "We can order room service for three."

"Three?"

Inga nuzzled his neck.

I hooked a finger in his belt. "And then we'll see about dessert."

Chapter Thirty-three

I parked across the street from Toodle Realty and told Cleo to wait in the car.

"I need a gun," Cleo said.

"No guns. This isn't a hit. I'm a hootchie stalker."

She looked disappointed. "Who's the hootchie?"

"Mr. Toodle. Mrs. Toodle found a smudge of Passion Pink lipstick on his baby blue boxers. Her Frosted Peach lips don't go there."

Cleo wrenched open my glove box and dug around. "You gotta have a gun."

She tossed out pepper spray, the *Police Business* sticker I snagged from Rocco, and a Snickers bar.

"Take the Snickers," I said.

"Aha!" Cleo's big brown eyes lit. "What's this?" She wrestled a stun gun from the glove box and jammed it in her pants.

"Don't shoot anybody."

"I got your back, girlfriend."

I grabbed my camera, chugged across the street, and hid behind a bush outside Mr. Toodle's office. The hootchie was a busy guy. He worked at his desk all morning, made calls, met with three agents, and drank four cups of coffee. Black with two sugars. I kept notes.

At 11:58 Mr. Toodle's secretary left in her car for lunch. At 11:59 a woman in a short, silky rose-colored dress sashayed across the street. Her neck snapped to the right and to the left before scooting toward Toodle Realty. She wore four-inch heels. Her legs were bare. Her lips were Passion Pink.

I returned my attention to the window. Mr. Toodle sprayed a squirt of breath freshener in his mouth. I snatched my camera. Ready. Aim.

The office door was flung open and Passion Pink shimmied into Mr. Toodle's arms. He pulled her tight against him. Their mouths met.

Snap.

Mr. Toodle was a wet and sloppy kisser. Yuck.

He didn't waste any time. He hauled Passion Pink across the room.

Snap

Hoisted her round bottom onto his desk. Slobbered on her face while fumbling with her blouse. Yuck.

Snap.

"Your Cheatin' Heart" blared from my pocket. *Damn.* I fumbled for my phone and cut off Hank Jr.

"Pants on Fire Detective Agency," I whispered.

"Caught ya working. Who're you stalking today?"

"Some miserable three-minute Joe. I got one word of advice for this guy. Foreplay."

Uncle Joey chuckled. "Then you're almost finished. Meet me at D'Aria's. I'm buying lunch."

A voice shrieked from the other side of the bush. "There she is!" a woman gasped. "She's a—she's a—"

"Gardener," I said.

Large hands parted the branches. The guy chewed his nails. "What are you doing behind there, lady?"

"I'm trimming the bush."

I turned back to the window and choked on a breath.

"Damn girl," I murmured.

Snap. Snap. Snap. Snap.

"She has a *camera!"* The woman screeched. "The gardener is a pervert!"

"What the hell?" The man bellowed.

Uncle Joey laughed.

"Gotta run," I said.

"Look out!" the woman shrieked. "The pervert has an accomplice!"

I frowned. Cleo?

"She's got a gun! She's got a gun!" the woman shrieked.

I leaped from behind the bush.

"Cleo, no!" I shouted.

Cleo charged the man. A crazed film glazed her eyes. She brandished a stun gun.

"We're gonna die!" the woman screamed.

"Stand back!" The man with the chewed nails stepped gallantly in front of her. He scrunched his face, braced for the hit.

ZAAPPPP!

The man crumbled to his knees. Cleo raised the weapon to her ruby lips and blew.

"Hootchie," Cleo spat. "You're just like my liar, liar husband."

"That's not Mr. Toodle," I said. "He's inside with Passion Pink."

"Oh?" Cleo's eyes narrowed on the Toodle Realty door.

The man on the ground groaned. The woman hoisted him to his feet.

"Get them!" the woman squawked.

I grabbed Cleo's sleeve and pushed her toward the car.

"Run!" I screamed.

And we did.

◇◇◇

I found a parking spot a few blocks from the restaurant. Uncle Joey sat at a table by the window. We waved from the sidewalk.

"He's cute," Cleo flapped her hand. "Single?"

"Married," I laughed, "a bit of a crook and probably fools around. But he's the best uncle a girl could have."

"Hmm," Cleo said. She coasted through the door. I skirted behind her to Joey's table.

"Uncle Joey, this is Cleo," I said.

She flashed a smile and glitzy rose-colored fingernails. "I'm Cat's partner," she said.

"Partner?"

"Assistant," I said.

"I just took down my first hootchie." Cleo patted her waistband. "I'm good with a gun."

"He was an innocent bystander," I said.

Uncle Joey swallowed a smile.

The waiter appeared with a sparkling bottle of Dom Pérignon. He popped the cork and the bubbles spilled in our glasses.

"The good stuff," I said. "What's the occasion?"

"Lunch with my favorite niece. And her new partner."

"*Temporary* assistant," I said.

Cleo and Joey winked at each other.

"Cute," I said.

"Try the garlic shrimp," my uncle said. "I ordered appetizers."

I popped a shrimp in my mouth and the savory juices dribbled from my lips. I dabbed with a napkin.

Joey chuckled. "There's a smudge of dirt on your cheek."

"A professional hazard for gardeners."

"And the smallest hint of a love-bite on your neck."

Cleo jerked her neck around. "You go, girl."

I felt my cheeks heating up.

"Max?"

I didn't respond and Joey smacked his forehead. "Not the dead man."

"Dead man?" Cleo shuddered.

"His name is Chance Savino," I said.

"He's a vampire," Joey said.

Cleo crossed herself.

"Ha ha," I said.

"If you marry him you'll have devil children," Uncle Joey said.

"He's Italian," I said.

Joey shrugged. "He'll do."

He narrowed his gaze on me. "Tell Savino to give up smuggling diamonds. He can't hold on to them."

I waved a protesting hand. "He's not a smuggler. The FBI wanted to use the diamonds to bring down Eddie and his crime buddies."

"Right," Cleo grinned.

"I like your new partner," my uncle said.

I opened my mouth and closed it again.

Joey reached in his pocket and tossed a small black box beside my glass of champagne.

"What's this?"

"You had a couple rough weeks there. I didn't have a chance to give you your birthday present."

I looked at him curiously and opened the lid. Two brilliant pink diamond earrings set in platinum. They took my breath away.

"Happy birthday, Caterina."

Cleo choked.

I popped out the silver hoops and slipped the dazzling pink diamonds on my ears.

"I don't know what to say."

"Don't say you can't keep them."

Cleo jabbed her fork in a 'shroom. "She won't," she said firmly.

I leaned across the table and kissed his cheek. "Thank you."

Uncle Joey looked enormously pleased with himself.

"There's one thing I need though," I said.

"Name it."

"I want the diamonds back."

Joey groaned. "You aren't giving them to the Feds, are you?"

"No."

"I have a buyer. He'll pay top dollar."

I mulled the idea over in my head. "OK," I said. "Sell the stones." I fished through my purse and dropped a piece of paper on the table.

"I did some checking and came up with three research hospitals. You can split the money from the diamonds among them. I'd like the donations made in Rita Polansky's memory."

Joey smiled. "There will be a small handling fee, of course."

"Of course."

Uncle Joey's eyes focused beyond my shoulder and across the street. I followed his gaze and stiffened.

"That's Eddie Harr," I hissed.

"So it is."

"He's getting into his car."

"So he is." Uncle Joey lavished duck paté on crunchy toast. "Did I mention Slick Eddie owns a big interest in that business across the street?"

The neon sign flashed "Midwest Oil."

"He makes a killing with the gas prices."

I pushed my plate away. "Just when I thought I couldn't dislike Eddie more."

An ear-splitting boom erupted outside. I felt as if my chest would collapse. Screams pierced the café. Flying debris and an amazing amount of dust billowed out in the street.

Cleo dived under a table and disappeared. A quivering stun gun flashed beneath the table cloth.

"Where's Eddie?" I choked. "Is he—"

Another blast and I was under the table with Cleo. I couldn't breathe. I waited until the thunder stopped. I lifted the white satin tablecloth and poked my head out. The tables around me were empty. Everyone had scrambled for cover.

Except for my Uncle Joey. He poured us another glass of champagne.

To receive a free catalog of Poisoned Pen Press titles, please contact us in one of the following ways:

Phone: 1-800-421-3976
Facsimile: 1-480-949-1707
Email: info@poisonedpenpress.com
Website: www.poisonedpenpress.com

Poisoned Pen Press
6962 E. First Ave. Ste. 103
Scottsdale, AZ 85251